BETWEEN BEIRUT AND THE MOON

BETWEEN BEIRUT AND THE MOON

A. Naji Bakhti

Published by Influx Press

The Green House, 49 Green Lanes, London, N16 9BU

www.influxpress.com / @InfluxPress

First published 2020. Printed and bound in the UK by TJ International.

Print ISBN: 978-1-910312-55-1

E-Book ISBN: 978-1-910312-56-8

Edited by Kit Caless

Editorial assistant: Sanya Semakula

Typesetting: Vince Haig

Proofreader: Dan Coxon

Cover art and design: Jamie Keenan

For my mother and father

BETWEEN BEIRUT AND THE MOON

I heard this theory once that if you toss a newborn into a swimming pool he'll come out the other side kicking. I find that highly improbable. My father, or so I believe, has always been a strong advocate of the theory. Instead of water, however, he chose books. And instead of infants, he chose the entirety of his son's and daughter's combined childhoods. In more than one sense, my sister and I have been kicking through books for most of our lives. The idea was that if you expose a child to literature long and hard enough, he'll grow up wanting to be a writer, a critic, an editor or the J.R.R. Tolkien Professor of English Literature and Language at the University of Oxford. Of course, I wanted to be an astronaut.

'Don't be ridiculous,' he'd say, 'who ever heard of an Arab on the moon?'

'I'll be the first one,' I replied at once, instead of taking the usual route of trying to look as non-ridiculous as possible, for my father's liking.

'You're flat-footed. They don't allow flat-footed Arabs on the moon,' he remarked casually, his face hidden behind this morning's *An-Nahar Daily*, 'it's illegal.'

'Who said?'

'Jesus-Mohammad-Christ said, that's who.'

That was another thing my father would say with unerring regularity. As if Jesus' middle name had always been Mohammad and everyone in the world had thus far simply failed to spot this most obvious truth. One expected nothing less of a Muslim man who had forged an unholy alliance with a Christian woman against the wishes of his now irritated family and his now pissed-off god, whom, one would have thought, must have known in advance and ought to have had ample time to cope.

'How many times have I told you not to dash your son's dreams?' my mother cautioned, as she made her way towards the balcony, cigarette in mouth and all. She was being generous today. Usually, she would spend most of her leisure time in the living room creating a cloud of smoke in front of her and then struggling to make out the images being displayed on the TV. 'He can do anything he sets his mind to.'

'Next you'll be telling him he can walk on water. God knows we have a hard enough time getting from one country to another without being held back for a cavity search. They'll shove a fucking Hubble telescope, mother and father, up his backside before they let him get on that space shuttle,' he said.

'Mother and father' is a colloquial term used in Lebanon to express the idea of something whole or complete. For instance, the weight of the explosion knocked the man, mother and father, right out of the window, as men in Beirut occasionally are; or the building collapsed, mother and father, to the ground, as buildings in Beirut occasionally do.

A LESSON IN BUDDHISM

When, in school, I was grilled on the subject of my religion by my classmates, I would respond with a shrug as bewildering to my inquisitors as it was to me. I knew that church was for Christians and mosque for MusliMs I knew this because both Christian and church begin with the letters 'C' and 'H', and because both Muslim and mosque begin with the letters 'M' and 'O', if you should choose to spell Moslem as such, but don't. I knew that the mosque was the one that smelt of feet on any given day, but particularly on Friday; and not nice nail-polished lady feet either, but thick-skinned and hairy man feet. I knew this because my friend, Mohammad, was Muslim and he smelt of feet on any given day, but particularly on Friday.

Mohammad had devised a game, or so he told us. He hadn't. All he had done was learn it off of his big brother.

'Christian or Muslim?' he asked one day during break, extending two clenched and clammy fists and imploring me to pick one.

I picked Muslim because, in Arabic, it means *peace* and, I reasoned, no harm could come of peace. The Arabic word for Christian bore an uncomfortable resemblance to the Arabic word for crocodile, and I was not especially fond of crocodiles at the time.

Mohammad slapped me straight across my left cheek with his clammy right hand and ran. He hid behind the teacher's desk for what seemed like more than ten minutes and I eventually gave up looking for him and forgave him instead. The next day I asked him where he was all afternoon and he said he was hiding behind the teacher's desk for the first ten minutes and had since then found his mother, walked home with her, done his homework, watched *Boy Meets World*, went to sleep, woke up, brushed his teeth, skipped breakfast and walked straight to school.

'Nothing,' he said, before reciting the above activities to me in that same order.

From a distance I observed as Mohammad extended his still clammy fists to an older boy whom I had only known by name. Mohammad then struck the older boy, Boulos, across his right cheek. Boulos made an instinctive gesture as if to react. His arm was half-raised and in pole position to strike when he slowly and gradually began to lower it.

'You're Christian, Boulos. You can't slap back. You see. Those are the rules of the game,' said Mohammad, smiling triumphantly. 'I know it's not fair,' he continued, 'don't blame me. Take it up with your own god.'

It was true that my mother had never made to slap me across the face, nor had my father for that matter, but it was also true that the sole of her shoe had narrowly missed the tip of my nose and the top of my head on countless different occasions. Of course, on these occasions the sole of my mother's shoe had long since left my mother's foot and was making its own pilgrimage from her hand to whichever part of my body it had set out to reach. My mother may have been Christian but her shoe, almost definitely, was not Christian.

'Am I Muslim or Christian?' I asked my Christian mother over dinner. The family had been sitting before the TV set, each with a tray on his or her lap, for at least half an hour watching my father's favourite Comedy Sketch programme: *Basmeet ElWatan*, which literally translates to 'The Death of a Nation', or alternatively, 'The Smiles of a Nation', depending on the manner in which one chooses to read the title. The TV set was old with vinyl wood varnish and knobs rather than buttons and my little sister's nimble fingers rather than a remote control. The story which my parents had upheld thus far was that either my sister or I had hidden the remote control somewhere within the house when we were very young and forgotten about it. They had searched for the remote countless times before, of course, and were eventually forced to concede that it was lost forever. We, my sister and I, had to pay the price for our mistake by getting up to change the channel every time one of our parents decided they didn't like the programme they were watching. As I was almost twice my sister's age at the time, it often fell to her to change the channel.

'Technically, neither,' my father replied absent-mindedly, drawing a stern look from my mother and failing to notice both her stern look and my concerned expression.

'Both, Adam,' my mother said, seeking to reassure me in some way.

'Yes, but if I had to pick one, which would it be?' I asked again.

'I heard Buddism is alright. Try that,' my father said, smiling and winking to himself.

'How many times have I told you not to confuse your son?' my mother remarked.

'I'm only laying out his options in front of him, darling,' he replied.

The conversation then went in the direction of Buddhism and how they, the Buddhists, worship a short, fat and bald man, who looked remarkably like my uncle Gamal and who had spent most of his days naked and attempting to lift himself off the ground without the effort of moving his legs. He sounded, to me, like a more obese version of Jesus but without the long and fair hair and the glimmering blue eyes.

'Glimmering blue eyes? Where do you think Jesus was born? Sweden?' my father interjected, now turning his attention away from the TV set for the first time in the conversation.

'Australia,' my sister replied with an air of authority which belied her tender age of six.

'Why Australia, Fara?' my father asked tugging at one of her ponytails playfully. Only my father called my sister 'Fara'. It means mouse.

'Why not?' she said, adjusting her ponytail.

The general consensus was that, as God would not have consciously and willingly overseen the evolution of the kangaroo, he must've turned his back on Australia for a good few thousand years and so could not have sent his own son to that overgrown island two thousand or so years ago.

The only link my sister and I could find between Jesus and Australia, years later, would be Mel Gibson, an Australian actor and director, who directed the movie *Passion of the Christ*. My sister maintains, to this day, that her answer was prophetic.

'He was born in the Middle East. He was probably tanned, had a long black beard, thick black eyebrows and dark black eyes,' my father said, running his thumb and index finger over his thick, black moustache, 'like bin Laden.'

A week or so later, as he dropped me off to school, my father leaned over and explained that there were quite a few advantages to being a child of a 'mixed marriage', chief among them the ability to switch back and forth between both religions at one's own convenience. By that point, Mohammad's game had spread and most children, Muslim and Christian, had been slapped across their cheek at least once. Whenever we saw two of our classmates chasing one another during recess we knew that they were both Muslim and that the one being chased had just slapped his chaser straight across the face. The Christian boys, as you would expect, did not like this game very much, but none of them slapped back or chased their aggressor because they were Christian and Christians must turn the other cheek, or so Mohammad, and countless other Muslim boys, had told them.

'I want to play again,' I told Mohammad, who shrugged his shoulders and extended his arms to reveal both his clenched and clammy fists.

'Muslim or Christian?'

'Christian,' I said smiling.

'I thought you said you were Muslim.'

'I did. But I changed my mind. My mum's Christian. I can do that,' I replied, victoriously.

Mohammad slapped me across the face and stood there laughing with four or five other Muslim boys, all of whom had latched themselves onto Mohammad ever since he'd introduced his now popular game to the playground. I did not wait for Mohammad to finish his laugh before reaching over and slapping him with the back of my hand across his right cheek as hard as I could.

'That's not how it works,' he said. 'You're Christian, you can't slap back. Ask your god.'

I asked him, I thought, and he said it's fine by him if I go back to being a Muslim for the next few minutes. But I didn't say it. I didn't say anything. I slapped Mohammad again and again. The fourth slap knocked him off his feet. He made a helpless effort to punch back as he fell to the floor, swinging his fist in the general direction of my face. I pinned him to the floor and began to punch his face wildly. I imagined that he was an alien life form which I had come across in one of my journeys to outer space, whose sole aim was to spread a disease that would divide the entire human race into tiny little groups of men and women who fought endlessly amongst themselves and achieved progress only sporadically. None of his newly acquired friends came to his aid and they were joined by more spectators, mostly young Christian boys who were led to the scene by the mere smell of retribution.

As I sat there in the principal's office thinking about what I'd done, my mother and father were escorted to the leather chairs either side of the one I had been occupying for the best part of an hour.

'Sit, they're not just for decoration, you know,' the principal, Ms Iman, said, tapping one of the leather chairs on its back and looking up at my father.

My father does not take too kindly to being told what to do by anyone, especially marginally younger women, and would likely have been much more cooperative throughout the remainder of the meeting had she, the principal, politely asked him to please take a seat without tapping any one of the leather chairs on the back and without making a remark about their function in an office. I was glad she had done both.

'Are you happy about what you've done, Adam?' asked the principal, leaning forward and staring me intently in the eye.

She was one of those women who had once been startlingly beautiful but who'd since deliberately taken the decision to cut her hair short, develop myopia and age a few years in order to be taken more seriously by her male colleagues.

'Yes,' I replied, knowing that it was perhaps not the answer she was looking for.

'You see, the boy shows no remorse,' she said, addressing my parents and filling them in on the details of the incident.

'It seems to me that my son was involved in a fight with another boy. Now where is that other boy?' my father inquired.

'Your son broke his nose. He's in the hospital,' she replied, raising her right eyebrow.

'That hardly seems fair.'

'What, that your son broke the boy's nose? Or that the boy is receiving medical treatment at the hospital?'

'My son's arms are covered with little scratches which, clearly, have been left unattended,' my father said, putting both his hands on the desk before him and adjusting his seating position. 'This boy fights like a little girl.'

I chuckled and received a stern look from both my mother and the principal, who evidently thought that my father's remark was neither funny nor was I entitled to laugh at it. I looked at my arm and noticed the tiny scratches for the first time. They hurt more now that I was aware of them. A tear must've escaped me as both of their expressions soon softened.

'What do you want to be when you grow up?' the principal asked, looking straight at me.

Ms Iman's what-do-you-want-to-be-when-you-grow-up lecture was infamous throughout the school. There was not a student summoned into her office who had not been on the receiving end of one. It went something like this: what do you want to be when you grow up? A doctor/ engineer/ lawyer/ businessman/ teacher. And do you think doctors/ engineers/ lawyers/ businessmen/teachers punch one another in the face? No. Exactly, now apologise to your classmate.

To say that it is inherently flawed is an understatement. That the moral fibre of a human being is essentially tied to his occupation is ridiculous. Even as eleven-year-olds, we were well aware of that.

'An astronaut,' I replied.

'An astronaut?' she repeated, turning over to look at my mother who shrugged her shoulders and smiled politely. 'Whoever heard of an Arab on the moon?'

Out of the corner of my eye, I saw my father slap his forehead audibly with the palm of his right hand, then slap his right hand with the palm of his left one.

'The point is you shouldn't resort to violence every time someone insults your religion. It's why the entire country has gone to the dogs. Is that clear?' asked the principal.

'Yes, Ms Iman,' I replied, occupying myself with the elaborate pattern of the Persian carpet on the floor.

'Hold on. You've had a student spreading sectarianism around the school for the past month and you're concerned that my son has found an unorthodox way of putting an end to it?' my father asked.

'Unorthodox? It's completely orthodox, Mr Najjar, that's the problem,' she said, somewhat impatiently, 'this is not the first time your son has been involved in acts of indiscipline, or blasphemy for that matter. Just last week, he asked the Civic Studies teacher whether Jesus Christ existed in the same way that Santa Claus did.'

'Well, with all due respect Ms Iman, what the hell was Jesus Christ doing in a Civic Studies class at a secular school anyway?' my father asked.

'Calm down,' my mother said, nudging her husband in the ribs.

'And a month or so ago – tell your father what you said about the Prophet,' she demanded, addressing me and completely ignoring my father's question.

'I asked the Arabic teacher whether, after commanding Mohammad to read, God then smacked him on the back of the head with the Koran, like you did to me with *Oliver Twist*,' I said, staring bluntly at my father.

'In all honesty, son, if Mohammad was anything like you, then God must've done, yes,' he replied.

'I will not have blasphemy in my office,' said Ms Iman.

'Do you know who I am, Ms Iman?' My father had just invoked the quintessential Lebanese statement which often preceded an indisputable declaration of war between two mostly rational adults.

It doesn't matter if you're a second-rate citizen living from pay cheque to pay cheque, with a modest background, no ancestors to speak of and earning barely enough money to feed your eight hungry children, in Lebanon you will ask this question of anyone who rubs you the wrong way and wait for them to ask you it back.

'Do you know who I am, Mr Najjar?'

Of course, neither of them knew who the other really was. Neither of them really cared to find out. My mother, suspecting as much, stood up, apologised to Ms Iman, told her that I would be severely punished at home and asked for Mohammad's mother's phone number so that she may call her and apologise personally. I don't know what my mother said, but I never heard from Mohammad or his mother again.

When we got home my parents sent me straight to my room to think about what I'd done. A few minutes later my father opened my bedroom door, walked in, and locked it behind him.

'Your mother and I agreed that the only way to punish you is this,' he said, holding his black leather belt in his right hand.

'But I didn't,' I began to object and stopped as soon as I saw my father's index finger being placed firmly on his lips.

'Jump and scream,' he whispered, deliberately missing me and landing hard lashes on the bedsheets.

'Never be afraid to fight for what you believe in, or defend those with less courage or intellect than yourself,' my father said, lashing furiously at the bed, 'but always stop short of breaking your opponent's nose. You know you've gone astray – scream – when there's blood involved.'

'I'm sorry,' I said, bouncing as high as I could and screaming over his words.

'Stop that's enough, stop,' my mother implored, banging on the bedroom door.

'Do not hesitate to blaspheme if religion happens to stand in the way of truth or knowledge, but do not do so intentionally to provoke others,' he continued, inciting me to shout louder with his left hand, 'apologise – louder – to those whom you have wronged, but never wait long enough to be told to do it by others. It takes the gloss off of the apology.'

'Open this door right now or so help me God, I will burst through it,' my mother shouted.

For a moment, my father stood before me panting and trying to catch his breath; then he unlocked the door, swung it open, and walked past my mother without saying another word.

ALJAHIZ AND MONSIEUR MERMIER

Not too many men are fond of the time their father almost ended their life. It would be a sad tale to tell had my life actually ended, and I, in all likelihood, would not be the one to tell it.

Once, I asked my father if he could give me his copy of *The Miserly*, a book by the Arab philosopher Aljahiz, which was probably collecting dust somewhere around the house. He gave me a ten thousand lira note instead and told me to go buy my own version before hiding his head behind the *An-Nahar Daily*. He was looking to see if they had published the article he'd sent in the week before. Such was the chaos which engulfed the house that when my father declared a book lost, no one bothered to look for it.

All I knew about Aljahiz was that his tragic and untimely death had come about when an entire library of his own books fell on top of him one night and crushed him to death. It was how we'd all imagined my father would go, looking for a book to read and then suddenly being overwhelmed by a number of them launching themselves at him.

Many visitors who passed by our home on occasion, would take one glance at the piles of books stacked haphazardly around the house and put them down to my father's insatiable thirst for knowledge. It was not, however, my father's insatiable thirst for knowledge which cost us valuable house space, it was his insatiable thirst for books. I use the word 'house' loosely. Ours was not a house; it was a small apartment on the sixth floor of an old building in Ras Beirut, just off Hamra Street. The location was ideal, but the apartment itself was designed to fit one or two people at most. Certainly, not four people and an entire library.

When Monsieur Mermier, a Frenchman working for the UN, moved into the apartment facing our own on the sixth floor, my father jumped at the opportunity to invite him to our home. The Frenchman, he told me, is the pinnacle of cultured and intellectual men. Of course, he might have said the same thing about Englishmen, were we living next door to an Englishman.

'Your home is a sanctuary for literature, Monsieur Najjar,' said Monsieur Mermier, taking a sip of his Turkish coffee.

'And a dumpster for everyone else,' my mother added, offering Monsieur Mermier a tray of Arabic sweets and wiping the smile off my father's face.

Monsieur Mermier suggested that my father should open a publishing house, since he seemed to love nothing more, on this evidence, than the sight of books stacked on top of one another. My father dismissed this without deliberation.

After my mother went to sleep, my father took out a bottle of Arak, a slightly stronger version of vodka diluted with water to be just as strong, and offered Monsieur Mermier a few shots. They drank to health and Lebanon and success and new friends and peace and old friends and peace and France and Lebanon and Charles de Gaulle and Jacques Chirac and my great-grandfather and good health and Zidane's footballing skills and success and Barthez's bald head and Voltaire and Monsieur Mermier's mother and my grandmother and Lebanon.

Not long into their drinking binge, my father confessed that it was his lifelong dream to run a successful publishing house. And not long after that, it was Monsieur Mermier's turn to confess that it was *his* lifelong dream to invest in a publishing house. Neither of which ever materialised.

Despite him getting along well with my father, I was always mildly suspicious of Monsieur Mermier. For instance, he would regularly sit with one thigh resting completely over the other; it was a manner in which I had never seen a man sit before. Most men I knew, including my father, would place one ankle over their knee and sometimes hold it there with their hands. His unusual seating disposition led me to one of two conclusions: either Frenchmen do not have genitals or, more likely, evolution has exclusively granted them the ability to suck their genitals inward, whenever they so choose. Also, he called me 'le petit prince' which I did not like.

By the time I was five, I had grown accustomed to leaping over piles of books to get from one room to the other. Later, I stopped leaping and simply walked over the books as if they were part of the floor, infinite little rectangular tiles each with its own design forming some random grand pattern which made sense only to my father. During my adolescent years, I developed the much more pronounced technique of kicking through the books and landing them halfway across the apartment.

Two large 'towering blocks of literature', as my father often referred to them inspired by Mr Mermier's comments, stood on either side of the apartment door as you walked in. Occasionally, I would stack the books on the floor over one another in such a way as to emulate a spaceship and pretend I was on my way to the moon. My sister would join in by spreading her little body across the floor and pretending to be a star, with ponytails.

'Grow up,' my father would say every time he passed by my spaceship, which is why I never got to the moon before bed.

Beside the kitchen, there was an entire room which no one apart from the members of my family had ever seen. It consisted of nothing but layer upon layer of old books, which presumably my father had once read. It was locked for most of the time anyway and my father carried the key around in his pocket. Whenever my father wished to find a book which he suspected was inside the room, he would hand my five-or-six-year-old sister a flashlight and toss her inside. For the most part, she enjoyed the task until she came across a dead cockroach, or worse, a living one, at which point she would begin to scream and my watchful father would reach across, grab my sister by the shirt and place her on the floor between his legs.

'They're harmless, Fara. They're even smaller than you are,' my father would say, before taking out a can of Bygone and emptying it inside the room.

I pushed the door open one Tuesday afternoon, having just returned from school, and found my father attempting to slowly pull a single book out from underneath one of his two 'towering blocks of literature'. The house was unusually empty as my mother and sister were not yet home. He ordered me to stand beneath one of them and support its weight while he made an attempt to withdraw the book. The moment he tugged forcefully at the book, perhaps out of frustration, both columns came tumbling over my head. Though we lived in a small apartment, the ceiling was undoubtedly high, and had one of the heavier hardcover volumes of *Encyclopedia Americana* fallen on my head, some serious injury might have resulted to my skull. None of them did. I would later survive two full-fledged wars and one tiny one which would last four whole days, but I consider this incident to be the most life-threatening, near-death experience I've ever been involved in.

I leaped and screamed and swore and cursed and was excused for all I'd done when my father saw that the books had landed on the floor and not on my head. He clutched my shoulder with one hand and kissed the top of my head twice.

'Not a word of this to your mother,' he said, as we picked the books up and began to stack them into two perfectly aligned columns.

THE OLDSMOBILE

Ours was an aging, white, second-hand American-made car called Barney. The night my father bought it from Payless Car Rental, he took me by the arm and told me all about how he intended to take us for a ride around Beirut in the morning. The next day, he gathered us around him, rubbed his hands together and presented us with the keys to the 1988 Oldsmobile.

My mother muttered something, put out her cigarette and left the room.

The car had been christened Barney by my sister who, having not yet seen the car, decided that it deserved a name.

My father's choice of cars had been notoriously unpopular. His tendency to buy used cars and, in this instance, overused cars resulted not only in regular visits to the overjoyed mechanic but also the occasional car accident and the increasingly frequent exchange of sharp words between my mother and father. For the most part, they pretended that we could not hear them in the back and, for the most part, we were glad to pretend that we could not. My sister, who at five was not as keen an observer of our silent agreement with our parents, would now and then stick her head in between the front seats in order to adjust the air conditioning or the radio, at which point my parents would briefly fall silent. They would resume only after the last of my sister's ponytail had withdrawn itself.

The neighbours did not like our car because it was too big and it took up too much parking space. My mother did not like it because it was white and would get dirty far too easily, and because my father had bought it without first discussing the matter with her. My sister did not like it because it was infested with little cockroaches that would, frequently, climb up her own little legs, and because it seemed to trigger an argument between my mother and father every time they set foot inside. My grandfather did not like it because the only thing worse than an American-made car is a second-hand American-made car and because he had explicitly advised my father not to buy this second-hand American-made car. My father, and the mechanic, were very fond of it.

Whenever my father was asked what he'd seen in this overgrown excuse for a car, he would inevitably ramble on about luxury.

'It's like driving a limousine,' my father would say, until my grandfather informed him that driving your own limousine was very much missing the point of owning one.

It was not long before my father came to view the car as an extension to our home. Soon my sister and I found ourselves sharing the back seat with all manner of paperback and hardcover books each seemingly intent on making it their own with little regard for leg space. The greyish cloth which had served to cover the inner ceiling of the car did so only half-heartedly, creating something of an air pocket between itself and the ceiling, and now hung low enough to scrape the head of almost anyone insisting upon sitting fully upright. The remaining side-view mirror was soon knocked off by a speeding motorcyclist and the rear-view mirror by my father's angry swipe at it. Driving Barney, as a result, involved an active effort on my sister's part, who would sit on top of a stack of books, with her back to my father, and inform him of oncoming cars when the occasion called for it. During the months of the winter, water from the rain would find its way through the cracks and seep into the seats. The smell of wet, crumpled old newspapers, which we often placed between ourselves and the damp seats, coupled with that of the seats themselves, and the equally damp books, became a constant over the brief but full life of Barney the car.

Every Sunday my father would pack us all, my mother, my sister, myself and the damp literature, into the car and drive us to his father's house. On the way there, to distract us from the challenges of the car ride, my father would tell us stories about Bilyasho, which is Italian for 'clown' and is spelt: *pagliaccio*. Bilyasho was a character who also featured heavily in the bedtime stories my father used to tell us. Bilyasho would get himself into all sorts of trouble, and then get himself out of it by some happenstance. He never meant anyone any harm, but he always brought it upon those closest to him. All the other characters admonished Bilyasho at the end of each story but then they forgave him and laughed about his latest misdemeanour.

My grandmother would welcome us with a smile and open arms. My grandfather with a nod. He had lost most of his hair and teeth. What little hair he did have, he would make sure to dye brown which he, to my grandmother's amusement, insisted was his original hair colour; a habit which my father picked up in his later years. His remaining teeth too were brown. His penchant for smoking over more years than he cared to count ensured that they would remain so. My grandfather's smiles were as sparse as his teeth and neither was a sight which I ever got used to seeing.

According to my father, the only time my grandfather is supposed to have smiled, prior to that Sunday, was when he won the lottery. My grandmother neither affirms nor denies this; nor does she claim to have seen him smile on their wedding day or on the birth of any of his ten children, especially the last one. Whenever I asked my father where all the lottery money had gone, he would shrug his shoulders and tell me to ask my grandfather. I never did.

My grandfather tells the story of how he woke up one morning with his old license plate number ingrained in his mind, how he wrote it down so as not to forget it, how he went around Beirut looking for the ticket with that same number, how he couldn't find it, how he could not find it, how he wished he could, how he sat down at Wimpy Café on Hamra Street for a cup of lemonade with mint, how he settled for a ticket with a single digit off, how he called on Abou Talal to help carry the briefcase full of cash across Ras Beirut, how Abou Talal had advised him against withdrawing the money all at once, how he ignored him, how hot it was that day, how you could tell because of the large sweat stain across Abou Talal's shirt, how humid, how like Beirut in the summer.

My father tells the story of how his father took him, the eldest, by the arm and told him all about the lottery ticket and his plan to return with a briefcase full of cash, and Abou Talal, how he was instructed not to tell anyone, how he ignored his father's instructions at the earliest opportunity and assembled all three of his brothers and all four of his sisters and his mother, how his father opened the door to find them all awaiting his arrival, how Abou Talal wiped his forehead and how my grandfather smiled.

'Where did all the lottery money go?' asked my sister one Sunday, looking up at my grandfather, as my parents and I made our way past the odd collection of twenty or so assorted relatives standing up to greet us.

My grandfather smiled. My father did too. Everyone else let out a nervous laugh, or pretended not to have heard.

When he first won the lottery, *An-Nahar* supposedly ran an article calling him 'the man who won whilst the nation lost'. It was the early seventies and Lebanon was on the verge of a civil war that would last for fifteen years. In that time period, my grandfather Adam travelled the world, sometimes disappearing for weeks and months on end but always returning home to his war-torn country, his faithful wife and his steadily increasing number of children. Once, after a particularly long absence, my father asked him why he'd taken so long to come back.

'Traffic,' answered Grandfather Adam, then he threw my young father the keys to his new Mercedes-Benz. He had driven it all the way from Frankfurt.

In the years after the war, when Grandfather Adam's lottery money had almost run out, he arranged to go on the holy Islamic pilgrimage to Mecca, referred to as Hajj. He had, thus far, not been particularly renowned for his religiosity; his casual approach to alcohol, bacon and extramarital sex being some of several reasons why he was not. Grandfather Adam never divulged his motives behind that trip, or any other. My father mused, years later at the funeral, that it was a result of some misplaced urge to express gratitude to someone for those fifteen or so years of joy. It was not lost on my father that gambling too, of which the lottery is a variation, is forbidden in Islam.

Upon returning from Hajj with a black eye, my grandfather is said to have serenaded everyone who had come to congratulate him on a successful pilgrimage with the tale of how he had been involved in a fight at the Stoning of the Devil ritual. A man had stoned him instead of the devil and he had stoned back. It was one of those rare occasions in which he had opened up about his travels at all.

'Where?' my sister asked again, still staring at him.

'Everywhere,' my grandfather said, leaning over to the sound of a much quieter room.

He placed both his hands on my sister's shoulders and told her – for what must have been the ninety-second time – the story of how he woke up one morning with his old license plate number ingrained in his mind, how he wrote it down so as not to forget it, how he went around Beirut looking for the ticket with that same number, how he couldn't find it, how he wished he could, how he could not find it, how he wished he could, how he sat down at Wimpy Café on Hamra Street for a cup of lemonade with mint, how he settled for a ticket with a single digit off, how he called on Abou Talal to help carry the briefcase full of cash across Ras Beirut, how Abou Talal had advised him against withdrawing the money all at once, how he ignored him, how hot it was that day, how he could tell because of the large sweat stain across Abou Talal's shirt, how humid, how like Beirut in the summer.

'And then?'

And then he told her about how, on his way back with Abou Talal, he had been ambushed by two Christian militiamen who demanded the briefcase, how he had been forced to fling the briefcase as far and as high as he could while he held them off, how the briefcase had burst open in the air, how random people on the street had danced to the tune of paper falling from the sky and how, for a brief moment, it was raining liras on Hamra Street.

When the story was over my grandmother had her head in her hands and my mother was standing over my sister with an arm around her. My father looked at me and shrugged his shoulders. These were fabrications, he knew. But he would not stop my grandfather in full flow.

'Go into the bedroom, and let the adults talk,' my father said, 'all of you.'

He meant the kids. Including myself, my sister and twelve or so of my forty-two cousins who happened to be present on the day, no doubt also dragged to the congregation by their parents. The teenagers hung out in one corner of my father's old bedroom, and mostly ignored us. The twenty-somethings were not really kids but they too were happy to vacate the living room upon my father's command. They lingered by the door. Looking back, I sometimes think it was a consciously symbolic gesture, an affirmation of their status as those to whom adulthood was just beyond the threshold of my father's old bedroom door. But we were kids and I suspect that it was more an expression of their dominion over the younger ones: us. They kept peering into the bedroom and rarely poked their head outside to see if the atmosphere was ripe for an induction into adulthood. Only the toddlers ignored my father, mostly because they could not understand him, or anyone for that matter, but also because there were no consequences to their actions. They picked their noses or made funny little noises, they clapped their hands together or cried or crawled around on the ground between this uncle's legs or past that aunt's pointy heels.

The rest of us occupied the bed. We were the youngest of the bunch in my father's old bedroom, but we were the loudest and most comfortable around a bed. This subgroup of cousins included my Aunt Sonia's two younger girls, Yara and Lara, and my Uncle Gamal's eldest daughter, Ferial. We were all about the same age, apart from my sister.

Yara crawled towards the centre of the bed. She craned her neck, surveying the room with caution before leaning in my direction.

'You know that it's made-up nonsense, don't you?' said Yara.

'They're stories,' said Lara, above her sister's shoulder, 'he spent all the money on alcohol and traveling around the world. He wasn't robbed. It never rained Liras on Hamra Street.'

'I don't believe you,' said my sister, who sat so close to the edge of the bed that when she spoke the sheer force of her words almost knocked her onto the floor.

'Suit yourself,' said Yara, 'I'm telling you the truth. He did not come back permanently until he was an old man.'

'Some say he even stole the money. Him and Abu Talal,' said Lara. 'Think about it. How many people actually win the lottery? What are the odds?'

'You're liars,' said my sister, 'both of you. And you're going to hell because that is where liars belong.'

'You know your mother is going to hell, right?' scoffed Yara.

'She means that in the best possible way,' said Lara.

'Of course,' said Yara.

'No, I don't,' I replied, 'who said?'

'*Your* mother is going to hell,' said my sister, which is what I should have said.

'Our mother says so, and everyone agrees,' said Yara.

She ignored my sister because she was small and even though we were all sat on the same bed, she could easily be pushed off, and the conversation carried on without her input.

'Why?'

'She's a Christian,' Lara whispered, presumably so as not to unintentionally spread Christianity around the room.

'I doubt it,' I said.

'No it's true, I swear,' said Yara, 'she is a Christian.'

'I know that. I meant I doubt that she would be sent to live in hell.'

'You're not sent to live in hell,' said Lara, leaning forward and pushing her fringe back, 'you have to die to go to hell.'

'Why would anyone want to do that?' asked my sister.

'That's a long way away,' I said, also ignoring my sister's words.

'That's what you say now,' said Yara, 'but life passes by in the blink of an eye.'

'Who said?'

'My mother.'

'Ferial agrees, don't you Ferial?' asked Yara.

'It does,' said Ferial.

Ferial was a shy girl who wore glasses and the frizzy, wild hair which so distinguished my sister, but with less character and more poise.

'No, I meant about their mother going to hell.'

'I am not sure about that. I mean, I don't mean to be rude, but have you asked anyone else apart from your mother about this?'

'It says so in the Koran,' said Lara.

She and Yara exchanged brief glances. One of them nodded to the other.

'Shut up. Tell them to shut up,' said my sister, glaring at me, 'why haven't you told them to shut up yet?'

'It says in the Koran that our mother is going to hell?' I asked.

'Not exactly.'

'It's implied,' says the other one.

My sister jumped up onto the bed, now barefoot, and formed the letter 'C' between her thumb and index finger. She swung her hand from Yara to Lara and back again. At first, I thought that she had meant to form a hook with her index finger but had simply forgotten, or failed, to tuck her thumb in. But she hadn't.

'Whatever you say goes back to you,' she said, waving the 'C' claw in their faces.

'That's ridiculous,' said Yara or Lara.

'Yes, look,' said my sister, illustrating the dynamics of the gesture, 'It flows like water under my finger then slides out my thumb and back onto you.'

'Shut up, and sit down,' said Lara or Yara.

'No,' shouted my sister, attracting the attention of the older cousins, 'you're ridiculous and you shut up and your mother is going to hell. That's how it works.'

There was audible tension in the room because now that the adults were invoked, they were bound to make an appearance at some point which would not end well for anyone caught in a compromising position in that instant.

'That's not how it works,' said Yara, her voice now also raised.

'It says so in the Koran.'

'It does not.'

'Tell your sister to shut up and sit down,' said Lara.

They were both standing on the bed now, in their matching bright red shoes. Yara pushed my sister off the bed. And I stood up and pushed Yara off the bed, and then Lara for good measure. I spotted Ferial silently edging herself towards the corner of the bed and gave her a slight shove too. I felt a large hand on my shoulder. I spun around and felt the knuckles of a fist connect with my face and a throbbing below my left eye which is unusual because usually you do not feel the throbbing until after the adrenaline wears off but I did. It was Yara and Lara's older teenage brother, Omar, who had intervened to put an end to the commotion.

'Didn't your mother teach you not to hit girls?' asked Omar.

I thought about trying a funny retort to do with her being too busy planning her journey to hell, but I could not formulate the sentence fast enough – I could not decide if she was booking accommodation or already packing – and my eye was throbbing, so I just lay on the floor and avoided making eye contact. Which was also what I did when my father burst into his old room to find me sprawled there with my hands pressed against my eye.

'Jesus-Mohammad-Christ,' said my father.

He pinched the bridge of his nose then walked out without asking any questions. He muttered something to my sister about putting her shoes on.

'Still driving that piece of shit?' shouted my grandfather after him, as we made our way past the same odd collection of twenty or so assorted relatives standing up to bid us goodbye.

My parents got into an argument on the way back. They argued about my grandfather, then about me and my black eye and my sister, then about the car. The fact that my father had managed to park the car almost ten minutes away from the house, for lack of suitably large parking space, further infuriated my mother.

Behind our house which was not a house, there was a garden which was not a garden. It was a parking lot reserved for the tenants of the apartment building; and it was my father who had first dubbed it a garden on account of a single tall jasmine tree surrounded by a small plot of soil in an ocean of cement. On Independence Day, as my sister approached her fifth birthday, the children in her nursery school were handed young cedar trees in little pots and told to take them home with them. Upon spotting my sister walk into the house, holding the cedar tree in one hand and my mother's hand in another, my father scooped her up and carried her to the garden. My mother, my sister and I observed as he dug a small hole in the soil with his hands and planted the cedar tree right by the jasmine one.

My mother then scolded my father for giving his daughter false hope. What the children in my sister's nursery school were not told is that cedar trees are not meant to survive and grow indoors, or anywhere by the coast for that matter, and that the potted plants would soon after proceed to wilt and then die.

'You told the boy he could become an astronaut,' my father said, dusting the soil off his hands and clothes.

'That is different,' my mother replied.

'I'm just giving the tree a fighting chance,' he said, as he rolled down his sleeves.

For a week afterwards, the highlight of my sister's day was checking on the cedar tree in the garden on her way back from school. It had not grown an inch but it hadn't died either. Then one day Madame Hafez, the landlord and fifth-floor neighbour, ripped the plant from the ground and tossed it in the trash can. She was not French but she had insisted upon being called Madame. Her husband Doctor Farhat, who winced every time someone referred to him as Monsieur Hafez, was the old man responsible for planting the jasmine tree in the then parking lot. In the elevator, he crouched down so that his eyes were level with my sister's and apologised on his absent wife's behalf. She adjusted her ponytail and nodded.

In order to park a car in the parking lot with the single Jasmine tree, one had to squeeze one's car through a narrow passageway which separated the adjacent building from our own. This was not ideal for most of the neighbours even with their German, Asian and French models, but for my father, with his 1988 Oldsmobile, it was impossible. His attempt to force the car through the narrow space between the two buildings is how the first side-view mirror was knocked off. My father continued to pay the obligatory parking fee for a spot which served only to remind him that his car was too big.

'I'll sell it,' my father proclaimed, as we made the rest of our way to the house on foot, 'I'll charge them extra for the literary entertainment.'

'It's not about the car,' my mother said.

'He's an old man, haneen, he's not going to change for you or me or anybody.'

'It's not about him, either.'

'I'm not moving to London to live off your sister's charity,' he said, slamming the steel gate to the building shut, 'we've already been through this.'

'Australia, then.'

'God damn Australia,' he shouted, 'and the hour in which it was created.'

A sharp exchange of words in the elevator was soon followed by a sharper exchange of words in the dining room, which in turn was followed by my mother's angry swipe at the stacks of newspapers on the dining room table. The *An-Nahars*, *Alhayats*, *Alanwars*, *Alsafirs* and *Aldiars* along with *A History of Arabia*, *Sometimes I Dance*, *Echoes of a Western Word*, *The Druze Revisited*, *My Beirut Then*, etc. flew across the room as my mother stormed out of it. My father knocked the remainder of them onto the floor, flung the door open and left the apartment. My sister and I were no longer in the back seat of the car pretending not to listen.

For some time afterwards, my sister and I sat in silence. Then she stood up, launched herself towards the newspapers on the floor, and began kicking them, throwing them in the air, leaping, snatching at them as they, now liras, now Yaras,

now Laras and now Madame Hafez's non-French face, fell
to the floor again. She did this until she could not bear to
stand, then she stretched her body across the floor and I
stretched mine alongside hers.

MOTHER AND FATHER

As my sister, my mother and I sat around in a circle crammed inside a single bathroom, my father stood over us, cross-armed, listening intently to the sound of bombs going off in the distance. We could measure their proximity, my sister and I, by the intensity of the expression across my father's face. A cringe meant that it would land somewhere else, on someone else's house, on someone else's family. It was when my father looked up that we feared the worst. I could never quite tell whether he would look up expectantly or whether he would do so in order to better hide his facial expression from us. There was also the relatively insignificant fact that when the shelling dragged on for hours, the sensation of fear was inevitably replaced by the unbridled urge to go and shit or pee or excrete desperately unwanted wastes. Whenever a bomb went off somewhere very far away, he would look down at us and smile and ask us about school and deadlines and essays and football and literature and such, mindful of our need to go.

It was the war of '67 or '82 or '00 or '06 and Israel and Lebanon were at it again. I, like my father before me and his father before him, was crouched inside the safest room in the house beside my family and hoping to God that no RPG rocket or bomb would land on my home. The last man to hold a gun for war in our family was my great-grandfather Samiir who fought for the French army during the mandate. His medals of honour are a family heirloom, then in possession of my father. Upon winning the war, the French offered my great-grandfather the French passport and nationality, which he accepted. For a brief period of time I was an as yet unborn Frenchman, then Lebanon got its independence and my great grandfather opted to burn the French passport in celebration.

On a routine night within the walls of the bathroom, my mother looked over at my father and then at me.

'You're lucky,' she said, as mothers almost inevitably will, 'some writers spend their entire lives looking for inspiration. You're hiding from it in the bathroom.'

I wanted to shout back, to say that I never wanted to be a writer, to ask whether she was suggesting I stand on the balcony and let inspiration and stray bullets hit me in their stride, to exclaim that there was probably infinitely more inspiration in space than there ever would be in a tiny old bathroom in Beirut. But I didn't, because when you're hiding from death, you worry about him overhearing you saying nasty things to your family, and then interfering to stop the brawl.

'I want to go,' I said to anyone who would listen.

'Go where?' my mother asked.

'There,' I said, pointing to the toilet seat.

'Hold it in, you're a man,' my father scowled.

'I can't,' I said, but I did. I held it in for two hours.

'You can do anything you set your mind to,' my mother said.

'But I can't,' I said, now almost pleadingly. But I did, I held it in for another hour.

'Your little sister isn't nagging as much as you are,' my father said.

Until finally, after five hours, I let go. No man ever remembers the good old days when, as an infant, he would shit himself daily. If he did remember, he would be infinitely more modest.

'Jesus-Mohammad-Christ,' my father said, looking at my mother in disbelief, 'your son just shit himself.'

'What have you done?' my mother asked in a whisper.

Once the first tear rolled down my cheek, there was nothing I could do about the rest.

'I think I'd rather be out there,' my father said, cringing.

'Leave him alone,' my sister shouted, clenching her fists.

'It's alright,' my mother said softly, wiping the tears from her face and mine, 'it happens.'

A flat-footed Arab astronaut is one thing, but a flat-footed Arab astronaut who once shit himself is an entirely different prospect.

At that moment, my father looked up; both my sister and I ducked in anticipation. It was the closest one yet. We later learned that the bomb had landed on the building adjacent to our own. Our bedroom window had shattered completely and shards of glass could be found on our beds.

When the shelling stopped my mother took out the broom and began to dust the glass off the beds.

'I just cleaned those windows, you sons of bitches,' my mother shouted at the top of her voice.

It was an hour or so before we'd tidied up the house and replaced the glass with scotch tape. I put on my best clothes and followed my mother around the apartment, attempting to make myself useful.

My sister and I heard repeated banging coming from the halls so we rushed there in time to see my father's attempt to knock down Monsieur Mermier's door fail miserably.

'He won't answer,' he said, more to himself than to us, 'I've been knocking on his door for the past ten minutes.'

Monsieur Mermier had been dead for more than an hour. The debris from the adjacent building had rebounded into his living room and there was nothing we could have done about it. The neighbours, all of the neighbours from the first floor to the fifth floor, gathered inside Monsieur Mermier's apartment, not that any of them had known him very well while he was still alive. Some of them called the ambulance, some of them mopped the floor, some of them picked up the broken shards of wood and glass and placed them in a pile beside the garbage bin, but most of them just stood by the door and cried.

'He was so young,' one large woman said, in between sobs.

'Not that young,' my sister interjected, to the sound of one or two chuckles and a few odd stares.

'Young enough,' the large woman replied.

'Young enough for what?' my sister asked, only to be ignored.

'Was he Muslim or Christian?' enquired the large woman.

'He was French Chafeeka, what do you think?' said a much shorter and stouter woman.

My father grabbed me by the arm and pulled me to the kitchen. He shut the door behind us and locked it. For a moment I thought he was about to take out his black leather belt and lecture me on the importance of restraint and maintaining one's composure. But he didn't. He took out his bottle of Arak and poured us a shot each.

'To Monsieur Mermier,' he said, raising his glass.

Many years later, long after I'd left Lebanon to pursue a higher education in London, my father would write a heartfelt article in *An-Nahar* newspaper. It would be his final article before he retired.

'I curse the country,' he would write, 'I curse the country that bid our children farewell with a smile across its face and told them to never return. I curse the country that presented our children with two alternatives: death or immigration and instructed them to pick between the two. I curse the country that forced its parents to send their children to outer space, or worse Europe, and wave silently from afar. I curse the country that gave our children water but no future, soil but no belief, light but no hope. I curse the country that stripped our children of their parents, and us of them. I curse the country that made fools of us all and led us to believe that we would grow old watching our sons and daughters rise to greater heights amongst their fellow countrymen. I curse the country that robbed me of my afternoon Arak with my son. I curse the country that deprived me of the sight of his wispy beard slowly maturing into one which resembles my own. I curse the country that resigned my wife and I to that comfortable couch in the living room, staring past broken shards of glass into the empty void that is tomorrow. I curse the country, mother and father.'

He passed away not long after that but by then my father had suffered through the untimely demise of his upstart publishing house, a severe, unwarranted beating at the hands of militiamen, and the sudden gratuitous disappearance of a cat called Ninnette.

THE MACARENA

There is an article which my father wrote several years before I was born and which my mother kept hidden away from the dust in her table of drawers. She showed it to me as soon as she believed I was capable of appreciating it. Every so often I would forget about it, and my mother would produce it again; a little older, a little more fragile, but still readable. In it, my father claims that he only wants three things out of life: a book to carry his name, a tree to carry his seed, and a child to carry him when he can no longer carry himself.

A car never came into it.

We awoke the morning after Monsieur Mermier's death to find the Oldsmobile riddled with bullets and littered with broken glass and heavily punctured books and newspapers. My father stood before it scratching his ear, first with his thumbnail then with the car keys, and smiling. That was the closest Barney would ever get to a eulogy; my mother shaking her head and lighting cigarettes, my sister and I inspecting the bullet holes and my father scratching his ear.

As the tow truck was too large to squeeze into an already narrow street lined with well-washed cars on either side, Barney stayed. It soon became a landmark, as well as an intermittent home for a brown street cat with a collar, which my father named Ninnette after the porter's wife. Ninnette was a dark-haired, brown-eyed slender woman who wore a gold necklace around her neck and several gold bracelets around her wrist. She smiled back at anyone who did not ignore her.

Often I would find my father bent over in conversation with Ninnette, offering the cat a lick of his Cadbury Fruit and Nut bar, which he always kept hidden away in his coat pocket or in his back pocket if he happened not to be wearing a coat. Or else I would stumble upon leftovers from my mother's delicious stuffed zuchinni and vine leaves dish in the most curious of places such as underneath Dr. Farhat's blue Toyota or on top of the backup electric generator where she liked to perch herself during the cold winter months, and of course inside the Oldsmobile itself.

Such was the extent of the Oldsmobile's reputation, that residents of the same street would inform the Shawarma deliveryman, and other visitors, that they lived two buildings down from the old, white American. My sister was of the opinion that the street was not too far off being called the White American. It was true that the original, 'Sadat', so called after a former Egyptian president who briefly restored peace under dubious circumstances in the post Gamal Abdel Nasser era only to be assassinated by the Israelis or the Egyptians or God's will, was not a particularly popular name.

The porter, Saeed, who was also Egyptian and who would now and again beat both his sons and their mother, made a habit out of ringing the doorbell early in the morning, newspaper in hand, to ask my father whether today was the day that the White American would disappear forever. Saeed believed that he could turn a profit by getting my father to sell him the White American for cheap.

'Any news?' my father would ask, taking the *An-Nahar Daily* from Saeed's hands and sifting through it.

'Madame Farhat is complaining that the car hasn't been washed in a while,' said Saeed one morning in midweek, as my sister and I prepared for school.

'Then wash it,' my father replied, still going through the contents of the paper.

'But there are no windows and too many holes.'

'Shouldn't that make it easier?'

'Yes, Basha.'

'Basha' is an Ottoman term which Saeed reserved for any man who was not a porter. It means 'lord'.

'Anyone moving into that apartment?' my father asked, nudging his head in the direction of Monsieur Mermier's old home, without raising it to meet Saeed's eyes.

'Monsieur Mermier's belongings are still in there.'

'Yes.'

'I found this book in your American car,' said Saeed, scratching his chin and producing a tattered book from under his armpit, 'something about goats and reincarnation, it is a bit damp, but still readable.'

'Calves, not goats,' my father corrected. 'It is yours. Have it.'

In his early forties, my father developed an interest in the Druze, a peculiar religious minority which exist only in the mountains of Syria and Lebanon. The car, more than our home, contained remnants of that period of time when, to my father only, the Druze were all the rage. This fascination with the Druze seeped into the now increasingly enthralled porter who would seize every opportunity to learn more about them via the discarded literature of the White American. No one knew very much about the Druze and, it was said, the Druze did not know very much about themselves except that they believed in reincarnation and that they might learn more about their religion in the next life. Those who wrote books about the Druze devoted the vast majority of their books to dispelling myths about the Druze believers and their beliefs. *The Druze Story*, for instance, was written by a scholar, Elias Jabra, who had limited knowledge on the matter beyond what his brother had told him. The scholar's brother had shot and temporarily killed several members of the Druze community in the War of the Mountain between the Christians and the Druze in the eighties.

One such myth was that the Druze did not eat spinach because a holy calf once slipped on a pile of spinach leaves and broke its neck. Jabra had this to say on the subject: 'Most Druze would tell you that the slip is not the reason they refrained from eating spinach and that calves or goats for that matter are, as far as they know, not particularly holy. Some of them would even tell you that they do eat spinach, albeit in the same manner that a Hindu would eat beef, or a Muslim eat pork.'

A Druze classmate of mine, Basil – a rarity amongst the mostly Muslim and Christian students – would ask his mother to pack spinach and rice in his lunchbox every day, and every day his mother would. This went on for a month with Basil eating spinach and rice during the break and receiving a dirty look or two in the process. Until, finally, everyone proclaimed Basil a Druze atheist who did not believe in the holy goat.

During the lunar month of Ramadan, while my Muslim classmates fasted, Basil and I ate. While they thirsted, we drank. The Christians ate and drank too, of course. But they did not chew too loudly, nor burp, nor lick their fingers, nor soak their lips in burger sauce or mayonnaise, only their teeth, nor raise their heads to knock back a cold can of Pepsi on a hot sunny afternoon.

When the history teacher asked why Basil and I were not fasting, I said I was a Christian and Basil said he was a Druze. Ms Bache was a brunette who had dyed her hair blonde because it was turning white. Crow's feet had formed around her eyes which her choice of large, round glasses only served to highlight. She also wore a scarf around her neck at all times. No one knew what exactly was wrong with her neck.

'Are the Druze not supposed to fast?' asked Ms Bache in class.

Basil pushed out his lower lip and scratched his eyebrow in reply.

That month, Basil and I were invited to our first Iftar, the ceremonial stuffing of one's face at sunset to make up for all the hours of the day spent thinking about hot food and not eating it. It was another Mohammad who had invited us, a short white boy with freckles. His appearance gave the distinct impression that he was European, despite the fact that no one in his family had ventured outside of Lebanon except for his father's brief stint in England. Both his mother and father were very much olive-skinned and did not have a single freckle between them. As adoption is forbidden in Islam, everyone at school ruled this out immediately. They, instead, decided that Mohammad's grandmother was raped by a Crusader, a phrase which was often repeated to Mohammad whenever the occasion called for it. Mohammad's family had originated from the south, an area which was historically heavily populated with Crusaders. His insistence upon not inviting anyone who had claimed his grandmother was the rape-victim of a Crusader to Iftar reduced his guest list to three Muslims, a half-Christian and a Druze.

I told my parents that I was going to fast on the morning of the Iftar. My father had not yet received his newspaper from Saeed and was sat on the comfortable couch in the living room holding a book entitled *The Druze Revisited*. On one of the bookshelves behind my father, squeezed in between Emily Nasrallah's *Birds of September* and Youssef Saleme's *Yassin Had This to Say*, rested a framed photograph of him wearing his cap and gown and moustache. In the photograph my father is not smiling. A wrinkle parts his forehead and a dimple parts his chin. The photograph was the only one on display in the house. It was coloured and my father's tie was red.

Though my sister was very fond of this photograph, she wasn't allowed to pick it off the shelf because she was too young to carry glass around the house. I had memorised the titles of the two books either side of the photograph as I was often the one to return it to its rightful place after my sister had left her fingerprints all over the glass. When my mother caught on to this, she moved the photograph up a couple of shelves.

'I liked it better when you wanted to go to the moon,' said my father, flipping the page.

'I still do,' I said, in an attempt to sound defiant.

'Adam, I have no doubt that you can do anything you set your mind to,' my mother said as she tied my sister's shoelaces, 'but I'm making stuffed zucchini for lunch today.'

'Can I fast too?' asked my sister, looking up at my mother, who in turn glared at my father, who in turn glared at me.

'No,' my mother replied.

'Why not?'

'We'll discuss this again when you learn how to tie your own shoelaces.'

'Why does he get to fast?' asked my sister, pointing her small finger at me.

'He won't last 'til lunchtime,' said my father, now momentarily less interested in *The Druze Revisited*.

'Don't discourage him,' my mother said, furrowing her eyebrows.

The doorbell rang and my father opened the door to find Saeed holding the newspaper in one hand and a brown cat in the other.

'Any news?' my father asked, taking the *An-Nahar Daily* from Saeed's hands and sifting through it.

'I found this in your car, Basha,' he said, holding out the cat.

Ninnette purred possibly in anticipation of a slightly larger plate of stuffed zucchini and vine leaves than she was accustomed to, owing to the fact that I was still determined to fast.

'Take it back.'

'Of course, anything else?'

'Stop beating your wife.'

'Why, has she said anything?'

'She doesn't have to,' said my father, now reading through his own article.

'I'll ask her to keep her voice down.'

My mother insisted upon having a family meal around the dining room table in the afternoon, when my sister and I had arrived from school. This meant that my father and I had to clear the table of the newspapers which had once again found their way onto it. It also meant that my father had to carry one of the foldable balcony chairs into the dining room, as one of the original four dining room chairs had long since lost a leg. He then adjusted the TV set so that he could both see and hear *Basmet Elwatan* from the dining room. The smell of stuffed zucchini had filled the room. After a short-lived argument between my sister and my father over who got to sit at the head of the table, we eventually found a place for her on my father's lap. She soon tired of this and resigned herself to the empty seat to his right.

Though my mother remarked that I did not have to sit with them this time, as I was fasting, she insisted that this was how it was going to be from now on. It wasn't. The next time we would sit together around the dining room table would be Christmas, and the next time after that would be the following Christmas.

Over lunch, my father told us the story of his mother and how she would starve them during Ramadan.

'I begged her. I bargained. I said, "I'll only have one olive and a piece of flatbread, that's it." She made me fast for an additional hour, just for that.'

Then he asked me if I thought astronauts fasted on their way to the moon. And I said, I don't know. And my mother said, drop it. And my father said, they probably don't. And I said, why not. And my father said, because the sun doesn't set in space. And my mother said lunch was over. And my father said he wasn't done. And my mother told him to take out the folding chair to the balcony. And my father kicked the folding chair shut with his heel as he stood up, grabbed it with his right hand, chewed on his last bite of stuffed zucchini and launched the chair out of the balcony and into the air.

The chair hung for a moment, allowing my mother, my sister and I enough time to rush to the balcony and observe it in full flight. It landed on the roof of one of the few remaining Ottoman houses in Beirut, opposite our own building. Madame Hafez owned that house too, but it was inhabited by the grandson of one of the men who had fought for independence from the French. He was an old man who had refused to pay rent for some time. Madame Hafez/Farhat had decided to wait for him to die rather than enter into a battle about neglected rent payments.

'I'm proud of you,' said my mother as she dropped me off at Mohammad's place.

She said the incident with the flying foldable chair was not about me. She said it was because my father was afraid of confronting the possibility of something.

I reclined against the steel gate to Mohammad's building. Only a few patches of green remained to indicate that there had ever been any effort made to paint the rusted bars of metal which now guarded the entrance to the otherwise polished building.

'The possibility of what?' I asked.

Basil and the Muslims were already there, sitting around the dining room table. When the sun finally set, we ate pizza, from Pizza Hut. Basil told us he was glad the goat hadn't slipped on pizza. Mohammad's mother let out a high-pitched giggle and asked if he would like more. And I laughed.

Mohammad's mother laid out the prayer mats for us while we were eating and we all stepped onto them as soon as we were done. I imitated the motions: hands on stomach, hands to ears, knees on floor, head against floor and mumbled the words to 'Our Father Which Art in Heaven'. My maternal grandmother, Teta Mary, had taught me it. I was afraid to sleep in the dark and glad to have her somewhat coarse voice by my bedside, despite the fact that her sporadic attempts to unofficially baptise my sister and I with 'Holy Water' in my parents' absence often included a violent chase and generally ended in tears. Hers, not ours.

When my grandfather Nabil fell ill, many years ago, my grandmother made a pact with God. She promised that if he let her husband live for a few more years she would take a cab to Mount Harissa, climb, barefoot, up the long winding stairs leading to the holy statue of Virgin Mary, kneel before it, recite 'Our Father Which Art in Heaven' and kiss it. Having witnessed both her father and step father die of heart attacks, Teta Mary was determined not to let her husband go the same way. When my grandfather recovered from his heart attack my grandmother left him at the hospital, took a cab to Mount Harissa, climbed, barefoot, up the long winding stairs leading to the holy statue of Virgin Mary, knelt before it, put out her cigarette and kissed it. Then she lit another cigarette and recited the words to 'Our Father Which Art in Heaven'.

Basil stood on the prayer mat, hands in his pockets, while the rest of us knelt to the floor. For a one idle second, we were praying to the spinach-eating, holy-goat-denying, Druze boy from the mountains. While the rest of the boys pressed their pious foreheads against the floor, Basil turned around so that he now towered over his lesser classmates. He extended his arms to the side like that Christ the Redeemer statue except with the palms facing downwards. Mohammad's mother, who stood behind the newly minted Druze deity, blinked but did not say a word. She, Basil and I shared one private moment of unabashed blasphemy in a room full of velvet fabric and young boys in pursuit of higher spiritual ends. Then he decided that divinity was not for him, and found a place for himself on the velvet couch.

'It upsets my stomach,' he said, as Mohammad's mother looked on.

My mother was the first to pick me up. She stood by the door whilst I put on my raincoat and said goodbye to my friends and thanked Mohammad's mother for the pizza from Pizza Hut.

'He's a lovely boy,' said Mohammad's mother with one hand on my shoulder.

'Thank you.'

'That business with the other Mohammad. The punching and the slapping. I was sorry to hear about it. It was unfortunate,' said Mohammad's mother, pulling out a piece of paper from her pocket, 'we should be sticking together, you know.'

'Yes,' said my mother, squeezing my shoulder.

'I heard your husband had a bit of a confrontation with the principal.'

'You, know. Boys and their pride.'

'My husband was the same before he moved to London for a few years for his studies. He's a lot more patient these days. Like English men, almost.'

'Yes, of course,' said my mother, producing a smile which revealed her lower teeth.

It was a smile normally reserved for my father. It indicated that she was not happy but that she was not going to give him the satisfaction of knowing this. My father's response was to raise an eyebrow, scratch his moustache with his index finger and cough.

'I noticed Adam was a bit off with some of the steps during prayer.'

'The steps? Was he?' asked my mother, looking down at me.

'I could recommend a teacher who would rectify that immediately if you like.'

'I'm not sure that my husband would approve of leaving Adam alone with a stranger.'

'He's a good friend of the family,' said Mohammad's mother as she put the small piece of paper in my coat pocket.

'I think we'll be fine.'

As we made our way back home, my mother took the small piece of paper out from my pocket and tore it to smaller pieces.

'The next time that woman makes you pray in her house, you do the steps to the fucking Macarena,' she said, lighting a cigarette and throwing the torn pieces of paper behind her.

The folding chair was still resting on the Ottoman roof when my mother and I returned. The house was empty but for my sister, who was standing on the balcony above the remains of the photograph's broken frame.

'It wasn't me,' she said, 'I swear.'

That night we could hear Saeed shouting, raging, slamming doors shut, breaking glass, cursing God and his son and all the prophets whose names he could recall, and their mothers, and Ninnette. We could hear Ninnette too.

'Are there no men in this building?' her voice came from the garden.

My father shifted in his seat. My mother put her hand on his forearm.

'Enough,' said my mother.

From that balcony, you could see Ninnette and the folding chair and the jasmine tree. From the other, you could see the White American and a fraction of the Mediterranean Sea. When there was no electricity in Beirut, as was often the case, you could spot the sun set behind a haphazard collection of war-torn buildings and half-baked attempts at invincible skyscrapers, or hear the echoing sound of afternoon prayer or the hoarse voice of the grocer as he pushes his cart down an empty street every Sunday at five: 'I have carrots, *I have zucchini*, I have vine leaves, *I have zucchini*, I have parsley, *I have zucchini*,' and once, 'I have no one, *zucchini*, no one cares, *zucchini*, it's everyman for himself, *zucchini*.'

My father never attended a graduation ceremony. When he had completed his courses, he collected his certificate from the secretary's office. That year the Israeli army made it to the middle of Beirut, on land. He walked home through Hamra Street with his eyes closed and his certificate in his back pocket. He passed Wimpy Café where a Lebanese civilian had stood up, pushed his chair back, pointed his gun at an Israeli general's head and shot him as he sat there eating his burger. It was Ramadan, the day before Eid. It was hot and my father had not had anything to eat yet. He waited for the sun to set then he sat around the dinner table with his brothers and sisters and his mother, and he ate couscous. Uncle Gamal asked my father whether he would join him for the customary fireworks. My father shrugged. The photograph was my mother's idea. It was taken a few weeks after my sister was born.

'What's going to happen to the folding chair?' asked my sister, as my father walked us to school.

My father adjusted his newspaper. He produced a Cadbury Fruit and Nut out of his back pocket. It was melted and he had eaten half of it. He split the rest of the chocolate bar between my sister and me.

'What's going to happen to the chair?' asked my sister, licking her fingers.

I spat out the raisins and the nuts. Then my sister spat out the raisins and the nuts.

'You know that jasmine tree in the garden,' said my father, 'when you are my age, its branches will extend into the balcony and seal everything else from view.'

My sister and I returned home later that afternoon to find that the photograph had been restored to its rightful place on the shelf between Emily Nasrallah's *Birds of September* and Youssef Saleme's *Yassin Had This to Say*, and that Barney had disappeared forever. My father told us the story of how it had been applauded on its way out by all the inhabitants of Sadat Street, including Madame Hafez and the old man in the Ottoman house. My mother maintained that no such thing had happened. Not long after that, Ninnette too disappeared forever. She took her two sons with her, and Saeed started leaving the newspaper on the doorstep, as was the norm before Barney had made its temporary home on Sadat Street. It was years before my father spoke to him again, choosing instead to disregard the Egyptian even as he held the door open for us or offered to carry the groceries or take out the garbage. A few days later, my father spotted Saeed relieving me of my hefty school bag as I nudged open the gate to the building. He strode towards us, slamming the door to the lift shut behind him. My father reached for the school bag, snatching it off Saeed's shoulder and flinging it back onto mine. Then he barked something about books and burdens and illiterate men, which I can no longer piece together from memory. He did this as Saeed shuffled silently to the side, never once opening his mouth to explain that he was in fact literate, that the weight of books was no problem at all for his muscular back and that he hoped he would be reincarnated into a better man (for surely he was now a converted Druze due to my father and the White American).

Ninnette, the cat, lingered for a bit, like the smell of the damp literature, where the Oldsmobile had once been.

THE DON

Autumn, not spring, is my mother's favourite season. Quite apart from the fact that the leaves begin to fall or that the clouds take it upon themselves to put the sun in its place, my mother favours autumn because the English word itself contains the initials of all four members of our family including her own. When there was nothing to be done, my sister and I would joke about being reunited with our long-lost brother Usama. In the weeks after my grandmother's death, I would often find the *An-Nahar* open to the obituaries page. This I assumed was my mother's way of coping with her mother's death.

Teta's father was told by a witch doctor that her original name, Samiha, would bring bad luck upon the family. It was changed to 'Mariam'. Teta's father died of a heart attack soon after. She kept her new name and her friends at the orphanage referred to her as Mary. Palestine was under British occupation at the time and English names were in vogue.

Fadia, her mother, once brought stuffed zucchini and vine leaves to the Catholic orphanage in Haifa, for Teta and her sisters. Fadia could not afford to raise her daughters on her own but she could afford to cook them a meal every now and again, which she did in the hope that the warm food would compensate for her absence. The nuns in charge seized the food and said that they would distribute it equally amongst the girls of the entire orphanage. Teta's response was to start a lawless gang within the orphanage, comprising of her three younger sisters and two other girls. They called themselves the 'Zucchini Bandits' and it all lasted for one night. When, next morning, the nuns found the empty pots under the girls' beds, they chased them through the rooms of several innocent orphan girls who had been looking forward to a hot plate full of zucchini and vine leaves over lunch. Then Teta jumped on one of the beds, leapt through the window and was out of the orphanage. She ran barefoot through the streets of Haifa past a blur of street vendors and olive and cypress trees and shoe-shiners and faces she said she recognised later as those of her children and grandchildren and the familiar sound of bullets and that of waves crashing against the shores of her hometown and steamboats carrying her countrymen from its shores to those of Beirut and she knew that she would not live out her life in that town. She ran until she could no longer stand then she spread her body across the floor next to a church.

She awoke in her mother's arms.

'They were delicious,' said Teta, looking up at her mother.

Her mother was remarried to an Englishman, named David, who died in bed, also, of a heart attack. Some of the neighbours blamed Teta, because they too had heard the witch doctor's words, but most of them knew that the Englishman just could not handle Fadia. Teta had nothing to do with it this time.

To Fadia, there were only ever two countries: Haifa and non-Haifa. And Haifa was the larger of the two. She would live and die there, in the city she knew but could no longer recognise. Teta Mary and my grandfather left everything behind with Fadia. They did not take pictures, only a wooden chest adorned with fragments of seashells which contained some jewellery, official documents and a few items of clothing. It was only going to be for a short while, until things smooth over in Palestine. By the time the steamboat reached the shores of Beirut, they understood that they were never going back.

After my grandfather passed away, Teta was sent to live in Thirleby Road, in Victoria, London, with my Aunt Sarah and her English husband. They would regularly lose Teta and find her hours later ambling along the South Bank. She would not get very far but she insisted that if she walked long enough, she could smell the sea water. They drove her to Brighton once. My aunt said that was her favourite day. On the way back, my grandmother said that it reminded her of Haifa. My aunt smiled and placed her long and wiry hand in my uncle's, who smiled back without taking his eyes off the road. Then my aunt heard Teta Mary suppressing sobs. What's the matter? asked my aunt. That was a lie, said my grandmother. I can't remember Haifa. I cannot remember anything before that steamboat.

I mentioned to her over the phone that I did not want to die in Beirut like Monsieur Mermier and that I wanted to

travel to London, on my way to the moon. I said I would
visit and bring fresh zucchinis. She said that London is cold
and rainy, and that I would not like it anyway.

With both her parents now deceased, and her siblings all
living abroad, my mother's blood ties to Lebanon had been
reduced to three.

'I'm an orphan,' she had said after the funeral and
perhaps this preoccupation with the obituaries was her way
of making sure that she was not alone in being one.

Then I realised that my father too was fond of the
obituaries section, mainly because plenty of the articles in
there were his. Now in his mid-forties, he found himself
losing people he had considered to be pillars of his own
little piece of society. He wrote one about Sabah, a renowned
singer and actress, who with the aid of plastic surgeons and
increasingly younger partners, had fought time admirably
and lost on a technicality. The song in which she uttered
the lines: 'Where's Mahmoud? Where's Maarouf? Where's
Elias? And where's Hussien?' was meant to speak to the
pluralism of the country but was understood instead as a
tribute to her former husbands. There was another article
about Ibrahim the vagabond who roamed Hamra Street and
never asked for money, even declining to take it when it was
offered. He had appeared immediately after the war, but no
one, including himself, knew from where. It was said that
he was a tortured former captive of the Syrian regime or the
Israeli Mossad or Iran. When people asked him who he was,
he responded by debating the merits of communism versus
those of capitalism. In the end, capitalism always won and
he said, 'it's the worse of two evils'. Then he would pull at

his grey beard, in a calm sort of way, and walk away. Once, a barber called him in from the street and gave him a haircut. For weeks no one knew it was him until a news anchor covered the story: 'Ibrahim the vaga-Bond'. Ibrahim died in a rain storm on Hamra Street, the first to hit Beirut in many years. Everyone knew it was him.

I read one about my father's, and my own, former PE teacher who wore his shorts closer to his nipples than his knees and whose rough beard combined with the absence of hair elsewhere gave the impression of one whose head had been fitted the wrong side up. Don Amin, my father wrote, would offer one 'well done' a month and occasionally take it back if the recipient were to let him down in the future. The latter part was not true. I was not sure why my father saw it fit to include this minor deviation from the truth.

'It speaks to the essence of the man, who Don Amin was,' said my father.

'What about his cedars, and his chewing gum?' asked my sister.

'What about it?'

'He was always chewing gum,' she added, 'the only time he wasn't was when he screamed so hard at a boy in class that his gum fell out and the boy pissed himself.'

'Did he pick it back up?' asked my father.

'No, he stepped on it to make his point.'

Don Amin regularly volunteered this piece of advice to his male students: 'Bouncing a basketball is like masturbating, boys, except it's a ball not a stick and no one's watching to see whether you're doing it right.' He sounded like gravel on a dry Thursday afternoon.

The Don scared a number of boys out of puberty for a good few years with that lesson in technique. At the time, I understood it as a thinly veiled criticism of refereeing standards in the game. Then I came to see it as a critique of religious indoctrination. Recently, I've decided that neither interpretation speaks to the essence of the man.

He began teaching in an Italian school, which is where he got the title 'Don'. He started off as a History teacher who stood on tables and attempted to breathe life into dates and names.

'The borders of Lebanon were drawn by French and British children in crayon on a white piece of cardboard titled the "Middle East".'

Then he had a stroke and the doctor said that he had to get out more. He gave up the classroom for a whistle and a pair of trainers. This suited him well. Don Amin would stop other teachers in the hallway, between the lockers, the backpacks and the pimples, to discuss this student's turn of pace or that one's ability to read his or her opponent.

Much of what I knew about Don Amin, I had heard from my father. In his stories, Don Amin was regularly cast as an unwitting master of comedy, a man whose every word or deed was an unintentional attempt at meta-humour. I saw a lot of Don Amin in him and, in the years ahead, I would recall my father with chewing gum in his mouth and a whistle hanging around his neck.

My mother wasted no time in picking me up from school. She would stand outside the gates in her hooped, bluish-green, sleeveless shirt and loose black pants. She'd swing my backpack onto her shoulders and ask me about my day, my teachers and my grades as we walked home. My father asked about my day too. But he didn't carry my bag and he often arrived an hour or so late.

One Thursday afternoon, I watched the playground slowly empty down to the last student. Even Basil, whose parents were much older than mine and who Don Amin referred to as 'August rain', had been escorted home by his older brother. Beirut does not know rain in August.

'Is he always this late, your father, Gibran the pimp?' asked Don Amin, as he sat down on the ground next to me. The Don called my father Gibran after the renowned early twentieth-century Lebanese-American poet and writer, Gibran Khalil Gibran. He called my father pimp because he didn't like it when people were not on time.

'No, Don.'

'Don't cover for him,' he said, attempting to light his cigarette. 'He's a pimp for being late.'

'Yes, Don,' I said, now looking at my shoes, black leather with an achingly uncomfortable sole and thin laces.

'You need new shoes. Proper gym shoes.'

'My doctor says I have to wear these. For my flat feet.'

'Nonsense. Who's your podiatrist?'

'Dr. Takkoush.'

'I know him. He was my student. I know his dad too. He was also a doctor. A dick doctor, you know,' he paused to allow me a giggle, I did and he continued, 'I went to his clinic several years ago. Couldn't get it up, you won't understand now, but remember me when you're my age. You know what he asked me?'

'What?'

'He asked me if I had unresolved issues with my mother. I'm a man in his sixties literally standing there with his dick in his hands and he brings up my mother. God rest her soul,' said Don Amin, now banging his lighter against the wired fence behind us. 'Do you have a lighter on you?'

I took out a red lighter which I had hidden away in my Eastpak. My classmates and I had taken to playing with lighters during the break. The game entailed running one's fingers through the flames without getting them scorched or burnt. It beat getting slapped around by Muslims all over the playground. Basil also used the Don's to light his own cigarettes.

On the brick wall opposite the wired fence hung a framed portrait of the incumbent president, in a glass casing. A still fresh-faced, balding, green-eyed, broad-shouldered man, distinguished for his lack of a moustache or any facial hair whatsoever. He was only the second president to hold office after the civil war, and a former general in the army. He started off as a symbol of a functioning democracy. When he was told that he would have to move into the presidential palace, he refused, citing the palace's distance from the sea as the sole reason. He was an avid swimmer and his love of Beirut was tied in with his love for the sea. Then he moved into the presidential palace, overstayed his welcome and grew a moustache.

'You shouldn't have that,' said Don Amin, lighting his Cedars and tucking the lighter away in his shirt pocket. 'Anyway, the Takkoush boy was teased mercilessly for being the son of a dick doctor. I fended them off, the kids, as you would expect. But they kept coming back.'

'What happened then?'

'Nothing. The little pimps grew up,' he said, taking a puff of his Cedars like it was a Virginia Slims Menthol 120, 'and their little pimp worlds grew up with them.'

He fell silent.

'You hear that?'

'Hear what?'

'Nothing.'

I laughed because I had come to regard his words and his slight slur – which my father mimicked well – as the marks of a comic genius.

'What about now?'

'Not really.'

'The sound of time. Passing. Is your father going to compensate you?'

'For what?'

'For wasting your time like this.'

'I don't think so.'

I laughed again.

'It's a crime.'

'What is?'

'Wasting a young man's time like this. An old man like me has plenty of time. But youth has no time at all. It's a crime. Can you hear it now?'

'I don't think so.'

'The voice of time. Telling us that there's more. More time, more waiting, more words, more voices, more love, more traffic, more loud arguments, more slamming doors and laughter, and beautiful women and handsome men, more childish giggles and wrinkles, white hairs and milk teeth, more of the stuff of life. Can you hear anything still?'

I stopped laughing. I listened. And when he stopped speaking, there was an uncomfortable silence.

'Nothing,' I said.

'No truer word has ever been spoken,' he said, laughing.

I took pride in having made my father's comic genius laugh. I puffed out my cheeks and I rubbed my nose.

My father arrived soon after, his sleeves rolled up, his forehead dripping with sweat and his tie hanging loosely around his light blue shirt collar. Don Amin told him off for being late and for listening to Dr. Takkoush's advice about the black leather shoes.

'Didn't I tell you the story about his father, the dick doctor, and his obsession with mothers?'

He also called my father a pimp and the son of a pimp. He did this while smiling and embracing him. My father kissed the Don's bald head and gave it a light tap. Then Don Amin retold the story of Dr. Takkoush senior and his failed attempt at armchair psychology. The two men talked politics.

'He's a swimmer.'

'Let's hope he doesn't drown.'

They laughed.

'Are you considering rejoining the party? We could do with having you back. Frankly, I'm sick of the direction which Malik wants to take us in,' said the Don.

My father shook his head. Mr Malik was my Arabic teacher.

The Don lit another cigarette and gave me a wink, before returning the lighter to his pocket.

'Your son reminds me of you at his age. Margaret Thatcher told me that he wants to be an astronaut.'

Margaret Thatcher was Don Amin's nickname for Ms Iman. My father placed his hand on my shoulder. He ruffled my hair. He was unaccustomed to doing this and he immediately placed his hand back on my shoulder.

'You know how boys are,' he said. 'They want to fly to the moon before they can drive to the end of the street.'

'The Arab Armstrong,' said Don Amin, now fixing his stare on me. 'God knows we need some inspiration from somewhere.'

My father cracked his joke about NASA shoving a Hubble telescope up my ass before they let me ride a rocket to the moon. Don Amin did not seem to hear him and I basked in the silence which greeted my father's attempt at humour.

'Will you write my name on a moon rock?' he asked, after a minute or so.

I nodded. Aside from the fact that I had not the first clue what Don Amin's full name actually was, I did not understand why anyone would want their name written on a moon rock. But in that moment, I would have written Don Amin's name on my birth certificate if he had asked for it.

'They should call it Camel,' he continued, running his hand through his beard.

'Call what Camel?' asked my father.

'The space rocket. Camel One.'

I laughed because I liked the idea of riding a Camel to the moon. And my father laughed because Arabs and Camels do not belong on the moon.

That night I snuck out of the house and walked for half an hour to Ramlet AlBayda. It was the only public sandy shore left in Beirut, courtesy of the warlords who ran the country after the end of the civil war. The other bits had been either privatised or wiped out altogether in favour of a Movenpick, a Four Seasons or a Phoenicia. On one side of the Phoenicia stood the St. George Hotel, or what was left of it. The war had been particularly cruel to the St. George, perhaps because it was located at the heart of West Beirut, a predominantly Muslim part of the city. On the other side of the Phoenicia stood an abandoned, shell-pocked former Holiday Inn building known for its distinct view overlooking Beirut and, Grandfather Adam swore, parts of Nicosia. It was used during the war as an outpost for snipers in what my mother and father referred to as 'The Battle of the Hotels'. The Muslims fought the Christians, and the Christians fought the Muslims, and the Christians fought the Christians, and the Muslims fought the Muslims over the complete control of a hotel or two in the name of their respective gods who, in turns, forsook them and forgave them their sins. The Palestinians, the Syrians and the Israelis too contributed to the dirtying of the bedsheets. I held my breath, Beirut fell silent, and I heard the towering Holiday Inn building wheeze. And I heard Basil cough and swear.

'Two snipers. One king size bed,' said Basil, elbows dug securely in the sand and cigarette swinging up and down between his lips.

'A tale about love and war brought to you by the makers of *A Room with a View*.'

Basil chortled and dropped his Gauloises. He buried it in the sand then took another one out of the packet.

'My father smokes so many of these, he doesn't notice when entire packets go missing. He's a social smoker in the same way that you're an astronaut,' he said, offering me one and lighting his own.

'Later.'

'Yuri Gagarin doesn't smoke.'

'Who?'

'The first man to go into outer space. Yuri Gagarin. Russian Soviet.'

'I want to go to the moon,' I said, taking the now warmish Almaza from the plastic bag and popping open the bottle cap using Basil's lighter, 'tastes like piss.'

Almaza was the national beer before Lebanon was an independent country. There used to be this running ad on Tele Liban which featured the transparent green Almaza bottle on a table with a constantly changing background. It was my first lesson in history. 'I was here when you got your independence in '43, and we celebrated,' said a deep, reassuring, if slightly patronising, voice. 'I was here during the earthquake of '56, when Georgina Rizk was voted Miss World in '71, when you plunged the country into civil war and we hid, and when it was over and we celebrated. Whatever happens, we celebrate.' Heineken bought it not long after that.

'Get your own beer and lighter then,' said Basil, snatching both away from me and taking a sip of Almaza. 'What's on the moon anyway?'

'Not Beirut.'

'Not anything. It's a desert. Go to Saudi Arabia.'

This was not the first time a desert had been suggested to me as an alternative to the moon. My father had made a similar suggestion a number of years back, except instead of Saudi Arabia, he chose the Sahara. Basil ran his index finger through the flames of his lighter as we both lay on our backs looking up at the towering skyscrapers behind us. He did this more out of habit than for entertainment purposes.

'Or Dubai,' I said.

'What about Dubai?'

'It was a desert too, before all the skyscrapers.'

'You think the moon will be like Dubai?'

'No. I'm just saying Dubai was a desert.'

'Listen, habibi, when NASA gives you that application form, lead with this. '"Dear NASA,"' said Basil, now putting on a voice with a higher pitch than his own, '"the moon reminds me a bit of Dubai."'

I flicked a used needle away from my elbow and spread my arms out. Ramlet ElBayda, or White Sands, was littered with them.

'I didn't say that. It's not a desert.'

'What then?'

When I closed my eyes, I did not see Armstrong's moon landing or Sagan's *Cosmos*, Moore's *Atlas of the Universe* or Aldrin's *Reaching for the Moon*. I saw Saint-Exupery's Sahara Desert with the little prince. I saw Monsieur Mermier on asteroid B-612. I saw him watering the rose, cleaning out the volcanoes, pulling up the baobabs. I saw him holding the prince's sheep in a box and watching forty-four sunsets in one day.

'Asteroid B-612,' I said without looking at him.

I followed a beam of light as it guided boats to the old ports of Beirut, we breathed in the stench of dead fish and listened to the waves wash them ashore. This new lighthouse had been built recently after seaside residents complained that the beam of light from the old one would enter their bedrooms and keep them awake at night. It looked like a rocket. The old lighthouse, which was thinner and taller and cloaked in black and white hoops, was now too far away from the sea to effectively guide anyone.

Basil lay on the white sands, eyes closed and mouth open. As I pressed my knuckles against the sand, in an attempt to sit up, I heard laughter in between the waves.

'Mermaids,' said Basil with one eye now wide open.

Three Christian girls, the crosses around their necks glimmering in the moonlight, walked hand in hand towards us. They kicked at the waves and pushed and pulled at each other. The blonde one lost her balance and fell into the water.

'You've ruined my top, Christabelle,' she said.

'It's water. Get over it,' said Christabelle.

'She can't get over it,' shouted Basil in their direction, 'it's Gucci and Gabbana.'

The third one, who most resembled a mermaid with her wet hair, thin torso and wide hips, laughed with one hand on her mouth.

'It's Dolce and Gabbana,' said the blonde one, as the three girls approached us.

'That's what I said, isn't it Adam?'

I nodded.

'Look,' said Christabelle, 'they're little boys.'

In the light of the skyscrapers, the girls looked like women. The youngest of them, the mermaid, would have been about eighteen but even she had the glow of a woman about her as she stood over us.

'This one is a mute,' said the blonde, pointing her finger in my direction.

'He's not a mute,' said the mermaid, smiling, 'he's a late bloomer. Look at him.'

'That's right, he is,' said the blonde, 'you do things at your own pace, don't you?'

'I guess,' I said, now looking straight at them.

'Look at those eyelashes, Christa,' said the blonde, waiving her French manicured nails about, 'I'd kill to have those eyelashes. And those thick eyebrows.'

'He'll make a handsome one, once he grows into that face,' said the mermaid.

Basil took a sip of the piss-warm Almaza and the mermaid snatched the bottle away.

'It's bad for you,' she said, tipping the rest of the beer down her throat.

'And needles aren't?' said Christabelle, laughing through her full lips.

'This one's the real heartbreaker, aren't you?' said the blonde, now looking at Basil.

'There's only one way to find out,' said Basil, smiling without revealing his teeth.

All three women laughed at this. He had a knack for saying funny things at the right moment, or else for saying things in a way which made them sound funny at any given moment. The mermaid grabbed Basil by the wrist and led him to the edge of water. She jumped head first into a strong wave as it crashed against the shore, wrenching him forward. She reappeared splashing her tail against the waves and flicking her wet hair behind her, signalling for the girls to join in. They did, even the blonde. I stood there with my toes dug firmly into the sand. They swam away and I could barely make out their shapes in the moonlight.

'Christa,' I shouted, cupping my hands so that my voice would carry further, 'you're the most beautiful one.'

Basil dragged himself back to shore, coughing and wheezing. He was still a goat-worshiping mountain boy at heart and the sea did not agree with him.

'She's not,' said Basil, still coughing. 'What are you on about?' The phrase 'she's good but she's not mermaid good' became ever-present over the next few weeks. Basil and I randomly compared girls our age, who had no interest in talking to us, to the mermaid women at Ramlet ElBayda. We would remember details that were not there, like the running mascara on the mermaid's face or the wink she gave Basil. We talked about the blonde's wispy voice and we estimated that she was at least thirty-five because she'd dyed her hair blond and because they must have been partly white before she dyed them and that's why she did. On a school trip to Der ElKamar in the mountains of Lebanon, less than an hour away from Beirut, Estelle pinched both of us on our necks. Estelle pointed out that we were being sexist. She had developed this habit early on in life. Her mother had encouraged it at first because she believed it showed character. Then Estelle got very good at it.

'You're just annoyed that we didn't ask you to join us,' said Basil.

'Yes. Who would want to miss out on seeing mermaids?'

'You'd have scared them away with your feminism,' said Basil, and walked off.

I laughed and Estelle pinched my neck again.

She mumbled a retort in French which would have gone above Basil's head even if he had somehow acquired a passing command of the language – or nuance in any language.

Estelle had cheeks which belonged to a fuller face and a stare which belonged to her mother. It said, I'm better than you but it's not your fault. She too was French and it was, in some terrible way, almost fitting that she and her French mother would move into Monsieur Mermier's old apartment. She said that she had never met her father but that she knew he was Lebanese and handsome in that Mediterranean manner. She showed me the pictures she had of him and I said that he was handsome. Then she showed me pictures of her mother when she was young and I said that she was beautiful, and meant it.

Basil sauntered towards Moussa's Castle and we followed him in. The castle itself was unremarkable. It mostly exhibited old weapons and artillery, some of which were said to have been used by the former princes of Mount Lebanon, like Amir Basheer AlShahab and Amir Fakhereddine AlThani AlMaani. The latter, we were taught at school, had risen to such heights that he challenged the reign of the Ottoman Empire and almost brought the Sultan to his knees. The Ottomans have no record of Fakhereddine. Historians estimate that he was at best a prince over Der ElKamar and a couple of other neighbouring towns and at worst a glorified tax collector.

Ms Iman walked behind the students and Don Amin led the way alongside an old man with a white beard and long, frail white hair.

'Prince Fakhereddine himself,' said Estelle, to sniggers from Basil and myself.

When we got to a wax figure of a boy being whipped by his teacher in front of a class full of other wax boys, the old man turned around.

'This is me,' he said, pointing his quivering index finger at the wax figure of the boy, 'I'm Moussa. Welcome to my castle. Any questions?'

He spoke of how it had taken him sixty years to build it single-handedly and how no one believed he could do it.

'Best sixty years of my life.'

Moussa explained that he had built the castle for the woman he loved and that she had rejected him and went off with a richer man. He told us about his teacher who had whipped him in front of the other boys for drawing a picture of his castle in class instead of focusing on the maths lesson. Then he recounted the story of his trip to his teacher's house, when he had finished building the castle. All those things he had wanted to say to him, all the images that returned to his mind when he knocked on the door. The teacher had passed away many years before.

'There's hope for you yet, Najjar,' said Don Amin, raising his eyebrows and chewing on his Chicklets.

'The opposite of ignorance is not knowledge, boys and girls,' said Moussa, with a smirk materialising across his face, 'it is innovation.'

His words were a rehearsed piece of theatre but they were no less genuine for it.

'Who's that?' asked Estelle, gesturing in the direction of another wax boy with his face pressed against the wall in the corner of the class.

'That's Moussa's distant cousin, Moustafa,' said Don Amin, 'he wanted to build a skyscraper. It didn't work out quite so well.'

The next day Don Amin did not show up to class. For a week, Ms Iman told us that he was in the mountains with his family, because that was where he was from. Then Serene, a Druze girl, gathered us around her during break. She stood beneath the president's portrait and spoke in a whisper such that those of us at the back heard nothing and those of us in the front heard nothing because those of us at the back kept asking Serene to raise her voice.

'There is something you should know,' she said, with one eye on the door leading to the playground.

'What?' asked Basil.

'It's about the Don,' she said, pausing for effect. 'That story the teachers and parents and journalists wanted us to know is not true. He didn't die of a stroke.'

'Raise your voice,' came the voice of a pubescent boy at the back.

The smell of damp socks wafted through the crowd and disappeared once he had lowered his arms. This was not news. We had long since figured out that the Don was not still in Der ElKamar.

'How did he die?' asked Nadia.

'He died of suicide,' whispered Serene, whose thick and full eyebrows moved to the rhythm of her speech.

'Who?' shouted a tall girl behind me.

She smelled of aluminium foil and her mother's perfume.

'The Don,' shouted damp socks.

'You mean he killed himself,' said Estelle.

'Yes,' said Serene, now holding my gaze. 'He jumped off the rooftop of his building in Rawche.'

'Not the Rawche Rock?' asked damp socks.

'It's possible.'

The rusty steel fence which surrounded the school was chest high. A security guard whose name everyone knew but had forgotten patrolled the perimeter of the fence. He had a deep voice which he often used to scare us away from the fence or to hold long, and audible, rants about the necessity of fences.

'Nonsense,' shouted a Mohammad sitting on the green bench to Serene's left. There was always one or two within earshot.

'How do you know this?' I asked.

'The neighbours,' she said, 'but you can't tell anyone.'

'We won't,' said Basil.

*

'Did you know that Don Amin jumped off a rooftop?' I asked my father, as he sat at the dinner table scribbling on a blank piece of paper.

My mother was out visiting Grandmother Mary's grave. At first, it was every other weekend. Then it was once a month. Then it was on Mother's Day. Then it was every other Mother's Day.

'I'm writing an article about him now,' he said, without looking up. 'It wasn't a rooftop. It was the Rawche Rock.'

'You could've told me,' I said, standing behind him.

'Why? Do you have a monopoly on dead people?'

'No, but it would've been nice to know.'

'Nice to know that your gym teacher committed suicide?' he asked, holding his pen still for a moment.

'Yes,' I said, refusing to back down.

'I'll tell you when the next one jumps off a building or a rock,' said my father, having resumed writing. 'Don't tell your sister.'

I told my sister.

'Is it true?' asked my sister, tugging at my father's shirt.

'That what?'

'That he killed himself.'

'Who killed himself?' asked my father, postponing the inevitable.

'Don Amin.'

'Who said he killed himself?'

'Adam told me.'

'What are you deaf?' asked my father, putting his pen down and turning to look at me. 'Or just an ass?'

'Don't call him deaf,' said my sister.

'I'll call him whatever I want to call him. He's my son,' said my father, flicking through the papers in front of him, 'and you're my daughter. Don't tell me what I can and cannot do.'

Your children are not yours. They are the sons and daughters of life's longing for itself. Gibran Khalil Gibran said something like that. I knew that quote by heart at the time. Mr Malik, the Arabic teacher, had drilled it into our heads. And I would've said it. Except Gibran seemed wasted on my father.

'What are you trying to protect her from?' I asked my father, standing to his right with my sister's head barely visible above the dinner table from the other side.

'I don't have to tell you.'

'A man was blown to pieces next door. You think it will terrify her to find out that her gym teacher threw himself off the balcony?'

'We live in a country where people die in a variety of ways,' he said, scratching his chin with the tip of the pen, 'what would you have me do about it?'

'Why did he do it?' I asked, after a moment of silence.

I had believed in the Don in the same way that he had believed in my camel ride to the moon. It diminished me to know that his words would forever have to stand alone without the man who had uttered them. It was a sentiment which, by reading his article, I found my father shared. Or maybe it was one which I had arrived to after reading my father's article.

'He was too busy throwing himself off the rock to tell me,' said my father, crossing a line out.

'Why did he do it?' asked my sister, raising her right hand in the air and moving her wrist in such a way that it appeared she was attempting to change the light bulb. 'It's stupid. He's a stupid man. He throws his life away. And poor Monsieur Mermier dies trying to stay alive.'

My sister narrowed her eyes and grew a few centimetres. My father looked at me as if to confirm that the minor growth spurt was not some optical illusion performed by a little girl; then he turned his head towards her.

As she changed the light bulb, my sister stomped her right foot, each time edging her little body closer to my father's. There was my father sitting at the dining room table with his pen in his hand writing an article about a deceased man, and there was my sister doing the traditional Lebanese Dabke. She danced and stomped her feet and twirled her wrist until her little chest pressed against my father's elbow.

'It's not for you to judge the dead, *Fara*,' said my father, placing his hands under her armpits and lifting her onto his lap.

'Are you going to mention it in the article?' I asked.

I meant my Camel ride to the moon.

'Why would I do that?' asked my father. 'It doesn't speak to the essence of the man.'

A smile flickered across my father's face as he said this. Then, with one hand around my sister, he added, or removed, or modified a line in his article, and I knew then not to ask any more questions.

The official cause of death was a stroke. Don Amin died of a stroke at his home, in his armchair, with his silver whistle hanging around his neck.

In his article about the Don, my father wrote that 'the words of a dead man echo throughout space because they have lost their source, because they are homeless, orphans and widowers all at once' and that 'the great among us leave that empty space behind them which makes their words echo louder'. He never mentioned the actual words themselves except to say that the Don was capable of bestowing a 'well done' upon those who had done well.

In my room, I told my sister about the day I beat up Mohammad, the sectarian. I told her about Ms Iman.

'What do you want to be when you grow up?'

I told her about the pretend whipping I received afterwards.

'But it seemed so real. I was outside listening,' said my sister, eyebrows raised.

'It wasn't.'

I went into my father's room, searched for the black leather belt and dragged it behind me into my room. My sister jumped, and I lashed against the bedsheets either side of her.

Every time she landed on the bed she would leap higher and laugh louder.

'Again!' she shouted, inciting me to lash the bedsheets harder.

There was a moment when she was so high up in the air that I was sure she would refuse to come down.

'Come down, darling,' my mother would say.

'Come down, *Fara,*' my father would say.

'Come down, you indiscriminate lump of mass,' gravity would say.

'No,' she would reply, ponytails rising, 'not until you apologise.'

We did this for some time, I lashed and she laughed and leapt in the air and her ponytails bounced and twirled, until I landed one of my lashes on her left arm. My sister then clutched her left arm in midair causing her to lose balance and land with her head against the edge of the bed.

My father burst into the room still clutching his pen. He knocked the belt out of my hand, picked up my sister and lifted her over his shoulder.

'What's wrong with you?' asked my father, holding my unconscious sister and kicking the belt under the bed.

I sat in the bright white waiting room at the hospital. I watched as my mother rushed through the door and into the emergency room. I could see my father pacing and angrily gesturing in my direction. I could see my mother grab his wrist and push it downward. I could see my mother kissing my sister and placing her arms around her small body. I could see my mother walk in my direction, crouch beside me and tuck her skirt under her legs.

'I know you were just playing,' she said, and I felt my eyes burn and the room blur.

I was six when they brought my sister home from the hospital. My father said, 'She's your responsibility, Adam', then he held her two small hands together in his and made her clap.

'Yes,' I said.

'Your sister is fine.'

'Yes.'

She was speaking to me as if I were half my age but I didn't mind. My father stood cross-armed with his back to us, conversing with the doctor and sharing an anecdote or two. I walked past my mother and into the emergency room where my father was.

'It was an accident,' I shouted, standing close behind him.

'Jesus-Mohammad-Christ,' said Father, turning around

with force. His elbow smacked against my eyebrow as he did so and warm blood trickled down my eye.

I did not feel the cut on my eyebrow and had I sustained it in the playground, I probably would have ignored it and kept playing. My mother held my head in her arms as the doctor applied Fucidin on my eyebrow. My sister, who had cried in intervals up to that point, stopped to observe. And a cluster of doctors came in anticipating a brawl of some sort which did not happen. When I blinked tears ran down my cheek, so I stopped blinking.

'When I die, cry over my dead body,' said my father. It was a common enough Lebanese expression but it seemed personal under the circumstances.

'Two kids in one day, Najjar,' said the doctor, as he applied Fucidin to my eyebrow. 'That's not very good parenting, even for a Lebanese father.'

YURI GAGARIN

A couple of days later my sister returned from school with her cast signed. She had fractured her wrist too but it took the doctors a while to realise this, as she was crying and would not properly communicate with them. Most of her classmates wrote 'get well soon' or 'you rock' or 'ponytail madness', in English, with a smiley face or heart and a signature underneath. Except for this one kid who wrote the digits '112' and signed it as 'the police'. This my father seemed to find more outwardly funny than the best episodes of *Basmeet ElWatan*.

'Jesus-Mohammad-Christ,' he gasped, between laughs, 'Jesus-Mohammad-Christ.'

My mother did not find this at all amusing and she pressed my sister for details of the boy, or girl, who had done this, as we all sat around the TV set.

'What's his name?'

'I don't know.'

'What did he look like?'

'I don't remember.'

'You do. What did he look like?'

My sister held off for longer than I expected. Then she came clean and told my mother that it wasn't a kid at all who had signed her cast but her English teacher, Mr David Aston. Mr Aston was a fifty-something Englishman from Southampton with hair parted to the right and eyebrows that stubbornly refused to yield to either side. He would speak very slowly and had come to Beirut in order to reignite his love life or inspire young Lebanese students, or both. He and Don Amin did not get along. The Don called him Mr Bean, which as far as the Don's nicknames go, was not particularly his best. Mr Aston did look a bit like Rowan Atkinson, with his long, lanky arms and gangly figure, but it wouldn't have made a difference to the Don if he were round and short. To the Don, every Englishman was Mr Bean and every couple of Americans were Dumb and Dumber.

'It is funny, a bit, that you think policemen even care about kids getting punished,' said my father, now standing in front of Mr Aston's class, flanked by my mother, my sister and myself and addressing the Englishman.

'I'm not sure what you're talking about,' said Mr Aston. 'If you're referring to the digits on your daughter's cast, then I think we should go inside.'

We all followed Mr Aston inside the classroom and my sister sat in her assigned seat.

'You don't have to sit there now,' said my father.

My sister looked at Mr Aston and he nodded.

'This is not London,' said my father. He had the habit of referring to the whole of Great Britain as London, which got worse with age. Much later, he would ask me what the weather was like in London while I was making my way across Grafton Street in Dublin. This was not a habit that was exclusive to my father.

'I am well aware of that,' said the Englishman, adjusting his necktie. 'Please take a seat.' It was a thin, red wool tie that looked as if it had been snipped at the end.

Mr Malik, the Arabic teacher, paused for a moment by the door on his way from class to his office. My father almost seemed to forget the Englishman and focused his eyes solely on the round, limping figure by the doorway. My mother offered Mr Malik a brief wave and a fleeting smile. Her smile was further emphasised by her dimples, which gave the impression of quotation marks on either side of her face. Far from making the smile itself less sincere as quotation marks sometimes do, they made it loud, almost like a smile which you could hear, one with a voice and intonation. Mr Malik nodded back and limped on.

'We'll stand,' said my father, slightly taken aback by the sudden appearance of the Arabic teacher, as my mother sat down.

In hindsight, it was obvious that some complicated history existed between my father, my mother and Mr Malik. Though back then I simply assumed, that like me and my classmates, my father had found the sight of the man to be strikingly grotesque.

'I'm not accusing anyone of anything, Mr Najjar.'

'You think I beat my wife and children,' said my father, tearing his eyes away from the now empty doorway.

'Nobody said anything about Mrs. Najjar.'

'My children then.'

'I didn't say that,' said Mr Aston, breathing in. 'It might be best for the children to wait outside.'

'They stay. Why did you write the police's number on her cast then?'

'My concern,' said Mr Aston, sneaking a glance at my eyebrow, 'is for my students' well-being.'

'Her well-being is well,' said my father, 'end of story.' He only ended stories early when speaking in English.

'Mr Aston, you seem to have misread the situation,' said my mother, looking calmly at the man, 'my husband does not beat up the children. And even if he did, the police wouldn't do anything about it.'

'I'm sure that is the case. I won't pretend to know more about Lebanon than the Lebanese.'

'You're English, Mr Aston, aren't you?'

'Yes, I am,' he said, pleased to be moving away from the subject.

'Then why haven't you gone through the standard procedures for a case like this?'

'Truth be told, I have,' said Mr Aston, smiling for the first time. 'Ms Iman kept saying she'd call you in, but she never did.'

My father ran the palm of his hand across his face.

'I'll take it from here,' said Ms Iman, as Mr Aston left her office and shut the door behind him.

'He seems like a good man, if a bit odd,' said my mother, adjusting her position in the black leather armchair.

My sister and I sat in the centre, with my father to my left and my mother at the other end. The office had remained as it had been, down to the patterns on the Persian carpets, except for a new water cooler and a calendar in the shape of a cedar tree behind Ms Iman's desk which read: 'Courtesy of Plaza Pharmacy.'

'He was a pastor before he decided to do this.'

'I can understand your hesitation in hiring him,' said my father, leaning back.

I smiled at Ms Iman. I did not mind being in her office when I was not on trial for blasphemy or thuggery. She smiled back. I expected to be offered a soft drink or orange juice. I was not.

'My condolences for the death of Don Amin. We all miss him here. I know you two were close,' said Ms Iman, ignoring my father's remarks, 'I read your article in *An-Nahar*.'

'Yes,' said my father, scratching his moustache, 'thank you.'

'The two of them look like they've been in a car accident,' said Ms Iman, pointing to my sister's state and my eyebrow.

'We don't own a car anymore,' said my sister.

'The Israelis,' I said, looking from my mother to my father and back again.

'The truth is my son and daughter were playing in the bedroom. He unintentionally lashed the belt at her arm and she hit her head against the edge of the bed. Then my husband accidently elbowed him in the face, around the eyebrow,' said my mother.

'Can I have some water?' I asked.

'Do you still want to be an astronaut?' asked Ms Iman, smiling again and looking at me through her eyeglasses. She handed me a cold cup of water. Ms Iman looked the same, except now she had developed more lines around her eyes and her cheekbones had become pronounced. This was a further attempt to be taken more seriously by her male colleagues.

'Yes,' I nodded.

She paused for a long second, and in that moment I heard her say: 'And do you think fathers of astronauts elbow them in the face?'

'How are you getting on in physics and chemistry?'

I shrugged and placed my fingers over my eyebrow. I wasn't getting on at all in physics and chemistry. Our teacher, Mr Abu Alam, did not have a high opinion of Basil or myself.

'Do you understand, you two?' he would ask.

'Yes.'

'You understand the soles of my highlander flip-flops. That's what you understand.'

Occasionally, he would take his highlanders off, for laughs, and wave them at us in class, using them to point to a Lambda on the whiteboard or a Mole on the chalkboard at the other end. Then he would drop them to the floor and flick them the right side up using his toe. It became something of a ritual.

'If he keeps this up, I'm going to have to ship him back to England,' said Ms Iman.

'Really?' asked my mother.

'He's managed to convince the biology teacher that it is her duty to cover that chapter on evolution, even though it wasn't included in the official curriculum.'

'He seems like an alright pastor to me,' said my father, putting his hands together.

'He's not a pastor,' said Ms Iman. 'He's a teacher.'

*

The biology teacher, Ms Mayssa, was a woman on a mission. Like Sabah, and my great-grandmother Fadia, she had been married a number of times. The first two died of a stroke and a sniper's bullet, respectively. The last one was mayor of Jib Janine, a town in the south with a population of nine thousand. He resigned and left the town in the safe hands of the other eight thousand, nine hundred and ninety-nine inhabitants, to live with her in Beirut. When they separated, he went back to Jib Janine and no one heard from him again. The Don called her 'the Black Widow'.

'So you're saying we're all monkeys,' said Basil, before giving me a wink.

Basil and I would sit next to one another in Ms Mayssa's class because she was the only teacher, apart from Mr Aston, who did not mind our side talks.

'No, that's not what I said,' she replied.

'We share a common ancestor with monkeys,' said Estelle, in an attempt to clarify.

'So you're saying my grandfather's a monkey,' said Basil, giving me another wink.

'In a sense, yes,' said Ms Mayssa, tucking her hair behind her ear. She was older than Ms Iman, but shorter and whiter, with freckles.

'Cut it out, Wednesday,' I whispered. Estelle and I had taken to calling him after that particular day of the week because we all agreed that it always came out of nowhere, like 'August rain'.

'Your grandfather may be a monkey, Ms Mayssa, but mine isn't,' said a Mohammad, in the corner.

'You misunderstand,' she said.

'If anyone's grandfather is a monkey, Mohammad, it's yours,' said Basil, turning around to face him.

Mohammad imitated the cry of a sheep. The conversation then went in the direction of grandparents as farm animals, featuring an amalgam of animal sounds. When the class was quiet, you could hear the hum of the overhead fan. It was synonymous with exams because that was the only time when the class was quiet. Ms Mayssa leaned against the wall, by the whiteboard. She never used the chalkboard at the other end of the class. The walls were not really walls, they were Gipson boards. We would knock on them and hear someone from the adjacent class knock back, occasionally forming a ballad across the wall.

'Maybe this was a mistake,' she said aloud, 'I did not think this through.'

'That poor mayor of Jib Janine,' said Estelle, looking from Basil to me.

'What?'

'Can you imagine being on the receiving end of that line?'

'What's on that floppy disk, Ms Mayssa?' asked Nadine, who looked twice her age.

I expected Basil to make a joke about Mohammad's floppy disk, but he didn't. He sat still and narrowed his eyes.

'Pictures of monkeys,' said Ms Mayssa, 'and humans.'

'Dear God,' I said. But in my mind I said Jesus-Mohammad-Christ.

Then Ms Mayssa displayed the slides of monkeys, apes, humans and everything in between on the whiteboard. For the majority of the slides, I could hear the hum of the overhead fan. The last slide was a picture of the Earth from the moon and imprinted upon it were the words of Neil Armstrong: 'I put my thumb up and shut one eye, and my thumb blotted out the planet earth. I didn't feel like a giant. I felt very, very small.'

When the slides were over, Ms Mayssa looked at me. I smiled, meekly.

'Yu-ri Ga-ga-rin,' chanted Basil, clapping his hands at every syllable. He was joined by Mohammad, who had tired of making animal noises, and Estelle, who raised her eyebrows as she did so. Soon the entire class was singing Yuri Gagarin's name. Basil gave me wink.

My father sat on the comfortable couch in the living room watching *La Yumal*, another comedy sketch show, which translates to 'Never a Boring Moment'. In the corner of the living room, the paint on the ceiling had begun to peel off again. Every other summer we would repaint it and it would peel off by winter. My father gave up on the whole matter and resigned himself to the fact that this corner of the ceiling will never fully be painted. In the eighties, an RPG rocket had landed in that corner of the living room, tearing through the ceiling as it did so. My father hired a local carpenter, Mehdi, to patch up the ceiling because he was the only man available and willing at the time. To the man's credit, he admitted that he was not a professional and that this would have to be a temporary solution. Mehdi said that he would come back with his cousin to fix the ceiling for good. Mehdi disappeared during the war. He was kidnapped, or killed, or immigrated to Montreal with his wife and son. My father would say that he spent half his life waiting for my mother, and the other half waiting for Mehdi.

'God damn you, Mehdi, wherever you are, and your cousin,' said my father, wiping the plaster off his shoulders, 'and your mother, and your father, and your grandfather and your grandmother and your wife, Ward, and her lover, Majid, and that godawful son of yours, Karim. I hope, to God, he is Majid's.'

My father believed in God most, not when he was in trouble, but when he wanted trouble inflicted upon others.

'Leave the boy out of it,' said my mother. 'It's your own fault for not hiring a professional to begin with.'

It was a game my parents were fond of playing. They pretended that he was lazy and she irritated when it came to matters of home improvement. This was the greatest trick that my parents ever pulled on us. Most of the time, we did not even know that there was no money to mend the ceiling or buy a new car or fix the leaking fridge.

'I'm bored,' said my sister.

B*asmet ElWatan* was not on that night.

'The class chanted my name today,' I told my mother, spotting an opening.

'Why would they do that?' asked my father, still watching *La Yumal*.

I filled my father in on the details of Ms Mayssa's class on evolution and her slides of monkeys. Then I told them about the final slide and Ms Mayssa's Armstrong quote. A war of ants erupted on the TV screen and the noise filled the room. My father got up to adjust the antenna. My sister stood on the dining room chair and held one antenna in different directions while my father fiddled with the other one.

'The American astronaut?' asked my mother.

'Not this again,' said my father, grabbing the other antenna from my sister's hand and pushing it backward. 'What's he doing in a class on evolution, anyway?'

'A testament to how far we've come since our tree climbing days,' I said.

I had prepared the answer ahead of time.

'Some people say it didn't actually happen,' said my father.

'Who?' asked my sister, now balancing her right arm up on her left one.

'Some people.'

'Why would they say that?'

'Because they believe it, why else?' said my father. He banged the palm of his hand against the TV set.

'It doesn't make sense.'

'Something to do with the American flag blowing in the wind.'

'What's wrong with that?' I asked.

'There's no wind on the moon.'

'Who said?'

'Jesus-Mohammad-Christ said, that's who.'

'That's not true,' said Basil, the next day as he, Estelle and I sat outside class during break.

The portrait of the president hung above us. The glass casing had gone missing. There was a rumour going around that someone had drawn a penis on it. Whoever it was had chosen not to draw a penis on the actual portrait and instead settled for adding the letter 'F' before the signature at the bottom which read 'Art of Metis and Sons'.

'Of course it isn't. The moon landing happened,' said Estelle, holding *The Prince of Tides* to her chest.

'Where else do you think America gets its oil?' asked Basil.

'Iraq?' said Estelle.

Estelle's thumb and index finger twitched as if she were pinching the air.

'Nonsense.'

'Why else would they bomb Iraq?'

'To rid the world of an evil dictator.'

'Whom they installed in the first place,' said Estelle, placing her index finger on the dimple in her chin. 'You're an idiot.'

'They made a mistake. And they admitted it, alright. It takes courage to do that.'

'He even speaks like an American,' I said.

The sun was out and I could see the sweat under Basil's armpits. Estelle wiped her chest.

'Besides, there were never dinosaurs on the moon to decompose. Where would the oil come from?'

'Aliens,' said Basil.

SHAWKI AND ESTELLE

The Arabic teacher whose classes were always the last of the day often complained that we lacked focus, determination and motivation, holding up two chubby fingers and a thumb. Everything about Mr Malik was round. His fingers were round, his glasses were round, his face was round, his mouth was round and when he puffed out smoke from his lit cigarette, it too was round. He had fought during the war for the Syrian Social Nationalist Party, a secular party, with a shady past, that ran their own militia. Imprinted on his face was a permanent scowl and his left eye always narrowed more than his right when he was looking at you. We suspected that he was a sniper at one point. Mr Malik had us memorise entire poems and recite them in class. It was a different poet every week. He would give us the name of the poet and we would go off in search of stanza or two to satisfy him. It was mostly the boys who recited the poems while the girls looked on.

> *'O moon of the darkened bedroom*
> *I kissed him once, just once*
> *as he slept, half hoping half fearing he might wake up*
>   *O silksoft moon*
> *his pyjamas held such softness*
> *Ah how I'd like a real live kiss*
> *how I'd like to be offered*
> *what's under the covers'*

Basil stood in front of the class and recited Abu Nawas' 'Ode to the moon'. As he did so, his right eye twitched. I believe he was restraining himself from winking. Mr Malik had explained that Abu Nawas was an eighth-century Arab poet with a knack for the controversial. That was only partially true as Basil pointed out to me on the day.

'He's part Persian. His mother sold him to an Arab. Can you imagine being sold by your own mother to an Arab?' asked Basil.

'No wonder he's a paedophile,' said the white, freckled Mohammad.

'And a drunkard,' added Basil.

'Maybe he was reaching back to his lost childhood,' said Estelle. 'Trying to find something in those boys that he hadn't found in himself as a child.'

'Or he just likes little boys,' said Basil. 'Look at Round Malik over there, his mother never sold him to an Arab and he can't keep his eyes off me.'

'Nothing wrong with looking,' I said, coughing.

'Besides, you're hardly a child,' said Estelle.

'Good,' said Mr Malik, when Basil had finished reciting the poem. Normally, he would ask us to explain the stanza, or 'put it into context', before we returned to our seats. He didn't this time. And Basil stood in his place, unsure of whether to make his way to his desk.

'I'd like to put the poem into context,' said Basil.

'No need,' said Mr Malik.

'I think it's important.'

I raised my hand.

'What do you want, Najjar?'

'I think it's important too, sir.'

'Make it brief,' said Mr Malik, staring at Basil.

'Abu Nawas was sold into slavery by his mother. He liked to touch little boys in their private places.'

Basil and I sat in the black leather chairs of Ms Iman's office. She hadn't arrived yet. We had been ushered in by Mr Malik. I pointed out the Persian carpets.

'Abu Nawas would have liked these,' said Basil, nodding his head.

Ms Iman walked in with her glasses in her hands. Her eyes flickered back and forth before settling on me.

'I think we can resolve this without my parents,' I said, joining my hands together and placing them on my stomach.

She leaned against her desk in front of us. As we gave Ms Iman our version of events in Mr Malik's class, she leaned more heavily on the desk. Her skirt rose above her knees, exposing her thighs.

'Is that all?' she asked when we were done.

'And we all know, Mr Malik is a paedophile himself,' said Basil, shrugging.

'I will not allow you to speak of another teacher like that in my office,' said Ms Iman, now standing straight.

'I'm sorry. I didn't mean anything by it,' said Basil. 'He just is, that's all.'

'What do you want to be when you grow up?'

On the off chance that Basil said he wanted to be a lawyer, I could not see Ms Iman explaining to him that his accusation was slanderous and that he would require more proof to make it with certainty.

'A good man,' said Basil, because it didn't really matter what he said. That was the answer she always heard.

'And do you think good men go around spreading nasty and harmful rumours about one another?'

'They're not rumours if they're true,' said Basil.

Ms Iman told us that we would have to apologise to Mr Malik for calling him a paedophile, which we had not done to his face up to that point. She called Mr Malik in and ordered us to stand outside the office while she spoke to him inside. The slamming of lockers and the sound of hundreds of students walking through the hall, prevented us from hearing the conversation inside Ms Iman's office.

'Why did you insist he was a paedophile? She was going to let us off with a warning,' I said, smacking Basil on the back of the head.

'Because he is.'

'You don't know that for sure.'

'I do.'

Then we heard Mr Malik from inside Ms Iman's office. The whole school heard him.

'You would rather believe those two dipshits outside over the word of one of your instructors?' shouted Mr Malik. 'I never thought you were good enough to be principal. This entire pimp's school will be remembered as a footnote at the bottom of one of my books.'

'I didn't say that you are a paedophile, Mr Malik, please compose yourself. I only want you to be aware of the rumours.'

'I am. Is that all?'

'The boys are waiting outside for you. They want to apologise.'

Basil and I shared a quick, worried glance.

'They can stuff their apology,' he said, as he pushed the door open. He stormed past us, turned around briefly to give us a round stare, then walked on like his legs were two hands of a maths compass. The left leg went first then the right leg circled it and so on.

'He's either going to eat us or fuck us,' said Basil.

'Ms Iman's thighs are no match for Ms Kristina's,' said Mohammad, when we told him about Ms Iman's rising skirt.

We nodded in agreement. Estelle pinched our necks.

The maths teacher was in her early twenties and half Greek. She would often walk in to find the boys in class doing the Zorba. This she laughed off for the first few times then one boy, Youssef, brought a dinner plate to class and broke it against the floor. She sent him to Ms Iman's office and the whole thing was called off. After that, the only time she allowed us a short-lived Zorba was when she mentioned a Greek mathematician in class. Pythagoras was popular for a time.

Ms Kristina came to class dressed in shorts and a very thin top, even in the winter. She would walk in and start drawing figures on the board. But she did not stand still as she did this. She would move around, twist and turn, and by the end of it there would be shapes and geometrical figures of all sizes on the board. A circle would contain about four triangles and three squares, and none of us could tell you how it had happened.

'Which one is the equilateral triangle again?' asked Mohammad.

'The one with the three equal sides, Mohammad, you know this.'

She crossed her legs when one of her students let her down.

'What about the Isosceles triangle?'

'Two equal sides,' said Wael, a tall, thin Christian boy with an ability to calculate large numbers in a short space of time which astounded the teachers.

'Five hundred and twelve times six hundred and twenty-seven,' said Basil.

'Three hundred twenty-one thousand and twenty-four,' said Wael.

She uncrossed her legs. Basil led a round of applause. The school had been an all-boys one up until the end of the civil war. The fairly recent influx of girls was encouraged but the girls were finding their place in what was still a boy's world.

Mr Malik's head popped in. He was holding the doorknob and leaning forward. He asked to speak to Basil and me, privately.

'You're going to get it up the ass,' whispered Mohammad.

'If we do we're coming back for you,' said Basil, 'and I hope he's got AIDS.'

Mr Malik filled his office. It was smaller than Ms Iman's. There were no leather armchairs or Persian carpets. There were only books. I could see *Birds of September* and *The Miserly* on the rusting, metal bookshelf to my left. Behind him, pinned to the board was Mahmoud Darwiche's poem.

> *Write down!*
> *I am an Arab*
> *And my identity card number is fifty thousand*
> *I have eight children*
> *And the ninth will come after a summer*
> *Will you be angry?*
> *…I have a name without a title*
> *Patient in a country*
> *Where people are enraged*
> *My roots*
> *Were entrenched before the birth of time*
> *And before the opening of the eras*
> *Before the pines, and the olive trees*
> *And before the grass grew…*
> *…Write down!*
> *I am an Arab*
> *You have stolen the orchards of my ancestors*
> *And the land which I cultivated*
> *Along with my children*
> *And you left nothing for us*
> *Except for these rocks…'*

Beside that hung what appeared to be a red, spinning swastika. This was not Hitler's; it was the Syrian Social Nationalist Party's. It looked like a disorientated swastika with an identity crisis. It was the emblem of one of the few remaining secular parties in Lebanon, except it did not believe in Lebanon. Its entire dubious existence was based on the idea that Lebanon is a colonial fabrication and that modern day Syria, Lebanon, Jordan, Palestine and Cyprus are linked historically and geographically as one. This region was referred to as the fertile crescent. The SSNP eventually allied themselves with Hezbollah which muddled their cause further. The juxtaposition of both the poem and the emblem made little sense to the informed observer. At the time, I accepted the board as it was, ignorant of the fact that the SSNP had rejected Arab Nationalism, much like it had rejected the notion of an independent Lebanon.

'What's your problem, you two?' asked Mr Malik.

'You want to castrate the poets, sir,' said Basil, 'it's unfair.'

'What does that have to do with your accusation, Abu Mekhi?'

'I'm saying, sir, that the poets were human. They played, they laughed, they drank,' said Basil, 'and they touched children.'

I nudged Basil in the ribs. He did not acknowledge it.

'Are you going to stop this nonsense you two are spreading about me or am I going to have to show you what it means to be a paedophile?' said Mr Malik, slamming his significant fist against the desk.

'Yes, sir,' I said. Basil nodded.

The chair creaked underneath the weight of the paedophile.

'Tell your father I read that article about the Don in *An-Nahar*,' said Mr Malik, standing up so that the poem and the swastika were hidden behind him. 'Tell him it is dire shit.'

The Don referred to him as 'Comrade', in his presence, on account of the fact that they were both members of the SSNP, and 'bastard', in his absence, on account of the fact that they disagreed about the direction in which it was moving. The Comrade gave us two weeks of detention.

'I will, sir,' I said, as Basil and I stood up to leave.

'Not you, Abu Mekhi,' said Mr Malik. 'You can leave, Najjar.'

As I made my way out of the doorway, Mr Malik cleared his throat.

'How is your mother doing, Najjar?' he asked.

'Alright, sir.'

'Give her my best.'

'I will,' I said. But I didn't.

'And shit article, don't forget that.'

'Yes, sir.'

'Dire shit.'

'Yes, sir. Dire shit, sir.'

Minutes later, Basil appeared by the classroom door. Ms Katerina gave him permission to come in. He placed his hand on his buttocks and pretended to limp all the way to his seat. Estelle laughed and was joined by several others in class. Ms Katrina put her fingers to her lips, then turned around and began to erase the shapes on the board. I asked him why Mr Malik had told him to stay and he flicked his wrist, mimicking the movement involved in throwing something behind one's back; as if to say it was already in the past.

Estelle and I walked home together. I had told my mother that our house was not as far as she made it out to seem. I told Estelle we could walk it easily. On the way, she told me that she was going to be alone for the weekend.

Estelle's home remained a mystery to me. She had never invited me in and I had never asked to be invited. The memory of shards of glass and rubble in the aftermath of Monsieur Mermier's death was still fresh. I imagined that she would skip past them every evening on her way to the bedroom, that she would get her socks caught in a splinter of wood or step on a piece of glass and scream, 'Maman!'

'She's a busy woman. Always in conferences. But I'm proud of her,' she said.

'I'm proud of my mother too,' I said.

'She's in a conference now. In Marseilles.'

'And what did your father do? Before he left,' I asked.

'Nothing. What do dark, brooding Lebanese men do?'

I looked at Estelle. She was whitest in the sun. Her hair glowed. I looked at the hair on her arMs She did not shave or wax them, but they were light and blond.

'We apply excessive amounts of gel to our hair until it falls off,' I said.

She nodded and smiled wistfully.

We stood outside the door of her apartment. It was locked. Estelle couldn't find her key, she banged against Monsieur Mermier's old door. I invited her into my house. My mother was picking up my sister and my father sat on the couch reading a newspaper. Estelle thanked my father for allowing her to wait inside for her mother.

'When's she arriving, your mother?'

'Not until Thursday.'

'Why don't you jump from our balcony to yours?'

Estelle looked at me.

'You're right,' said my father, 'he should jump.'

Estelle, my father and I stood on the balcony. The idea was that I would leap from our balcony to Estelle's, walk in, unlock the door from the inside and let her in. We heard the zucchini man.

'That's unusual,' said my father, 'he doesn't normally show up on weekdays.'

'I really appreciate it,' said Estelle, smiling.

My father removed his Parker pen from his shirt pocket and drew out the details on a newspaper. It was the sports page. I was to step on the first pile of books, then the second, presumably higher, pile of books and leap from that onto the next balcony. The two balconies were not far apart and an actual leap was unnecessary. My father insisted.

I ran up the first time and slipped on *Echo of Lost Words*. I ran up the second time and slipped on *Daily Matters which No One Cares About*. I started to run up the third time and my mother walked out onto the balcony, holding my sister's hand. My father explained the plan.

'Why don't you jump?' asked my mother.

'I'm an old man,' said my father.

'I can jump,' my sister volunteered, only to be ignored again.

'If anyone should be jumping, it should be me,' said Estelle.

'No,' said my mother, 'your parents – mother – isn't here. We cannot give you permission to do something like that.'

I looked at my mother, my father, my sister and Estelle, and I ran up for the fourth time. I stepped on *Rainbows in the Desert* then *Contemporary Ink* and landed on Estelle's balcony.

'Are you alright?' asked my mother.

'Did you break a leg?' asked my father.

I stood up and dusted off my cargo shorts. I had been forced into a roll on the ground to lessen the impact of the landing. My first instinct was to land on my knee with one arm on the other knee, like superheroes often do, or like footballers pose for pictures. Somewhere in midair common sense kicked in and I allowed myself to roll.

I climbed into Estelle's bedroom from the window. There was not a single shade of pink to be found. The room was neutral. It looked like a hotel room, and I slowed my walk. I wasn't intruding on someone's private space. I could hear the laughter from my house. As I turned to leave her room, I spotted a piece of paper taped to her closet. Written on it, in French and in a blue marker, were the words: 'What would Prince Charming have for occupation if he had not to awaken the Sleeping Beauty?'

On her desk lay an open notebook, she had scribbled Basil's name in the margins. I looked for my name. It was not there. I flipped through the notebook. It was not her diary. I glanced across the room. There was no diary.

I ran past the living room where Monsieur Mermier had died. It was unrecognisable. A different TV set, white walls, all new couches. One of them was still wrapped in nylon. I could not tell you where exactly we had found the body or the glass. I saw the blood in a pool on the floor. Had I ever seen the body? Why had Estelle wanted me to embarrass myself? Did she know that her notebook was open? Did she remember what she had scribbled? What would Monsieur Mermier have thought of her?

'My hero,' said my mother, as I opened the door, and she wrapped her arms around my neck.

'Turns out I had the key all along,' said Estelle, as she dug both her hands into her pockets and then held out the key, 'but we thought we'd let you open the door anyway since you went through all that trouble.'

I looked down at my shoes then at her, then walked past my father and into my room. I heard laughter coming from the hallway. I later found out those were Simone de Beauvoir's words taped to the closet. Also, French.

Detention went by quicker than we expected. The school was unaccustomed to dishing them out and Basil and I spent the first period with Ms Kristina and the second with Mr Malik.

'Maybe it was just a coincidence,' said Basil, pursing his lips.

'No. You know what she's like.'

'A girl.'

'Sophistique. Chic. French.'

'Croissant.'

'Baguette.'

'Fromage. Tour Eiffel. Champs-Élysées. '

'Saint-Exupery. Zidane. Voltaire. Charles de Gaulle. Jacques Chirac. Barthez.'

'Oui.'

'Better than you and me.'

Ms Kristina never gave us anything to do. She would sit and correct papers, often leaning forward to decipher this or that student's handwriting. Basil and I would spend the first hour making up stories about Momo the Child Molester. They were these macabre little stories about a failed Child Molester who would follow a child around for weeks only to fall at the final hurdle. Basil was always better at drawing the story out and adding the details. I'd have the last word. They would regularly end with Momo saying something like 'never mind, he was too old anyway'. But Basil made the stories real, frequently giving the Child

Molester a redeemable feature, though not necessarily profoundly humane or relatable. My favourite was the one in which Momo the Child Molester gets electrocuted trying to molest a child. I do not recall the details of that story, but in the end it turns out Momo was an organ donor. I was irritated at the time because by killing Momo off, Basil had robbed me of my final line. This manifested itself in a heated debate about whether or not anyone would want the organs of a deceased child molester. Basil argued that it could prolong the life of a child, or his parents. I argued that I would not place in my chest the heart of a man who would place his penis in a child. I was confident I was on the right side of this moral dilemma but then Basil noted that we had not yet decided what the epitaph would read. And I had the perfect line.

Mr Malik gave us assignments to start on in detention and submit in class the next day. I relished the writing, it was reading the work aloud which I struggled adjusting to. The audience consisted of a reluctant Basil and a belligerent Mr Malik, neither of whom gave the impression of being enamored by my way with words. I soon discovered that an audience of two is the most difficult of all. Any attempt at an Iambic pentameter was met with a nod of approval from Mr Malik and a shake of the head from Basil. Piss-taking metaphors which eschewed substance for humour often elicited Basil's trademark wink and bite of the tongue, and Mr Malik's glare.

'He's doing this on purpose you know,' said Basil, 'getting her to go first, then stepping in to ruin it. I don't mind seeing his ugly face on any given day. But it's the contrast that kills you.'

On the last day of detention, Mr Malik asked us to write a short essay each entitled 'Why I Write'.

Basil said he did not write at all. He said he only wrote because he was told to. I told him to pretend that he had a reason for writing. He pretended not to hear me.

In class, the next day, Mr Malik stopped the session ten minutes early, took out my paper and ordered me to stand in front of class and read it. I shook my head. He nodded.

'We don't have all day,' he said, shoving the essay against my chest as I stood in front of class.

I saw a red circle around an empty space at the top centre of the page, and the words 'no title' underlined twice above it.

'I write because if I screamed at the top of my voice, my father would lump me with a book entitled *The Life and Times of Antoun Saadeh* by an author named Wahid Saleme,' I said, holding the paper with both hands. 'I write because if I were to whisper in my friend's ear, she would put finer words on a poster and brandish it in my face. I write because voice is measured in decibels and ink in decades. I write because my pen is limited. When I asked it to fly to the moon, it refused. When I asked it again, it insisted that birds fly in the sky, pens write on paper and clouds write stanzas in the sky and look like paper to the naked eye. When I asked it for the third time, it dried up and stopped speaking to me. I write because Shawki pushes me to do so.'

Shawk means passion, a deep yearning. The pronunciation of which differs only slightly from that of the Arabic word for thorn, the kind often found in one's side. I looked up at Estelle. Her chin rested on her fist. The class was quiet. I could hear the hum of the overhead fan. Even Basil tilted forward.

'He said to me once: "Adam."' I winced, and heard the stuttering laughs. 'He said, "writing without shawk, Adam, is like eating without hunger. Tasteless."'

Basil crossed his arms.

'So I called him Shawki.'

Estelle grinned. Her lips parted wide enough for me to see her canines, and long enough for me to see her wisdom teeth which had not yet pierced their way through her gums. Nor would they for many years.

'For those of you who do not know Shawki: he is an old man in his early seventies. His beard is white and long. He is small in stature and bald. He stands hunched over behind me whenever I hold a pen in my hand and surveys the white paper in anticipation. He pokes me with his cane and sometimes, he'll fall over and I have to interrupt my train of thought and pick him up with both hands. But the train doesn't stop. You ask: "Where are you going with my thoughts train?"'

I grimaced at this. Mr Malik allowed himself a snort.

'And the train whistles back, cursing you in the process. And as he curses you, he namechecks your father and your mother and your sister and your brother, Ussama, and your generous wife and her miserly neighbour and Madame Hafez and her husband, Monsieur Hafez. And Monsieur Mermier. And your old friend Estelle.'

I looked up at Estelle again. She gave no sign of being taken aback at the mention of her name.

'I write because I do not know how to paint, or sing or carve or knit or box or play an instrument or chop a tomato or peel a potato or fly to the moon. I write because if I stopped writing, the sun would cease to rise and the animals would cease to breathe and the Earth would cease to revolve. Because the Earth revolves around the tip of my pencil. I write because I am a militiaman who forgot his RPG at home, and took to the streets armed with an unsharpened pencil which he found in his mother's purse while he was looking for chewing gum. I write because there are very few verbs and very many nouns. I write because…' I read the last paragraph in one breath.

Mr Malik waived his hand for me to stop.

'Enough. Return to your seat,' said Mr Malik. 'Give this to your father. Tell him there is more life in this than the dire shit about dead people he hands in to *An-Nahar* on a weekly basis.'

'Tell him to shove his bachelor's degree in Arabic Literature up his barely literate backside,' said my father, after I'd relayed Mr Malik's words, 'but this is good.'

'Sweet boy,' said my mother, laughing. And at first I thought she meant me, but she had not. She meant Mr Malik.

'Such a sweet, sweet man that Malik. Give him a hug from me when you see him next, will you?'

Mr Malik was many things, and chief amongst them round, but he was not sweet. He was so round in fact that any attempt to describe the man as anything other than that ended with those same words bouncing off his round frame and rebounding onto the wall like a bullet ricocheting off the hinges of a door or the metal railings on a balcony.

I nodded but had no intention of giving Mr Malik a hug. My father ignored the exchange and proceeded to examine my paper. He held it up against the light, as if to check if it had been forged. He stared at me again, squinting as he did so, his newspaper resting on his lap. I held his stare.

'This is better than good,' he said.

A couple of weeks later, my father chucked his *An-Nahar* at me in the morning.

'Two writers in the family now,' said my mother, smiling. She had eyelashes which curled to the point of a near perfect circle, forever caught in a loop.

'When can I publish an article?' asked my sister.

I opened the newspaper in front of me. It was large and unwieldy. Two or four sheets fell off.

'Fold it,' instructed my father.

I folded the paper. I read my own words on the twelfth page. They were more authoritative, wiser, more assured. I read my name. Adam Najjar. I read the title: 'I Write Because'.

'Who chose that?' I asked.

'One of the editors. You didn't title it.'

'I don't like it.'

'Remember to title your stuff then.'

I read the article next to it. 'To Live in Beirut on a Monday'. I stopped halfway. I reread my article. Mine was better. I grinned.

I took the article with me to class. Mohammad and Wael told every single teacher that I'd had an article published in *An-Nahar*.

'Waste some time while we wait for the referee's whistle,' said Mohammad.

I thought it was a good line, because I was in that frame of mind.

Mr Abu Alam read the article, allowed himself a half-smile, and said, 'I didn't think you had it in you.'

Ms Mayssa led a round of applause in class. She talked about the importance of believing in oneself and to keep

A. Naji Bakhti

pushing ourselves so that we may one day achieve our dreams. She said the Don would be proud. She didn't read it.

Ms Katrina asked me to give her the newspaper. I did. She read the article out loud then cut it out in the shape of a triangle and pinned it to the board.

'Isosceles,' said Mohammad.

Ms Katrina crossed her legs.

Ms Iman nodded her head in my direction during break, which she did not normally do.

Mr Aston asked me to translate the article for him. He said he hoped that he had played some small part in this. I said he had. He said he would like to take this opportunity to thank the class for making him feel at home. Truly, at home, he said. I said he was welcome.

'Terrible title,' said Mr Malik, spotting the triangle-shaped article pinned to the board.

'The editors chose it,' I said.

'Najjar,' said Mr Malik, 'the boy of the hour. Your turn to recite.'

I walked to the front of the class. I was not aware who the poet was for this week. I looked at my article behind me. Mr Malik tapped his pen against his desk.

> *Write down!*
> *I am an Arab*
> *And my identity card number is fifty thousand*
> *I have eight children*
> *And the ninth will come after a summer*
> *Will you be angry?'*

It was the only poem I could think of under pressure. I spoke the defiant words of the Palestinian poet, Darwiche, which had remained pinned to the board in Mr Malik's office behind the round teacher's desk, far away from the hardened eyes of any Israeli soldier.

'Palestine is lost,' said Mr Malik, swinging his hand back as if to slap me, 'God help all Arabs if you lot are the future.'

Basil laughed for the first time that day. When the bell rang, Mr Malik called Basil over and they walked to the Arabic teacher's office together. They appeared to be engaged in a heated debate. Basil was gesturing in exaggerated fashion towards the heavens and Mr Malik was almost imploring him to maintain his composure. Mr Malik pointed to his own forehead then placed his index finger on Basil's forehead. As they turned the corner, Mohammad made the observation that Basil was hobbling as if he too had the legs of a maths compass. This was not entirely true but I did not deny it or leap to Basil's defense.

Several years later, Mr Malik was asked by one boy in another class if he still had his sniper gun. He said he did. Then he was asked, as a follow-up, whether he still rides his motorcycle from the war days. He said he didn't but that he did ride the boy's mother. He was sacked on the same day. The truth is that he would have gotten away with it, but the boy happened to be the son of a member of parliament and his mother, the wife of a member of parliament. Mr Malik would have known this.

One Sunday in April, Estelle knocked on the door. My mother opened the door. She called my name. I stood on the doorstep. And Estelle stood on the doormat. I didn't ask her to come in. The house smelled of stuffed zucchini.

'Maman found a better job in Paris,' said Estelle, 'she wants us to move there.'

'When?'

'Tomorrow morning. I've never been to Paris.'

'Do you think you'll like it more than Beirut?'

'It is Paris. If I don't, there's something wrong with me.'

I nodded.

'What about your father?'

'Maman says we were never here to find him,' said Estelle, and she told me I was naïve with her eyes. 'I think she just wanted me to carry something of this part of the world with me.'

I nodded.

'When you said Shawki, in the essay, you meant the Don. Didn't you?'

'Will you come back home?'

'Who knows? Maybe. Yes. I will.'

Estelle wiped a tear off her face.

'When I die, cry over my dead body.'

'That's stupid,' she said, 'don't say stupid things. It doesn't suit you.'

I didn't apologise for the article or my outburst. She didn't ask me to. We hadn't spoken for months. She winked at me and opened her arms. I leaned in, she pinched me on the back of my neck. I smelled her. Not Chanel or Dior, just Ariel, maybe Persil and Garnier Fructis. Not like Basil. Estelle once said that he was so olive-skinned, you could taste the olives. He did smell of olives, with a hint of Labneh and some mint and a dash of thyme and sweat.

'I'll let you know if I ever spot your father walking down Hamra Street.'

She laughed and I never saw her again.

I would come across five or six men who looked like her father in Beirut. I spotted one in Verdun. He was tall and imposing and he wore a leather coat that extended to his knees. I spotted one on Rawche. He was wearing flip-flops and pink shorts and he too was tall, but much skinnier and less imposing. I spotted one on Mar Elias. He wore a suit, not tailored. It was loose and his tie was longer than it should have been. He had a face with no clear outline. I saw one on Mar Mkhael. He was young, younger than the man in the photo would have been at the time. He was drunk and ungroomed. Then I stopped looking.

THE REVOLUTION

In Mr Aston's class, I explained that Estelle had left for Paris. Mr Aston said that he had not been informed of this. He made a note of it on the attendance sheet in front of him. Mohammad said that I should follow her. Basil said he had known about it. He leaned in closer to my desk and asked me if I had patched things up with Estelle. I shrugged. Mr Aston turned to Mohammad and told him to shut the window because of the racket outside. It was Friday and afternoon Azan was at its loudest. Mohammad froze. He looked like a goat caught in headlights. Mohammad was the only boy in class who had any facial hair. He had managed to squeeze out a goatee and keep it there for weeks. Basil too could grow something of a moustache but he had chosen not to. Mohammad reached for the window but did not shut it.

Opposite the school stood a mosque and adjacent to the mosque stood a church. Every so often, when the Azan rang throughout the streets of Beirut, the church would join in by ringing its bells. The other teachers cited this as an example of the pluralism of Beirut. And the first few times you heard that sound, it was. But only the first few times.

'Mohammad, we haven't got all day,' said Mr Aston, 'we're covering Gatsby and the American Dream today.'

Nadine looked at Mohammad. Wael looked at Mohammad. And I imagine if Estelle were there, she would have surveyed Mohammad with interest too. Mr Aston, who had been leaning against the teacher's desk, and supporting his weight with his knuckles, straightened his back. Basil got up and shut the window. It was one of those old roll-up windows which had been painted and repainted. The glass bore the effects of the sloppy paint jobs over the years, a white stain here which had turned yellow or a splash of dried paint there with the marks of fingernails running through it. Some long ago student had attempted to reverse the damage done by the reckless painters with their fingernails, but childhood dreams and maths lessons had no doubt stood in the way. The rope upon which the entire operation depended was also visible. Basil had only to give the window a little push and the rope took care of the rest.

Mr Aston gave Basil a nod. The Englishman had walked halfway across the classroom with the intention of shutting the window himself, possibly realising that he had asked too much of the class. For the next hour or so, he talked about Gatsby's green light which 'year by year recedes before us'. Mr Aston's passion shone through, he slammed his fists, he clapped his hands, and pointed and wagged his index finger in equal measure. And even as he did so, there was something resigned about his voice which the odd flicker of the eyelids betrayed. I was not, at the time, in the habit of observing too many world leaders in the midst of their stirring speeches. Though I imagined that they must not have sounded too different to Mr Aston's that day. The only speech which I could recall was Saddam Hussein's during his trial in court, not long before he was sentenced to death.

'I am not here to defend me,' the vicious dictator had said, pointing his index finger in the direction of the judge, 'I am here to defend you.'

Mr Aston's glimmering blue eyes alternated between Mohammad and Basil for the duration of the session. When he was done, Mr Aston let his head drop. Basil and Mohammad exchanged glances.

Twelve minutes before the end of class, we heard a bomb go off. It felt closer than it was. The glass from the three windows shattered and Serene sustained a cut on her forearm. Wael stood on his seat, flailing his arms in the process, and the rest of us ducked and covered our heads with our arMs Serene was stunned silent. She gasped at first but she did not cry or shout afterwards. Even her eyebrows had seemed to fail her, flickering inauspiciously then flatlining.

'It's a bomb, habibi, not a mouse,' said Basil, craning his head more than usual to look up at Wael, 'get down from there.'

The politician, and member of parliament, targeted by the car bomb would survive the incident. He would need a walking stick for the remainder of his life, but he would use that stick as a political tool with which to beat his opponents.

Mr Aston, however, did not handle the car bomb as well as the intended target. He swore loudly then he apologised profusely, then he gestured for the class to remain calm. Moments later, the class door swung open and slammed against one boy's desk. Mr Aston swore again. The boy's name was Ali and, sensing the opportunity, he swore too.

'Damn the father of that pimp's whore of a bomb,' said Ali.

Ms Iman's head appeared through the door as she scanned the room for any injuries. Ignoring both Ali and Mr Aston, she spotted Serene and led her out of the room with one arm around her shoulder.

Mohammad sat upright and eyed Basil. There was such an air of smugness about the former, that when Nadine coughed suddenly, I concluded that she must have choked on it.

'I don't blame you,' said Mohammad the next day after class, running his fingers over his goatee.

'For what?' asked Basil.

'Shutting the window.'

'Why would you blame me for that?'

'You saw what happened. The bomb, the shattered glass, the gash in Serene's arm.'

'You're blaming me for not predicting the future,' said Basil, looking at me and not Mohammad, in disbelief.

We could hear some of the older boys playing football on the makeshift asphalt pitch behind us, and the voice of a short, skinny Egyptian boy who had recently moved to Beirut with his Christian parents. They had found Egypt a bit stifling and chose Lebanon as their place of refuge. Abed was not very good at the sport itself, but had a deceptively deep, strong voice coupled with an Egyptian dialect and was allowed to commentate on the match.

In the late nineties, an Egyptian football commentator by trade, Methat Shalabi, captured the spirit of the World Cup for the Arab-speaking nations. His voice rang throughout the city like Azan, as everyone in Beirut tuned in to listen to Methat Shalabi commentate on France's annihilation of Brazil in the '98 final. Brazil's capitulation, France's dominance, Ronaldo's despair and Zidane's Marseilles roulette. Shalabi immortalized them all.

'That Algerian boy can play,' he would say about the star of the French national team. 'Give him back, Chirac.'

Abed stood in the middle of the makeshift pitch and the older boys just played around him. Pretty soon he found himself a loudspeaker and his voice became synonymous with school breaks. He had memorised the name and age of every single boy, and even seemed to know strange, intimate matters about some of them. On one occasion, he debated the merits of one father's decision to take a second wife and whether polygamy is justified in today's world. The goalkeeper, whose father had recently ventured into polygamy, dropped the ball and fluffed a clearance not long after that remark. The older boys accused Abed of being the son of an Egyptian intelligence officer and he did not deny it. So they let him speak his mind. He cleared his throat before mentioning the car bomb which had kept a significant number of players off the pitch because their mothers were reluctant to send him to school on the day.

'We all love our mothers,' said the Egyptian boy, 'but sometimes they can be a little bit overbearing.'

Now pitchside, Mohammad raised his voice even louder so that he could be heard above Abed.

'You shut the window. It blocked out the Azan. The glass broke,' said Mohammad. 'You do the maths.'

'So you're saying God did it?' asked Wael.

'Yes,' said Mohammad, running his fingers over his goatee, 'but only because our Druze friend shut the window.'

'I only shut it because you froze up,' said Basil.

'I didn't freeze up. I could have done it if I wanted to.'

'Habibi, you couldn't have done shit.'

'Who the hell is Aston to tell us whether or not we can listen to the Azan?' said Wael.

'You're Christian, Wael,' I said.

'It's the principle.'

'Surely, *that* should have been a foul,' rang Abed's voice through the loudspeaker. 'This sort of thing happens sometimes when there is no referee.'

'Six hundred and twenty-seven times two hundred and sixty-five?' asked Basil.

'One hundred sixty-six thousand, one hundred and fifty-five.'

'Who made you Druze minister of foreign affairs anyway?' asked Mohammad.

'I'm not defending him because he's foreign, you dumb, ape-descendent, Muslim goat. I'm defending him because he's not wrong.'

'I'm the goat? Your mother worships goats. She prays for the goats to protect her son before she goes to bed, every night,' said Mohammad, 'and sometimes I answer her prayers.'

Basil shrugged at this.

'What do you do with that Child Molester in his office all the time anyway?' asked Mohammad.

'None of your business,' replied Basil, clenching his fists.

'That's alright,' said Mohammad, placing a hand on Basil's shoulder, 'we already know.'

At this Basil launched his fist in the direction of Mohammad's jaw. He missed and Mohammad landed an uppercut which knocked Basil off his feet and onto his back. I kneed Mohammad in the stomach but was dragged by the collar from behind before I could do anything else. I was on the floor and Wael had his hands around my throat. I thought about throwing him a particularly large equation to solve, but it seemed unlikely that maths was the answer. Someone caught Wael with an arm around his neck and lifted him off me. By the time I got to my feet, I could see boys from all over the playground at each other. The older boys had stopped their game of football and were exchanging blows indiscriminately.

'Najjar is back to his feet and he scans the pitch for his next target,' announced Abed, before adding, 'Najjar's father is, of course, Muslim and his mother, Christian. He thinks he might be a Buddhist.'

The younger boys revelled in the chaos. One of them, a short curly-haired boy with severe dandruff, swung a fist in my direction. His thumb was tucked inside his fist. I shoved him out of the way.

'Revolution!' screamed Basil, fist in the air, rushing past me and leaping onto Mohammad who was now sprawled on the ground.

A couple of young boys followed him into battle. One had black hair and black eyes and his nose so protruded from his face that it was almost ahead of Basil. I felt my elbow connect with a chest and I did not turn to see whose.

'It is *mayhem*, ladies and gentlemen,' said Abed, still standing in the middle of the pitch untouched, 'this is not the game we know and love.' Then, 'Where has that round thing gone off to?'

A few of the girls joined in too, but they only pushed and scratched each other. Serene extended a leg to trip one of the younger boys. Once he was writhing on the floor, she jumped on top of his back and pulled at his fringe. I felt a hand on my shoulder from behind. I ducked and turned. It was Basil. He already had a noticeably swollen lip.

'I made out with Estelle a couple of times before she left,' he said, 'we didn't tell you because we thought you wouldn't like it.'

Later, he admitted that he only told me because he was afraid that Abed might announce it into his loudspeaker.

I put my fist through his gut. He sat on the floor and I sat alongside him.

Then we heard the Don's whistle. The entire playground fell quiet. If anyone could come back from the dead, the Don could. We looked around and saw that it was Ms Katerina holding the whistle and surveying the playground from atop one of the green benches. The ground remained still and silent, except for Abed who had abandoned his loudspeaker and was juggling the ball in the centre, still unscathed.

The Persian carpet, the Plaza Pharmacy calendar, the leather armchairs were unchanged. Basil held an icepack to his right cheekbone, his upper lip red and swollen. My neck was covered in Band-Aids. Wael had dug his fingernails into my neck while he was being dragged away. He and Mohammad had joined us too. Wael could only see out of his left eye. Mohammad had escaped lightly. He was bigger than most. Ms Iman sat behind her desk surrounded by Mr Abu Alam, Ms Katerina, Mr Malik and Abed. The Egyptian commentator was there on account of the fact that he was the only uninvolved, neutral party in the whole playground. Though his stay in Ms Iman's office was short-lived.

'He has to go,' Mr Abu Alam said, arms crossed, 'the Englishman has to go.'

He was wearing shoes, not highlander sandals. He kept a pair of Clarks in his desk drawer for times like these. He did not have socks on.

'These boys are trouble,' said Mr Malik, 'I've been telling you this for a while now. They've dragged my reputation and the reputation of this school through the dirt.'

'They messed up,' said Ms Katerina, 'but Mr Aston disrespected their religion. What were they supposed to do?'

'Not beat each other up, Katerina,' said Mr Malik, 'stay out of this if you're going to make it more complicated than it is.'

'The Englishman has to go,' repeated Mr Abu Alam.

'I agree,' said Mohammad.

'Shut up,' said Mr Abu Alam.

'What about Wael?' asked Ms Katerina, crossing her arms.

'What about him?' asked Ms Iman.

She turned her head towards Wael, not Ms Katerina, as if he were the one making a case for his own innocence.

'He is a Christian who was defending his Muslim friend's right to listen to Azan,' said Ms Katerina. 'Shouldn't we be encouraging this sort of thing?'

'He had his hands around my throat,' I said.

'That's true,' said Wael, nodding. 'I also elbowed a younger boy in the face and poked one of the football boys in the eye.'

He was more afraid of being left out of the collective punishment than anything else.

A hint of a smile flashed upon Ms Iman's otherwise straight face. She may have found Wael's willingness to die by the sword admirable or, possibly, amusing.

'Either way, you can't blame the entire playground debacle on these four,' said Ms Katerina.

'What do you think, Abed?' asked Ms Iman, glancing at the short Egyptian boy, before casting her eyes on the four of us again.

'I think that a foul is a foul only when the referee blows his whistle. Otherwise, it's a claim for a foul and that's not the same,' said Abed, beaming.

Mr Malik placed his hand on Abed's shoulder and guided him to the door. He ushered him outside then slammed it behind him. He mumbled something about not having time for cryptic, football trivia then crossed his arms and glared at Ms Iman, who promptly took the lead.

'Who threw the first punch?' asked Ms Iman.

'Mohammad did,' said Basil.

'Only because he missed,' said Mohammad.

'He called my mother a goat-worshipper.'

'Isn't she?' asked Ms Iman.

'That's not the point.'

'What about you, Armstrong?'

'I was defending the goat-worshipper's son,' I said.

'Aren't you going to call their parents?' asked Mr Malik.

'And have four sets of angry parents with different religious backgrounds in my office?'

'It could start another civil war,' said Mr Abu Alam, with a half-smile.

'If you learn one thing,' said Ms Iman, 'from your entire experience at school, let it be that it is easier to make another boy bleed than it is to make him think.'

'I'm not sure I understand what you mean by that,' said Basil.

'Me either,' said Ms Katerina.

'I can make you understand, Abu Mekhi,' said Mr Abu Alam, waving an imaginary sandal in the air.

'What will we have done, if we raise a generation like the last?' said Ms Iman.

'We are past that now,' said Mr Malik.

'At the centre of our galaxy,' said Mr Abu Alam gravely, now clearing his throat, 'there is a black hole.'

There was no overhead fan in Ms Iman's office, but had there been one we would have heard it hum as if from afar. Mr Malik's rolling of his round eyes, a previously soundless regularity, emitted a *squish* loud enough to turn a head in his direction. It was unusual to witness Mr Abu Alam approach physics and chemistry, or rather astronomy, with the intent of delivering some somber and salient pedagogy. Wael's neck twitched in anticipation of a flying sandal which never arrived.

'A few relatively young stars exist around this supermassive black hole,' continued Mr Abu Alam, looking upwards as if at the stars but finding only a ceiling without an overhead fan.

Wael looked up too and received a smack on the back of the head from Basil.

'Their existence has dumbfounded experts for years. They believe that the black hole should, in theory, have prevented those young stars from ever having been formed,' said Mr Abu Alam, theatrically joining his fingers together. 'In astronomy, it is referred to as the *paradox of youth*.'

Squish.

Ms Iman suspended all four of us for a week. She also blamed us for drawing a penis on the glass casing of the president's portrait.

'Mohammad doesn't even know what a penis looks like, let alone how to draw one,' said Basil.

'That's right. Basil's the expert on penises,' said Mohammad, which earned both of them an extra week each.

She hadn't noticed the 'F-Art of Metis and Sons'. She warned that any more misdemeanours and she would expel us without hesitation. Abed's skill on the ball earned him the grudging respect of the older boys, who allowed him to join their matches from then on. Over the coming weeks, we would hear his voice less frequently and, when we did, it was often through heavy breath just after he had been subbed off. Eventually, he did the honourable thing by announcing he would resign from commentary for good through the loudspeaker before kicking it halfway across the asphalt pitch. Abed had moved up in the world and there was no going back.

My mother told me that I would sell Chicklets on the streets for five hundred Lebanese liras a packet, and live off the goodwill of others for the rest of my life. My father refused to speak to me for a week. He did not communicate with me through my mother or sister. He went about his daily routine without acknowledging my presence. The first couple of days, I said 'hello', 'thank you' and 'goodnight'. I quickly realised that it didn't matter so I stopped.

On the third morning, I stood outside the bathroom door. I needed to excrete desperately unwanted wastes.

'I have to go,' I said.

My father did not reply. I banged on the door with one hand on my crotch.

'I need to go, now.'

The door swung open and my father stood in front of me in his stained white flannel shirt and blue chequered shorts with a green towel around his neck. The smell of Gillette wafted through the door. He still had some shaving cream on some parts of his neck. One half of his face was unshaven. He wiped his mouth with the towel and blinked at me.

I slid through and swung the door shut behind me. I slipped my boxers off and stood over the toilet.

Nothing.

My father kicked the door open and I sprayed the mirrors above the toilet seat with my urine. It was his way of telling me to hurry up. I put my boxers back on and left the bathroom. My father walked back in. I switched off the lights.

'Damn your pimp father to hell,' said my pimp father. 'May he be violated by the son of a pimp's dog.'

I pictured it.

To my young mind, the Pimp seemed an omnipresent power, a divine presence or, at the very least, an astute businessman and wealthy benefactor. This was how I explained away the fact that his name often preceded that of institutions or edifices or people or domesticated animals. It was the Pimp's world and I accepted this early on without much deliberation.

My mother put her arm around my neck and dragged me to the kitchen. I skipped over a puddle of water on the floor by the fridge. She made me a halloumi sandwich and watched me eat it. Then she made me another one with tomatoes and I ate that one too.

'Life is running,' she mumbled, a saying which both she and my father were fond of uttering sometimes in quick succession, other times independently and in starkly different tones.

When my father said it, in his willful dictum voice, I always assumed he meant that 'life is all about running from one place to another' and that we must push ourselves because 'tomorrow we will run faster, stretch our arms further and one fine day...' When my mother said it, in her sorrowful lament voice, I always believed it meant that 'life is running out' and that there is no outrunning it.

She waited until my father had left for work and taken my sister with him to the pimp school.

'Tell me, honestly. Is this the influence of a political party? Is that what this is?'

I shook my head.

'Revolution? You can stay home and revolt for free. You know better than to listen to the propaganda of these militia parties, don't you?'

I nodded without committing to it.

'Nothing good comes of it, Adam. They start recruitment early and then you're stuck.'

'It was a school fight. That's all. It had nothing to do with a militia.'

She breathed in.

'Adam, you can't keep doing this,' said my mother, 'you're not like the other kids in your school. Their parents have money. They have lands and companies and property.'

'That's not my fault.'

'No, it's not,' said my mother, leaning against the leaking fridge and crossing her arms. 'It's not your fault that we live in a rented apartment, or that we don't own a car or that your allowance is half that of your classmates. None of it is your fault.'

'Exactly.'

'Your father and I made that decision long ago. We chose your education over a comfortable lifestyle.'

I shrugged. When God said: 'let there be light', he meant let there be pimp's light.

'You think you would stand a chance of becoming an astronaut without the best education money can buy in this country?'

CANNONBALL

When we walked back into school, Wael and I were treated like returning heroes. Basil and Mohammad were still suspended. The younger boys had their own stories about who we were fighting and with what degree of success. One story had it that the four of us had stood up to Mr Malik and that he'd somehow managed to turn us against one another, using his paedophilia. This story relied heavily on a lack of understanding of the word paedophilia. Another story had it that the four of us planned to sneak into the school at night and draw another penis on the president's portrait, but were caught in the early stages, while fighting over who would take credit for the plan. Even the girls thought we were facetious enough to merit fleeting attention.

'You know I had a crush on you when we were kids,' said Nadine. 'I thought you were so cute with your astronaut dreams and your steely determination. Of course, it's not as cute now, but still beats future third-generation businessman.'

She was forever caressing her eyelashes with her index fingers.

'Thanks,' I said.

'Did anything happen between you and that French girl?'

'Estelle? No.'

'She was a weird one. Between her and goat-boy you had one hell of a group there.'

I shrugged my shoulders. I was in the kitchen again and my mother was telling me off for being the son of lower-middle-class parents living in a rented apartment and attending an expensive private school. In my mind, I was always eating the halloumi sandwich while she lectured me. It wasn't true.

'Do you want to be my boyfriend?' asked Nadine.

'Okay,' I said.

She stuck her tongue down my throat and then held my hand tightly.

Her father was a good surgeon but a failed politician. He owned land and property and, if you count the chauffeur and the housemaids and the cooks on minimum wage, people. I met him a couple of days later when I was invited to Nadine's house in Rabieh.

There were no tall buildings and stuffy apartments in Rabieh. There were houses and mansions and pools in backyards with bars inside them. I saw a cross on the door of every house and a housemaid cleaning the porch in front of every other one. Trees extended into the street and belonged to people because they grew in backyards. I saw an Aston

Martin with a Lebanese license plate and a Porsche Cayenne with an American license plate. There were gates and fences with signs that said 'Do Not Trespass' or 'Beware: Dog', and I thought 'you're bluffing'.

The maid, a short elderly woman from Sri Lanka, ushered me to the swimming pool outside. There was nothing special about Nadine's place, except that they had a balcony overlooking the pool but none overlooking the street and a single Roman column standing by the gate. Nadine threw her bag on the floor and ran upstairs. The Sri Lankan woman picked it up. I stood outside by the pool. It was one of those round ones. There was a trampoline on one side and a swing on the other. Neither had been used much. The nylon packaging which dangled off the trampoline's edge had been only partly removed, as if the trampoline itself was too large and a mere third of it was all that was required.

'I never had a son,' said Nadine's father, Dr. Antoine. He sat on one of the sunbeds and I sat on a chair beside it. He was short with thick-rimmed glasses and a moustache. His hair combed itself. He wore navy blue shorts with a pager attached to them.

'I never had a rich father,' I said.

It was a line out of Basil's textbook. Dr. Antoine laughed. He took a sip of his Johnnie Walker.

'What'll you have, habibi?'

The Sri Lankan housemaid stood behind him.

'Almaza,' I said.

'Where are you from, Najjar?'

'Beirut.'

'Where in Beirut?'

'West Beirut.'

'Aren't you Muslim?'

'I drink.'

'Your father doesn't mind?'

'No. We drink Arak together sometimes.'

He waved his hand. She disappeared.

'We don't have Almaza,' he said, 'she's going to bring you a Corona or a Heineken.'

'Cannonball!' Nadine shouted.

It was very American. A more authentic girl would have shouted 'Yala'.

She ran through the door in a blur. She leapt and clutched her knees in midair, pulling them towards her chest and spinning as she did so, then falling back-first into the swimming pool. Warm water splashed against my ankles and Dr. Antoine's. There were white lines on her shoulders from a different bikini. She already had larger breasts than the rest of the girls in class combined. Dr. Antoine clapped. He passed me a glass, I did not know of what.

'I taught her how to do the dive head-first. But she insists on doing this.'

'Where's your mother?' I asked Nadine.

'She's in Paris. She runs a business from over there. It's a clothing line.'

'That's what we tell her,' said Dr. Antoine leaning in and pinching my ear between his index and thumb.

Johnnie Walker travelled up my nostrils.

'Do you like it?' asked Nadine.

'Of course, he likes it.'

'It's alright.'

'Adam wants to be an astronaut,' said Nadine.

Dr. Antoine laughed.

'I know your father,' said Dr. Antoine, 'he's the journalist, isn't he?'

'Yes.'

'He was SSNP for a while in the eighties. He keeps writing about dead people now. Why does he keep writing about dead people?'

'I'll ask him.'

'I liked his earlier work,' he said taking another sip of his whiskey. 'It was listing, really, that's all it was. That was his thing, wasn't it?'

'I suppose,' I said, as I observed Nadine performing a near perfect breaststroke.

'Like a shopping list, but it made sense. Or it didn't. I don't know. But it got you thinking about ideas, not people.'

'Jump in,' said Nadine, splashing water in my direction.

'Living breathing ideas,' said Dr. Antoine, 'not dead people.'

The water was fresh and smelled of chlorine and Nadine's perfume. The Mediterranean was nowhere within sight.

'I don't have swimming trunks,' I said.

'The *docteur* will lend you some,' she said.

Her father was French educated, meaning he spoke French as a second language.

'She thinks it pisses me off when she calls me the docteur,' he said, staring at his daughter. 'It doesn't really. I am the docteur. I worked hard to earn that title. I did not work nearly as hard to become a father.'

'Later,' I said, splashing her with Corona.

'The newspaper has been shit for years anyway. It used to be the voice of the people. Now it's the voice of a few capitalists with more money than they know what to do with,' said Dr. Antoine. He poured himself some more. He spoke as if he wasn't sitting in front of his own swimming pool in Rabieh.

'It's corrupt,' I said, taking a sip of my Corona, 'everything's corrupt.'

I liked pretending to be a rich man who was pretending to be poor.

'The whole country is corrupt. I should have stayed in London.'

'London?'

Nadine floated on her back. She had somehow acquired Ray-Bans and they made her look older still.

'I got my degree from the University of Edinburgh. Best years of my life,' he said, scratching at the label of the bottle, 'have you heard the joke about the Saudi Arabian in London?'

'No.'

'So this Saudi Arabian student in London writes his father – this was before the internet – and he says "Dear Father, I love my Ferrari. But everyone in London rides trains." So his Saudi father responds with "Dear Son, I've wired you some money. Go buy yourself a train and stop embarrassing us."'

He extended his glass and knocked his head back and laughed in the direction of the sun. I did the same. Then we drank. And I had five more Coronas and a sip of the doctor's whiskey.

'Another?' asked the good doctor.

'No more,' I said, but I smiled and took another sip of his whiskey. It was a Jack Daniels or a Johnnie Walker. It did not make sense to me that whiskey would be named after men. It is one of those questions I asked myself just that one time and I never asked again. I asked it of other people after four or five drinks because it seemed like an insightful thing to articulate, but I did not privately turn it over in my head. Men. The patriarchy. Whiskey. Drink.

'Isn't this better than walking on the moon?'

'It is close enough.'

'I'm breaking up with you,' said Nadine, as she made her way out of the pool.

She sat on the edge of the pool first then swung her legs out of the water.

I tilted my head to the left so that another Roman column stood between the sun and my eyes. There were bullet holes etched across the column in the form of a ribbon, remnants of the civil war.

'Hail Caesar,' I said.

'What?' asked Nadine, wrapping a towel around her waist.

'I understand,' I said, tipping over the rest of a warm Corona I had left by the foot of the chair to try the whiskey.

'I hope you do it,' she said, 'I hope you spend your whole life working hard for it. I hope you become the first Arab to stand on the surface of the moon, all alone and against all the odds. And I hope you look back and realise that it was not worth it in the end.'

I had the urge to wash away the bitter taste of alcohol from my mouth, to bite off half an apple or to shove a vine of grapes down my throat. I swallowed my own saliva and I clicked my tongue and I heard my dry mouth curse Jim and Johnnie and Jack. I threw up. I wiped my mouth.

'I want to go home,' I said.

'I'll drive you home. I've got to go to the hospital anyway,' hissed the doctor.

Nadine ripped the towel off her body and threw it at her father. Then she turned and walked away. And I swallowed more of my own saliva and observed the bullet-ridden Roman column.

'That's enough,' shouted the doctor after her, launching his glass into the air.

It spun along a vertical axis, overtaking the sun at one point without flipping, before landing in the pool.

His left hand gripped the armrest as he bit his upper lip.

I craned my neck in time to spot the Sri Lankan housemaid bending over to pick the wet bikini off the floor. There behind her was Nadine's olive, bare backside. On her left butt cheek were two perfectly aligned moles such that if you were to tilt your head to the same side and at a certain angle, you might feel obliged to return the smile. She had walked past the maid towards the door leading into the hallway, now unburdened by the weight of the bikini or the towel or the water.

The doctor drove his grey Mercedes Benz well for a man who had drank a quarter of a bottle of whiskey. He gripped the steering wheel with both hands and watched the road ahead and said nothing for the length of the journey.

'Is this your home?' he asked, looking out the window.

'Yes,' I said, 'we don't have a swimming pool.'

I meant to say that from our balcony you could see a fraction of the Mediterranean Sea. When there was no electricity in Beirut, as was often the case, you could spot the sun set behind a haphazard collection of war-torn buildings and half-baked attempts at invincible skyscrapers, or hear the echoing sound of afternoon prayer or the hoarse voice of the grocer as he pushes his cart down an empty street every

Sunday at five: 'I have carrots, I have zucchini, I have vine leaves, I have zucchini, I have parsley, I have zucchini,' and once, 'I have no one, *zucchini*, no one cares, *zucchini*.' But I didn't.

'That's fine,' he said, rubbing his eyes with his knuckles. 'The world isn't split into people who do own swimming pools and people who do not.'

'Are you alright?' I asked.

He removed his foot from the brakes allowing the car to roll slowly. Then he applied his foot to the brakes with a little more force than necessary. I thought I saw him nod, but it could have been the brakes.

'Thanks for the Corona. And the Jack Daniels,' I said, as I slammed the car door shut behind me. 'And the ride.'

'Johnnie Walker,' said Dr. Antoine, as he rolled up the window. 'Pass my regards on to your father for me. Tell him to leave the dead alone.'

The morning Mohammad and Basil returned to school, having served their suspension, I sat in my seat nursing a headache. While my classmates stood up straight beside their desks with the national anthem echoing throughout the school, I pressed the palms of my hands against my ears and placed my forehead on the table. I could still hear the first stanza.

> *All of us! For our Country, for our Glory and Flag!*
> *Our valour and our writings are the envy of the ages.*
> *Our mountain and our valley, they bring forth stalwart men.*
> *And to Perfection we devote our words and labour.*

I felt Basil's nimble fingers flicking my ear. I waved his hand away. Then I felt another hand, this one meatier, on my shoulder. The sheer weight of the hand resting on my right shoulder made me sit up straight. I looked up to see Mr Malik with one eyebrow raised and his entire mouth shifted to one side of his face.

He nodded his head and my classmates took their seats.

'Apropos of nothing, are you not Lebanese, Najjar?' he asked.

'Yes, sir,' I said. I debated telling him that my father's grandfather was in fact fleetingly French, and that my maternal grandparents were both Palestinian. I did not.

'Would you stand up for the Marseillaise?' he asked.

'No, sir.'

'Would you stand up to ask God to save the Queen?'

'No, sir.'

'Is Deutschland, Deutschland uber alles?' asked Mr Malik. His words would not have felt out of sync had they been accompanied by music.

'No, sir,' I said. I was unsure what he meant by this, but I sensed that there was a rhythm to these questions and I knew not to interrupt the rhythm.

Mr Malik narrowed his eyes and thinned his lips. As a member of the SSNP, his entire political ambition was to do away with Lebanon.

I shrugged my shoulders. He gave me a slap on the back and hobbled back to his seat. Mr Malik had a very specific way of standing while the national anthem was being played every morning. He would never place his hand on his heart or pump his chest and belt out the anthem itself. He repeatedly told students off for doing the former and openly showed his disdain for the latter. Instead, he placed his arms rigidly by his sides and extended his neck forward. He glowered straight ahead but not in a determined sort of way. His eyes betrayed a sorrow, a resigned sense of something lost.

'His youth?' ventured Basil, on more than one occasion with the anthem blasting in the background.

'No, something more concrete,' I said, believing every word.

'His hair?' asked Mohammad. 'The vast majority of it, anyway.'

'A person, I think.'

'His barber,' said Wael.

Mr Malik sat behind his desk and scratched his nose.

'Ask not what your country can do for you,' muttered Mr Malik, to no one in particular, 'ask what you can do for your country.'

'Kennedy,' said Mohammad, nodding.

'Gibran Khalil Gibran,' said Mr Malik, rolling his eyes without moving his neck. 'The assassinated bastard stole it.'

This seemed to me at the time an attempt to instill national pride in young, impressionable minds. Had Mr Malik not proceeded to undermine his good work, I would have settled on that assumption.

'Our writings are the envy of the ages,' continued Mr Malik, now pointing the knuckle of his index finger in my direction. 'It says so in the anthem.'

'Yes, sir,' said Ali, failing to spot the hint of irony in Mr Malik's voice.

The implication was that the least I, a hungover, disinterested student, could do for my country is to stand up for its national anthem. Mr Malik did not articulate this because, as a teacher of Arabic literature, he revelled in planting hidden, but not subtle, meanings in his sentences; or because he was a Syrian nationalist/ SSNP.

Mr Malik then claimed that the whole tune was stolen from the anthem of a failed state in Morocco at the onset of the twentieth century.

With the anthem still ringing in my ears, I flung myself out of the uncomfortable, wooden green chair and burst through the classroom door, only to throw up at the feet of the Syrian janitor who had been leaning against the lockers outside class. Audible chuckles and several turned heads greeted my swift re-entry, but nothing would disrupt Mr Malik's resolve.

That session we were supposed to cover Qays' 'Majnun Layla'. The Bedouin poet who so loved a married woman named Layla that he went mad, wandering the desert for years until he was finally found dead by her grave where he had carved some of his verses on stone.

Mr Malik, however, would tell us all about 'Majnun Layla' on another day. Instead, he instructed us to turn our textbooks to the pages marked 'The Modern Era'. We did this, and he pointed to a text titled 'You Have Your Lebanon and I Have Mine' by Gibran Khalil Gibran.

Your Lebanon is an arena for men from the West and men from the East.

My Lebanon is a flock of birds fluttering in the early morning as shepherds lead their sheep into the meadow and rising in the evening as farmers return from their fields and vineyards.

You have your Lebanon and its people. I have my Lebanon and its people.

Yours are those whose souls were born in the hospitals of the West; they are as ship without rudder or sail upon a raging sea... They are strong and eloquent among themselves but weak and dumb among Europeans.

That is as far as we ever got with the text in class. Mr Malik never allowed us to find out more about Gibran's Lebanon, he never asked whether we agreed with him or whether we thought he was a bit too sentimental and idealistic. He never asked us about our Lebanon. He asked the janitor whose mop had made its way in and out of the class door repeatedly with the smell of detergents overtaking the room, as the latter listened in on Mr Malik's impromptu lecture. The barrel-chested janitor mentioned the glorious cedar tree, then he resumed mopping up the mess for which I was responsible. It was the same cedar tree which featured on the Lebanese flag and had often been mistaken for a Christmas tree.

Mr Malik did tell us all about his Lebanon which was not Lebanon at all. He even declared that in most of Khalil Gibran's writings the word 'Lebanon' had replaced the original 'Syria' which Gibran used to denote the region. For the next half an hour, Mr Malik proceeded to rip the country's fabric to shreds.

'You think houmous is Lebanese?'

It was on this day that I learned of the myth of Fakheridine: that the Ottoman empire did not have a record of the Lebanese prince who nearly brought it to its knees; that he did not exist at all in his modern incarnation; that old men with white beards tend to let you down that way. Mr Malik was almost as animated as Mr Aston had been throughout the Englishman's delivery of his Gatsby lecture. Except Mr Malik never moved from his chair. He stayed seated for the entire session. He threatened to stand up at one point, having grown tired of sitting, but the act tired him more so he waved a hand contemptuously and pretended to adjust his seating position. When he was done, all that was left was the cedar tree.

'What's your point?' asked Wael, gripping the edges of the table tightly.

Wael was a patriot at heart, he had not yet figured it out for himself.

Mr Malik surveyed the class. Then he looked up at the overhead fan and back down at Wael and sighed.

'Your father is a Phalangist, fascist, isolationist, separatist pimp. Isn't he?'

The Phalangists were a Christian party with its own militia during the civil war in the seventies and eighties. One of the founders of the party, Pierre Gemayel, had captained the Lebanese football team that went to the Berlin 1936 Olympics held in the Olympiastadion. He wanted to bring that discipline and sense of order back with him to Lebanon, he said. He was not speaking about the football.

The party soon distanced itself from Nazism and played a major role in the Sabra and Chatilla refugee camp massacre, facilitated by the Israeli army, which resulted in thousands of Palestinian casualties.

Women and children were rounded up and brought into the Camille Chamoun Sports City Stadium in Beirut. They were told they would be buried alive within the stadium. Then a bomb went off somewhere close by and the Phalangists and the Palestinians, alike, fled. The stadium itself was flattened by the Israelis. The history of the Phalangists spans stadia.

'Is he?' asked Wael.

The swastika in Mr Malik's office spun a few times.

'What about Moussa's Castle?' asked Serene, tilting her head to the side as if the Arabic teacher had spent the best part of the last hour insulting her person. 'That's Lebanese.'

Mohammad leapt up and slammed his hand against his desk sending a jolt through the classroom.

'That's it. And Moussa himself?' added the momentarily high-pitched descendent of some long-ago Crusader.

When Mr Malik left class, we read on, each silently in his own seat. Wael had forgotten his book so he stood over me and read Gibran from mine.

'What will remain of your Lebanon after a century? Do you think the atmosphere will preserve in its pockets the shadows of death and the stench of graves?'

Did he know?

'I say to you that an olive plant in the hills of Lebanon will outlast all of your deeds and your works; that the wooden plough pulled by the oxen in the crannies of Lebanon is nobler than your dreams and aspirations.'

'I really thought houmous was Lebanese,' said Serene, lifting the silence.

An image of Serene licking houmous from a spoon crossed my mind. Her tongue was extended, unnecessarily, outside of her mouth and the spoon was held at a certain angle such that instead of bringing the spoon to her mouth she had to lean forward in order to lick the houmous off the spoon.

'It is,' said Wael, 'forget that Syrian nationalist paedophile.'

The Sabra and Chatilla massacre conducted by the Lebanese Forces (the military branch of the Phalangists), with the aid of the Israelis, was in retaliation for the assassination of the son of the former football captain. The son, Basheer Gemayel, was a short, chubby, weak-chinned and physically unimposing man in contrast with his tall, broad-jawed and traditionally handsome father, Pierre. Basheer was also president elect at the time, a young thirty-something-year-old with charisma and oratory skills to rival Hitler's. It was Habib Shartouni, a member of the SSNP, who had assassinated him.

'You stand accused of killing the President of the Republic of Lebanon,' said the judge.

'I killed a Mossad agent,' said Habib.

Habib then retired to write poetry somewhere in Paris.

'Where's Basil?' I asked Mohammad who was seated behind me.

Wael, his eyes still rooted to the textbook, pointed in the general direction of the door and mumbled something about Basil having followed the Syrian paedophile out of class. The janitor slammed a pungent black nylon trash bag onto the desk in front of me.

CAPTAIN DRUZE

Serene was Druze. She was from the mountains and had the same accent as Basil, except it seemed more tolerable on her. We went to a pub called the Shipman's Crew. She said she had never been to the pub but that her father knew the bartender well. She said her parents would disown her if they found out she was going out with a Muslim. I said I wasn't a Muslim.

'Christian then,' she said, 'it's all the same. They will disown me.'

There were ropes hanging from one end of the ceiling to the other. Some of them hung low and others had been cut off in places, presumably because they had irritated the Captain at some point. There was also a miniature, rusty anchor on the wall behind the bar. The Captain would touch it on his way to the cash register, or the fridge or the tap.

'Not that either.'

'You're not Druze though, are you?'

'No.'

'Then we are back to where we started. Are you at least rich?'

'No,' I said. 'Have you ever had sex?'

'No,' she said. 'You're very straightforward.'

From my seat, at the corner of the small, dimly lit pub, I could see Mr Aston at the bar. He was looking at an empty drink and I told the Captain to bring him a new one. He was having an Amaretto Sour which was a common enough drink for a teenage Lebanese girl but unusual for a former English pastor.

'I'll bring him a drink when he asks for one,' said the Captain, wiping the table with his dirty cloth. His back was hunched because of a motorcycle accident in his younger days but you couldn't tell because he still managed to tower over most people. 'What are you having?'

'Almaza,' I said, 'two of those.'

'I don't do Almaza, anymore,' said the Captain. 'They were bought by Heineken. The hops are imported from Holland. I have 961 Beer, if you want the local stuff.'

961 is the country code for Lebanon. Dial 961 and a Lebanese phone number and you might get the voice of a man or a woman who will at first speak to you in Arabic with that soft Lebanese dialect, and, if you do not say anything back, they will ask you in French if you are fluent in French. Stay silent for a little while longer, and they will ask you in English if you would prefer to speak in English. Stay silent long enough, and they will insult you in all three languages, but mainly in Arabic. Almost exclusively in Arabic, if they are angry enough.

The Captain placed the two bottles of 961 on the table and opened the bottle caps. The bottle was dark and the label yellow. Serene slammed the bottom of her 961 bottle against the tip of mine which sent the lager shooting straight up the bottle. I tipped the bottle into my mouth and tried my best to drink most of it. I coughed and a bit of beer spilt onto the table.

'Nothing like Lebanese hops,' said Serene.

'What are you, twelve?' asked the Captain.

'Something like that,' she said.

'These are coasters,' he said, waving two coasters in my face, 'use them. The bottle goes on the coaster. The coaster stays on the table.'

'Aye aye, Captain,' said Serene. She could turn most things into a joke and her laugh was bright and high but also restrained and rarely, if ever, lasted beyond the time it took her to place a hand over her mouth.

'You know what your problem is?' she asked, as I leaned in to kiss her.

'What?'

'You're too eager,' she said, then she kissed me. 'You're an eager little boy. You should be more patient, little astronaut boy.'

'You know about that?'

'The whole school knows about that,' she said, placing a hand on my neck, 'the Don wouldn't shut up about it and now Ms Iman won't shut up about it either. You're the boy who won't grow up. The first Arab astronaut. The eager Arab astronaut.'

I laughed and tried to kiss her again, but she pushed me away with the tips of her fingers.

'Will you draw my initials on a moon rock so that they can stay there forever?'

'Why would they stay there forever?'

'Because there is no wind on the moon. For an aspiring astronaut, you don't know much about the moon, do you?'

She placed a hand over her mouth, preemptively, and I heard her muffled bright laugh.

'Did you hear about him and Ms Mayssa?' she asked, nudging her head in the direction of the bar. 'Apparently, she left the mayor of Jib Janine to be with him. And now they've had a big falling out and he's not doing very well.'

'The Captain and the 'Black Widow'?'

'Not the Captain. The Englishman. And don't call her that,' she said, as I rubbed the back of my neck. 'She doesn't want to move to London with him.'

'Why not?'

'I don't know. Maybe she still loves the mayor.'

'Of Jib Janine?'

'Yes. Or maybe she loves Beirut too much.'

'How do you know all this?'

'My mother told me.'

'How does your mother know all this?'

'The neighbours told her.'

'How do they know?'

'Don't be stupid. The neighbours always know.'

I propped my elbow against the bar and ordered another two cold 961s. The Captain mentioned something about coasters then handed me both.

'Did you dial 961, sir?' I said, offering a bottle to Mr Aston as he sat slouched over.

Mr Aston said that he did not accept drinks from minors. He said that I should be home, probably in bed. He said he had not dialed 961 because he was in Lebanon and you do not dial the country code when you are in the country.

'But what if you're at home and need to call Beirut?' I asked.

'Who says I'm not at home here?' he asked, taking a sip of the 961.

'Mr Aston, the Beiruti,' I said, raising my bottle in the air. Mr Aston ignored it.

'Home is where the heart belongs.'

I shook my head and stared into Mr Aston's blue eyes and the stars stared back at me.

'Is the boy bothering you, David?' asked the Captain.

Serene knocked back the last bit of 961 in her bottle. She shifted in her seat. I gave her a wink and she ignored it. She looked up at the ropes hanging from the ceiling, then she shrugged, then she pursed her lips, then she shrugged again and looked past me and crossed her legs and blew her nose and bit her lip then she gaped down at her bottle and she was lost in it. She did all those things, in some order, before I could open my eyelid. When I did, my eye felt heavy and I picked the crust out with my index finger and rubbed it with my knuckles.

'Home is where the soul settles and memories stay.'

I shook my head again. He squinted, the universe contracted, and gaped down at his bottle and for a moment he was lost in it too.

'I can tell him to go home,' said the Captain.

'First you make friends,' he said, waving the Captain away with his hand and taking another sip of the 961, 'then you make memories with friends, those memories happen in a place, that place develops meaning, and that meaning, given enough time, is home.'

He said this calmly while staring at an old thousand lira bill taped to the wall behind the bar.

'What happens when the friends leave?' I asked, pressing the cold bottle against my eye.

'Then they take a part of home with them.'

'Nonsense,' said the Captain. 'Home is about roots, about history. You don't choose home. You're born into it.'

Then the Captain recited that infamous Mahmoud Darwiche poem in English. The very same one which hung in Mr Malik's cramped office. It was the line about his roots being 'entrenched before the birth of time, before the opening of the eras, before the pines, and the olive trees and before the grass grew'.

It seemed everyone in the world knew that poem by heart, or had it posted on a board somewhere or their fridge or put in a frame where a photograph of their loved ones used to be.

A few years after he passed away, Mahmoud Darwiche's private possessions, including his briefcase, his typewriter and a few unpublished papers, were confiscated from his former home in Palestine by the Israeli authorities. My outraged father sat down to write yet another article about yet another dead man.

'To home,' I said, raising my bottle in the air again and Mr Aston did the same. The Captain placed two coasters on the bar in front of us.

With one hand in mine and another over her mouth, Serene led me into the one toilet and closed the door behind us. She began to bang her fists against the door rhythmically and I soon followed.

'Did you tell him anything I told you?' she asked, still banging her fists against the door.

'No.'

We did this for a few minutes, without looking at one another.

'Are you sure?'

'Yes,' I said.

'Yes,' she said.

'You better not be fucking in there, Najjar,' shouted the Captain, 'I know her father. He's Druze. He'll chop your dick off and force feed it to the goats when I tell him about this.'

Serene kept banging her fists against the toilet door and I did the same.

'Would he?' I asked Serene.

'Yes,' she said.

'Yes,' I said.

She laughed for some time without placing a hand over her mouth. When she stopped laughing, she sat down on the floor, crossing her legs as she did so. Some of her knuckles were bruised and she reached for the toilet paper and wiped the tears from her eyes.

'With a Druze girl? In the toilet of a pub?' asked Basil, the next morning outside Mr Malik's class. 'Are you mentally challenged, son?'

The Gauloises which had been moving up and down between his lips now stood still. Basil had developed the irritating habit of calling most men 'son'.

'We were just pretending,' I said, waving the smoke away.

'Tell me something, son of life. Were you wearing a space helmet while you were doing it? Because maybe that's what this whole astronaut thing is about. Maybe it is just a sex fetish. Maybe your whole life has been building up to this moment when you and a Druze girl get together in a shitty pub, and you do her from behind with a space helmet on. And that's it. We never hear about your space dreams ever again.'

'No. I wasn't.'

'Try it. Next time. See how it goes.'

'Do you think her father will chop my dick off and feed it to the goats?'

'It has happened before.'

Every so often the news would report an amusing story about a boy in a remote Druze village in the mountains who had had his genitals chopped off for having sexual intercourse with an unmarried Druze girl. The last one to be reported featured the father of the Druze girl in question, grinding the culprit's penis before feeding it to his goat. The goat was called Ramzi and animal rights groups were outraged that Ramzi had been fed the sinner's penis. 'If it is not fit for the girl then it is not fit for the goat,' was one group's slogan. No one remembers the boy's name. The father was never charged or sentenced, the police tended to turn a blind eye when it came to Druze and honour crimes.

'What's the point of having a Druze friend, if you can't make this go away?' I asked, as Wael walked past flashing the 'OK' sign with his fingers.

In Lebanon, the 'OK' sign means 'you're in trouble'.

'I'll take care of it, son,' said Basil, punching Wael half-heartedly on his shoulder.

Mr Malik discussed Al Maari in class, a blind, vegetarian, recluse of a poet who was known as a heretic in the golden age of Islam. When I looked over to where Serene would normally sit in class, I found an empty seat, and when I looked back ahead, I saw Mohammad biting his lip to keep himself from laughing out loud.

Halfway through class, I spotted a tall, balding man pacing outside the window. I gestured to Basil who gave me a wink.

Mr Malik said that Al Maari's epitaph read: '*This is what my father has wrought upon me, and I have wrought this upon no one.*'

'What do you think that means, Najjar?' asked Mr Malik.

'That life is hard, sir,' I responded.

'Not death?'

'No, sir.'

'Sir,' interrupted Basil, 'am I right in assuming that Al Maari's words were conceived of when he was still alive?'

Mr Malik shook his head and let out an exasperated sigh which was also a wheeze and which, due to the Arabic teacher's physique, appeared to give off the impression of a large deflating balloon.

'Yes, Abu Mekhi, you are right in assuming that the dead do not speak, or write back or conceive of any words whatsoever. Is there a point to this?'

'None, sir.'

The bald man was now lighting his fifth or sixth cigarette and it soon became clear that Basil's attempts at prolonging class were not going to yield any results beyond possibly angering Mr Malik further. This was proving counter-productive. He and I would have to deal with two fully grown angry men instead of one.

'Sir?' persisted Basil. 'Do you think that Al Maari would have had a different take on life if he had not been blind, and his face ravaged by smallpox, and a vegetarian?'

'Do I believe that Al Maari would have perceived of life differently if he had lived a different life? Yes, son of life, I do. Yes.'

Mr Malik slammed his book shut and dismissed us with a mixture of disgust and dejection in his eyes.

The balding man approached me after class and extended his hand. He introduced himself as Serene's eldest brother, and told me that he wasn't going to chop my penis off if that was what I was afraid of.

'We were just pretending.'

'I know,' he said, leaning against the wall, 'but you should be more careful, it is not every day that a man pretends to have sex with a Druze girl and gets to keep his dick.'

'It won't happen again,' I said, with my hands pressed hard against one another.

'I'm counting on it,' he said, pulling at his earlobe.

Mr Malik then burst out of class, his gut hanging over his belt, with Basil close behind him. His forehead dripped with sweat and his sleeves had been rolled up, as they always were, except that he had rolled them up with more purpose on this occasion.

'Don't touch that boy's penis,' shouted Mr Malik, from across the hallway, pointing his finger straight at Serene's brother.

'I wasn't going to.'

'You said he was going to chop it off,' said Mr Malik ambling towards us, but turning his head to look at Basil.

'I assumed he would, wouldn't you?' asked Basil.

'Are you sure?' asked Mr Malik, standing face to face with the much taller man.

'If I wanted it off, it would already be off.'

'Where's Serene?'

'That's none of your business,' said Serene's brother running his fingers through his beard.

'She belongs in class.'

'She belongs where her father says she belongs.'

I missed Serene.

'Do you know who I am?' asked Mr Malik.

'Do you know who I am?' asked Serene's brother.

'Go near this boy again, and you will have the entire armed militia of the SSNP at your door.'

For a week, I would look at Serene's empty seat then at Basil and receive a shrug of the shoulders. It was the month of Ramadan again. Mohammad was fasting, Wael was eating and Basil was smoking. The portrait of the president had been taken down, he had been ousted after being accused of 'raping Lebanese democracy'. The presidential seat was left vacant and so was the place where the portrait had been.

'You know it is a sin, right?' asked Mohammad, raising an eyebrow and staring up at me from his seat on the wooden green bench.

'What is?' I asked, biting off a chunk of Cadbury Fruit and Nut which I had stored in my back pocket.

'Having sex with an unmarried girl. An unmarried girl from another religion, let's not forget.'

'The problem with you Muslims around Ramadan is that when you eat less, you talk more,' said Basil, lighting another cigarette.

'Did you know,' said Wael, 'that the moon moves three centimetres away from the Earth every year?'

'What's your point?' asked Mohammad.

'What will Muslims do in billions of years when the moon is so far away? Who's going to be able to tell when it is Ramadan and when it isn't.'

'I'm talking about a sin. That doesn't depend on the moon's distance from the Earth.'

'He was pretending,' said Wael, turning to study my expression, 'he didn't actually have sex with her, did you?'

'Wael's worried he'll be the last virgin standing in the group,' said Basil, giving me a wink, 'when the world ends, habibi, it will just be you and your Virgin Mary left.'

I laughed at this and Mohammad did too. I spat out the raisins and nuts. I liked the process of sucking on the chocolate until it melted away in my mouth then spitting the rest out.

'Because you were the king of sex in one of your previous lives, were you Basil?' asked Wael.

'In this life and the previous ones. Who do you think invented the Kamasutra?'

'Bullshit. Name one girl you've slept with,' said Wael.

'Paulina.'

'Paulina?'

'Paulina the Polish prostitute.'

'Paulina?'

'And Marta.'

'Who's Marta?'

'They call her Marta the Moldavian man-eater.'

'Is she Moldavian?'

'No.'

'How will you confront your creator about all of this?' said Mohammad, resting his chin on his hand.

'I'll say I used protection.'

Ms Iman came walking towards us with her hands in her pockets. She nodded her head in the direction of the other boys and placed her arm around my shoulders. Wael gave me the 'OK' sign. She looked at me without saying a word, then ushered me forward.

'I know that you and Serene, the Druze girl, are friends,' she began, as we walked away from everyone within earshot. 'Have you spoken to her recently at all?'

'No,' I said.

'Do you know if she will be returning to school?'

'No,' I said.

'Did she say anything before leaving?'

'No,' I said.

'I know that this is a difficult time for you too. If you need to talk,' said Ms Iman.

I could see Mr Malik looking at his feet as we passed him by. He was standing outside his class, cross-armed, listening closely to a conversation, not ours. I waved to him and he nodded his head. When I saw him next in class, I waved to him and he nodded again. Even after he was sacked for his remark in class about riding a student's mother as opposed to his old motorbike, I spotted him hobbling along on Hamra Street a few times, left leg first then right leg encircling it, and I waved and he nodded.

'Are you going to call in my parents?' I asked.

'Do you want me to?'

'No.'

Ms Katerina walked over to Mr Malik. I smiled at her and she smiled back. She did not seem to acknowledge Ms Iman. I wondered if in the morning she would lay on her back and put her legs up and pull her jeans onto her waist with gravity on her side, or if she would roll the pair of jeans up and then slip her legs through one after the other. I wandered if she prepared her clothes the night before and put them on a chair next to her bed so that she can get up and throw them on in the morning. I wandered if she took her bra off before she went to bed, or if someone took it off for her.

'The truth is, we haven't heard from her or her parents, and we are getting a bit worried,' Ms Iman turned on her toes and placed both her hands on my shoulders. 'You are not a child anymore, and this is a serious matter.'

'I did not know it would be such a big deal,' I said, looking over my shoulder.

Ms Iman laughed, but it wasn't the polite laugh she had reserved for the Don's occasional crack or the punctual laugh which indicated she had seen or heard enough of a student or even the emergency laugh which she had in place in case anyone accused her of not having a sense of humour. The laugh was loud and unrestrained, not unlike Serene's in the toilet of the Shipman's Crew. She removed her glasses and wiped them with her top, then she scrubbed her eyes with her knuckles and put her right hand on my neck.

'The Don used to say that the two biggest deals in the region today are sex and religion, and unfortunately for us, they don't get along very well,' said Ms Iman, taking a step back and pursing her lips, 'but I don't have to tell you that, do I?'

'No,' I said.

'Will you be attempting to contact her?'

'No,' I said.

'Do you still want to be an astronaut?'

'No,' I said, then, 'maybe.'

My mother paced back and forth. My father sat on the comfortable couch looking at the floor, the answer to all his problems lay perhaps in one of the books scattered across the living room, in that undecipherable grand pattern which he alone could make sense of.

As it turned out, Ms Iman had called my parents. My mother glared at me then resumed her pacing.

'I cannot believe that you are reading. Your son is going to ruin his life,' she said, still standing.

My mother had steadily developed a deceptive standing posture mimicking a bent over seated position, not a crouch exactly, which she called upon in times of crisis to subtly emphasize an otherwise verbal point. She also slapped her thighs.

'He can do whatever he wants with his life,' said my father, now unfolding his newspaper which had been tucked under his arm up to that point.

'You're going to sit there and read your own article?'

She slapped her thighs again.

'What can I do? "Your children are not yours, they are the sons and daughters of life's longing for itself." Gibran Khalil Gibran,' said my father, his face hidden behind the newspaper.

I clenched my jaw.

'He almost got his genitals chopped off.'

'It's all part of his grand plan. Somehow this is all part of the road to becoming an astronaut. Isn't it, son? That's why he punches people, lashes his sister with my belt, and has sex in public toilets,' he said, peeking his head above the newspaper to glare at me.

'Pretend-sex,' I said.

'Jesus-Mohammad-Christ, I wouldn't boast about that if I were you. And don't interrupt me when I'm ranting,' he said. 'He's plotting his way to space. That was my point.'

'I'm plotting my way to space,' I said.

'Not everything is a joke,' said my mother.

My father got up and walked to the dinner table. He grabbed a book and threw it in my direction. It was entitled

Steps in Space. He had folded one page down the middle. I opened the book to that page as I dropped back into the comfortable couch.

Printed there were the names of the twelve men who had made it to the moon.

'Do you understand?' he said.

'Understand what?'

'Read the names aloud.'

'Armstrong, Aldrin, Conrad, Bean, Shepard.' I stopped and looked up at my mother.

'Go on,' barked my father.

'Mitchell, Scott, Irwin, Young, Duke, Cernan, Schmitt.'

'What do they all have in common?' he asked, leaning in.

'They're all astronauts.'

'They're all American,' said my father, and the edge of his mouth twitched. 'Astronauts don't ride to the moon on the back of rockets,' he continued, 'they ride to the moon on the back of nations.'

'What's that got to do with anything?' asked my mother.

'He needs to grow up. That's his problem. Stop pretending. And grow up.'

On these occasions, it occurred to me that my father might have believed in adulthood as a separate state of being, that he bought deeply into the notion that adults lead distinct lives from their childhood selves, that to grow is not to build on your childhood but to cast it aside in favour of the person you were always supposed to become. And this person was never an astronaut.

'He can do anything he sets his mind to.'

'No. That's the problem. You've made him think he can walk on water and now he wants to walk on the moon,' he said, pausing to scratch his moustache with such vigour that I was surprised it had not come off his upper lip altogether.

'I don't want to walk on water. I just want to walk on the moon,' I said, slamming the book shut.

'Become a teacher. And teach about going to the moon. Become a writer. Write about going to the moon.'

'I don't want to write about astronauts going to the moon. I want to be one.'

'Write in first-person then.'

Serene showed up to class a month later. Ramadan was over by then. Mr Aston had not been to any of his classes for a week. When Ms Iman said he had gone back to London, the general assumption was that he had passed away, like the Don. It turned out he had in fact left for Southampton. He had had enough of Beirut, packed his belongings and walked away. Ms Mayssa cried in the middle of another PowerPoint presentation, and Nadine placed an arm around her.

Serene walked into Ms Katerina's class late. She sat down and looked straight ahead. When Ms Katerina saw her, she stopped drawing the circle on the board. Then she looked around as if to make sure that no one in class scared Serene off. The room fell silent, except for the eternal hum of the overhead fan. Basil raised his hand.

'Do you have a question, Basil?' asked Ms Katerina.

'Five hundred and twenty-five times one thousand six hundred and twenty-two?'

'Eight hundred fifty-five thousand five hundred fifty-five,' said Wael.

'That is incorrect, I think,' said Ms Katerina, taking out her calculator.

'I was distracted,' said Wael.

Serene smiled in my direction, after class. Mohammad said I should go talk to her and Basil slipped a condom in my back pocket.

'It is olive flavoured, found it in my father's wallet,' said Basil, before giving me a pat on the back. 'He's stopped smoking so now I'm stealing these instead.'

I walked over to Serene, took her arm and walked her into the nearest empty classroom I could find. Outside, Wael was asking Basil if and when he thought his father would resume smoking because he was considering indulging in a cigarette or two himself but was conscious about smoking his allowance away.

'They're dirt cheap,' said Basil.

I shut the classroom door. Chairs stacked on top of desks leaned heavily against the smeared walls and towered above broken overhead projectors which littered the floor. The lights were off and the room smelled of tuna sandwiches in aluminium foil and rotten, mouldy bananas. There was no whiteboard, and only one chalkboard. Pictures of famous men throughout history were taped to the walls featuring one of Einstein with his tongue out and another of Gandhi in his glasses and a Gibran Khalil Gibran self-portrait. There was also a picture of the former president and someone had given him a beard to go along with his moustache. And stapled, haphazardly, atop a picture of Stephen Hawking in his wheelchair was a recent one of Sabah.

'Did he throw himself off the Rawche Rock?' I asked.

'The Don?'

'The Englishman.'

'No,' she said, licking her lips, 'not unless there is a

Rawche Rock in Southampton.'

'Where have you been?' I asked, still holding on to Serene's arm.

'I wanted to contact you but I couldn't,' she said.

I nodded. Serene's face looked rounder but not fatter. I could still see her dimples but they were less pronounced and her eyebrows, too, seemed lighter.

'Stop staring at them,' she said, putting her hands over her eyebrows.

'My friend gave me this,' I said, taking the condom out of my back pocket, 'it is olive flavoured.'

Serene grabbed the condom from my hand, ripped open the green wrapper and threw it onto the floor.

'It is lime flavored, your friend is an idiot,' she said, 'open your mouth.'

I did and she placed the condom on my tongue. It tasted of rubber and lime.

'Did they beat you?' I asked, swishing the condom around in my mouth.

'Don't be silly. Would it worry you if I said they had?' she asked, tracing her right eyebrow with her index finger and thumb.

I nodded again. I surveyed the room: Shakespeare, Lincoln or Washington, Mahmoud Darwiche, Aristotle or Socrates or Plato, Dali and Mozart or Picasso and Beethoven, one of them was an artist and the other was a musician, Martin Luther King Jr., Pele with his right hand aloft, and Sabah. There was no Neil Armstrong or Yuri Gagarin.

'What would you have done about it,' she asked, 'if I said that my father had beaten me?'

'Beat someone up.'

The condom had lost its flavour.

'I heard you begged my brother not to beat you up,' she said, laughing before quickly placing a hand over her mouth.

I gazed out through the dusty window glass. There was a jasmine tree not far off and a green gate and a brown cat having a stroll and not a Druze within sight.

I spat the lime-flavoured condom onto the floor.

She smiled and kissed me on the cheek. It was a small peck, nothing more. She smelled of sweat and the insides of a pencil case when you leave the pencil shavings in for too long.

'You like to pretend you're tough, don't you?'

She lifted her skirt to reveal her bluish-red upper thighs.

'They did not want it to show,' she said.

And then after a pause, 'Nor do I.'

Basil and I went to the Shipman's Crew that night. We drank two bottles of 961 each, not Almaza, then we gathered the empty bottles and walked out. Basil launched the first bottle through the window shattering the glass, then I did the same with the second bottle and so on. It was divine justice, said Basil, and we were only administering it because God did not exist. If the barman had only kept his mouth shut and not blabbed to Serene's father then I would not have had to ponder the once imminent loss of my genitals. I would have been spared the indignity of being 'rescued' by Mr Malik and Serene would have been spared a beating.

'You sons of bitches, you cowards, you Israeli pieces of shit,' he shouted.

'Fuck your 961 and your Lebanese hops and your fake ship,' shouted Basil back hysterically, as we ran away, 'it's a bar, and you're a barman. And we're not at sea!'

'And your coasters,' I added, putting on the high-pitched crackling voice which Basil had employed earlier.

'And your coasters,' repeated Basil, 'fuck them too.'

The Captain chased us, at full speed, feet slamming against the ground, fists clenched, head held high and back arched forwards.

'My hops were entrenched before the birth of time,' I shouted upwards, catching my breath and looking firmly ahead, 'before the opening of the eras, before the pines, and the olive trees and before the grass grew.'

We ran past the Wimpy Café, except the sign now read Vero Moda, and you could not smell the rich Turkish coffee anymore. We ran past Piccadilly Cinema and a poster with the line 'Roger Moore as James Bond in *For Your Eyes Only*' which featured an enlarged pair of bare legs, a woman's, spread wide with miniature Moore standing between them in a suit, pointing a gun and looking overwhelmed. We ran past a large portrait of Sabah drawn across the entire length of a building adorned in bullet holes on Hamra Street. She was young and blond and smiled down approvingly at passing cars, entirely unaware that she was a piece of art not life.

We ran past a blur of thick, thin wires and naked wires, dancing from the roof of one shell-pocked building with its dried-up balcony plants and exterior, double foldable French wooden shutters onto the next shell-pocked building with its dried-up balcony plants and exterior, double foldable French wooden shutters and holes big enough for birds to build nests inside them; until we ran out of breath and the wires ran out of roof and so hung off the ledge of the last roof of the last building in Ras Beirut. And when we looked back we could not see the Captain and he could not see us and we did not know where to go from there because we thought he would get on his motorcycle and catch us or call the police or my father or Basil's but he did not.

Basil swung his olive-skinned and hairy arm around my neck, and laughed. He never wore a watch. He never asked me for the time of day nor accused me of tardiness except when he was in a foul mood and it suited him to do so. He slowed down his run and I slowed down mine then we sat on the edge of the pavement. I could feel a pain in my side and I breathed in the moist air of Hamra Street.

'You should start shaving properly,' he said. 'Your face looks like a radish field.'

He ran the back of his hand across my cheek and I swatted it away.

Above us was one of those electric ad boards which had been installed by the mayor of Beirut after someone from the ad company had bribed him into doing so. It shined a light on the street and the pavement and several nearby residential apartments and their assorted laundry. The second or third ad displayed a cold bottle of Almaza in the sand with luggage resting beside it and the Mediterranean in the background, as it always was.

'Open your doors,' it read. 'They're coming back.'

That summer Almaza ran an ad featuring teary-eyed mothers talking about their sons and daughters, working or studying abroad. It showed brothers missing their sisters, girlfriends pining for their boyfriends, or friends reminiscing about the absent member of the gang and how it was not the same without him. But it was alright because they were coming back in the summer, and they would all share an Almaza and that was fine. It was fine.

'She's over there in London freezing her ass off,' said one girl, in her yellow bikini stretched out on the sand, 'she belongs here with me.'

'I miss you, son, don't forget us,' said one mother in the ad, 'come back home, don't deprive me of that face.'

'He was just here,' said the father, 'he left five days ago.'

Basil leant back and rested his weight on his elbows, like we were still at Ramlet Elbayda. He placed his hands beneath his back and thrust his hips forward. He looked like he was about to give birth.

'If you had to worship one animal, though,' he said, looking up at a tourism ad for some Far Eastern country featuring elephants, 'just one. Which one would it be?'

'The goat,' I said, smiling.

'I'm serious,' said Basil, his eyes wide open, glued to the ad.

I turned over all the farm animals in my head and none of them was majestic enough.

'Apropos of nothing,' continued Basil, sounding like Mr Malik, 'it's the calf not the goat that the Druze are meant to be worshipping. This goat business is a total fabrication. So is the calf nonsense.'

I thought of the jungle, but I had never seen an elephant or a bear up close, nor did I aspire to. Also, from the pictures and images on TV, the elephant seemed to me too disinterested in the affairs of man, or anything else for that matter. For various, largely inexplicable, reasons, I would grow to dislike elephants deeply. Perhaps it is the way their trunks arch backwards when they bathe themselves in a pose reminiscent of a delicate wrist to a furrowed forehead or maybe it is the sound the trunk emits which deigns to scream for attention. They are arrogant, self-indulgent creatures, I reasoned, and I have no time for them. Insects I ruled out altogether on account of the fact that I could not bring myself to worship an animal whose entire survival was subject to a can of Bygon. Tigers and lions seemed too cruel, seals too sluggish and eagles too opportunistic. When at last I settled upon the whale because it is big and a rare sight, Basil had, like the elephant, lost interest.

'You?' I asked, locking my fingers and placing my elbows on my crouched knees. When Basil did not reply, I assumed that the conversation was over and with it the evening and so shifted my weight to one side and pressed the palm of my hand against the pavement in an attempt to stand up.

'He's having an affair,' said Basil, staring ahead.

His elbows had tired and he had leaned so far back that his head almost rested on the concrete pavers, but for his fingertips, which thinly prevented it from doing so.

'Who?' I asked, caught between sitting and standing.

'The pimp. My father. I found a picture of her in his wallet. I meant to steal a condom and a few thousand liras. Now I think I should have left the condom.'

I edged my body closer to his. He lifted his head and I slid down and placed my arm underneath it. We pretended to stare at the electric ad board which was no longer within our line of vision. There were no stars above and it was better to pretend that we were staring at something than nothing at all.

'The goat,' he said, and I did not ask him if he was serious. It was still dark when I returned home. The light had not yet snuck in through the grey, plastic shutters and bathed the dusty books. Basil and I spent most of the evening lying on the pavement and looking up at the ads. Almaza, Pantene, Ras El Abed, Garnier Fructis, Wassim's Hair Salon. One of us would make an animal sound and the other would choke on his Almaza, and wait for his opportunity to exact revenge. There was no power, apart from the odd private generator in select buildings and ad boards. As I stumbled my way back home down the middle of the starlit, empty road, a couple of barren street lamps adjusted their posture momentarily and saluted my footsteps without lighting them. For the most part, they stood repentant by the side of the road. One of them leaned forward as if permanently on the verge of whispering a secret into the ear of an oncoming pedestrian.

The Horse Shoe, a coffee house not a retailer for equestrian footwear, had shut its doors around midnight and left the cheap metal chairs and tables out on the pavement unguarded. I picked up one of the surprisingly light chairs and tossed it as far as I could, which was not very far at all. It tumbled, clanking its way across the street and into a stationary greyish-black Jeep. I am unsure whether it was the absence of Basil or the Captain, or the almost clumsy, awkward sound of hollow metal against asphalt – as opposed to that of glass shattering – but suddenly vandalism seemed altogether a less than satisfying endeavour.

From the first-floor balcony of a dwarfed building which bore the strain of rain and wind, but also intense sun, hung a water-soaked cardboard sign. It read 'Urgent: waitresses needed.' An aging man with a gruff beard and two stumps for legs sat on a cardboard box beneath the house with the scarlet shutters and swung his stumps first left then right then around and back again. I waved to him as the soft rain began to descend on our heads alone. He coughed out phlegm and continued swinging his stumps. Sabah's voice emanated from the brothel and rang through Hamra; she was most alive at night.

I was greeted with a gust of smoke as I eased the door to the apartment open. I had expected to find a still and fragile silence. A single spot of light burned bright. I reached for it with my fingers but it appeared to fade as soon as I did so. I made my way blindly through the darkness and the undying fog of war towards the ethereal light. There I found my mother and her cigarette. I blinked and my eyes were both dry and wet. She did not acknowledge my presence at first. She looked through me, as if I were part of the fog which might blur her vision but not impede it.

She did not ask me why I had just walked in or where I had been. She smiled a half smile and said that she had reminded herself of Yvonne. Yvonne was an elderly disabled woman who had lived across from my grandparents' house and lost her teeth to age, and her children to war. She sat on her balcony and smoked her way through the night, and the rest of the war. The light from Yvonne's eternal cigarette was a source of comfort to my mother who could see it through her bedroom window, even as the gunshots intensified.

'There is a lake in Australia that turns pink,' said my mother.

On the couch beside her, cigarette buds rose to fill half the bottle of wine wedged between the Palestinian cross-stitch embroidered pillows.

'Australia?'

'And sand so white it makes the snow in the hilltops of Mount Lebanon look like soot.'

'I don't understand.'

'We should have left,' stammered my mother, between one puff of her cigarette and the next.

'Where to?'

'We were very close,' she said, 'we were very close. After the first one then after the second one, then in a couple of years when they're both older. Stubborn old goat.'

Having had enough of goats, and other animal sounds, for one night, I began to retreat in the hope that my absence would go unnoticed.

A rustle sounded from amongst the books. I swerved and squinted but could not make out any shapes, apart from those of the bookshelves and the books themselves.

'Haneen?' asked my mother, straining her neck.

That is what my parents called one another when they thought we were not there or could not hear them. In the moment, I believe my mother thought I was not there or perhaps the smoke had become so dense that it shielded me from view once again.

Lebanese terms of endearment included 'hayete' or 'habibi', which meant life or love respectively. But 'haneen' was different. It implied a nostalgia of some kind, a sorrowful longing, often for the past, but also for a person.

There was no reply.

According to my Teta Mary, she and my grandfather Nabil did not mind my father so much when he was their daughter's Muslim suitor. They minded him somewhat more as her Muslim husband. Also, according to my Teta Mary, my grandfather was never going to go through with his threat to round a small battalion of Christian militiamen and storm the gates of my father's fortress, which was not a fortress. It was the small apartment on the sixth floor of an old building in Ras Beirut, the very one my sister and I were later conceived and raised in. Though it was an undeniable truth that he had in fact managed to round a small battalion (of three) Christian militiamen in pursuit of my mother and father who had planned to meet and get married in Cypriot Nicosia. It had to be Nicosia because civil marriage did not, and does not, exist in Lebanon, which makes interfaith marriage a difficult prospect.

My grandfather Nabil, who had battled a heart condition since his late forties, was a resourceful man. Barely a year before my parents eloped, my grandfather managed to pull off a minor miracle. He saved his only son from the clutches of the Christian Forces who had kidnapped the latter, having wrongly assumed that he was an undercover Muslim spy due to his frequent sojourns in West Beirut.

This was the mid-eighties, in the heat of the civil war and my uncle had believed that his life, like that of many before him, was lost and he resigned himself to his fate. He said his Christian prayers (mainly 'Our Father'), which the Christian Forces took to be an excessive commitment to the role, and asked for a drink of Arak. They brought him vodka and toasted his acting skills. The word 'Hollywood' was tossed about, and De Niro's name was taken in vain. My uncle thought about his fiancée in East Beirut, a Christian girl who was already pregnant with his child. He dared not hope that my grandfather Nabil would appear in the underground prison and save him from certain death. But, on some level, he must have known that if the news of his son's disappearance did not cause him an immediate heart attack, it would stir my grandfather into immediate action.

It did. Not two months later, my grandfather barged into the underground cell with a small battalion of armed Muslim militiamen. To hear my grandfather Nabil tell it, he merely hitched a ride. They were going in there anyway, and my tentatively devout Christian grandfather followed them in swinging Teta Mary's substantial white bra in the air. It was a sign of peace, a signal to the snipers that he was a family man not a fighting man. My drunk uncle was so distressed that he tried to claim that his name was Hussein and that he was in fact a Muslim spy, which perplexed the Muslim militiamen but not enough for them to actually put a bullet through his head before my bra-swinging grandfather could swoop in and whisk him away. My grandfather drove his son to the Beirut International Airport, which would later be renamed the Rafik Harriri Beirut International Airport, booked the first ticket to Dubai and from there to London, after the visa arrangements had been made. My uncle's fiancée followed him not long after that and he never returned to Beirut, not even to attend my grandfather's funeral.

Which is why, when my then would-be father heard that my then would-rather-not-be grandfather Nabil was threatening to round up a small battalion of Christian militiamen, the former wiped his forehead and booked two tickets to Cyprus where he and my mother were officially married. Not to be outdone, my grandfather Nabil booked four tickets to Cyprus, one for himself and three for the Christian militiamen, who were glad to see Cyprus for the first time. One of them stayed in Cyprus permanently having confessed his love for a Cypriot girl named Sofia, and tzatziki. The other two, according to my grandfather, might as well have stayed in Cyprus for all the good they did. My grandfather, and his party of militiamen, camped out at the airport for close to three days. And with airport security being what it was at the time, there were little to no issues with the matter. Except for one security official, Sofia, who would now and then ask if the Middle Eastern gentlemen were going anywhere or whether they planned to spend their entire holiday at the airport.

When my grandfather found out that my mother and father had managed to make their way to their scheduled airplane unnoticed, he sent word via Sofia that my mother was to make her way out of the plane across the runway and into Waiting Room C where she would be greeted and forgiven by her own father. He also sent an enclosed piece of paper in which he presented the alternative. To this day, I do not know what that alternative was. Neither my parents nor my grandmother ever disclosed the contents of that brief letter; and my grandfather never knowingly acknowledged its existence. He passed away when I was still only five or six and did not yet have the wherewithal to properly cross-examine him. Though I doubt that I would ever have. As I understand it, the letter contained, in my mother's own words, some 'heat-of-the-moment threat'.

I remember hearing the full unbarred version of the story. Whenever I wrap my arms around my knees and tuck them into my chest tightly, I can hear my mother's raspy voice, which by that point uncannily resembled my grandmother's, and see my father's uncomfortable stares and unsolicited intrusions as my sister and I crouched away hidden from the thunder and the RPG rockets and the Kalashnikovs. It was several years after the death of Monsieur Mermier. It was also the second time in six years that we had found ourselves hiding away.

The story was told within a series of other stories, meant to distract my sister and I from the terrible, colour-draining sounds and the equally terrible silences. For a few minutes, that story held my attention to such a degree that I cared a little less about the then immediate threat to my own life, and those of my family. I was reliving the earliest prenatal threat to my as yet unformed life. There before me were my parents now irreversibly trapped in the tiny, damp bathroom, with their own children hiding away from the threat of bullets and bombs, and there – in the retelling of that story – was the possibility, now discarded, that my very real mother and father could have never been. The impending threat of death-by-shrapnel seemed now to be less impending.

But to have once been a living being, to have once had a mother and father, and at once lost them; is that not better than to forever be a story about a letter which so disheartened my mother and so intimidated my father that they never became mine, and I never came to be? My mother shuddered when she recalled the contents of that letter and my father's eyes fixed more intensely on the ceiling, or perhaps past the ceiling itself. What strength, internal or external, had compelled my mother to defy the force of my grandfather's personality, the brutality of his words? It was not until sometime after those nights spent in the bathroom that my mother touched upon the subject again, in another private Arak-infused, smoke-basked conversation which lasted well past midnight but not a minute more after that.

ANDALUSIA AND THE MOORS

Alana was not Druze. I asked her. Alana was Canadian. She said she was Canadian and believed it. Her parents were both Lebanese but she had lived with them in Montreal for three or four years. She moved with her mother to Verdun Street. Her father would visit them a few times a year.

When I asked her if she was Muslim or Christian, she said again that she was Canadian. Then I asked her what her nationality was. She stared right through me and I never mentioned her nationality or her religion again.

Basil and I signed up to work as summer camp monitors. He said he knew someone on the inside who could get us the job and all we really had to do was make sure that a few kids don't drown at the beach and then get them home safe to their parents at the end of the day. Alana had had the same idea.

'I used to babysit my cousins all the time, in Montreal,' she said.

Alana looked bronze by the time she started working for the Octopus Summer Camp. Except for the bits around her eyes, still relatively white because of her aviator Ray-Bans which she would gently remove only to make a point and then return when the point was duly made.

Waist deep in sea water and with one of Don Amin's trademark whistles hanging around my neck, I watched as Alana lifted a three-year-old onto her back and ordered the rest of the children to follow her into the sea. She needn't have said a word, that day they would have followed her to the moon, or to Gibraltar at least.

'Oh my warriors, whither would you flee? Behind you is the sea, before you, the enemy.'

Tariq Bin Ziyad's immortal words did not feel out of place coming from her lips which were thick and full and hid her otherwise protruding canines well. Alana could have reconquered Andalusia for the Moors with an army of children and a three-year-old on her back. I was sure of it.

At Janna Beach Resort, she placed both her hands on my shoulders and tried to drown me. As I was standing in the sea and we were still in the shallow end, this did not work. Then she ordered the children to drown me, and they ran towards me, a wave of onrushing five-year-olds kicking through sand and shallow waters to try and drown me.

'Put far from you the disgrace from which you flee in dreams, and attack this monarch who has left his strongly fortified city to meet you.'

This did not work either.

Also, as she was making her way through to help them out, one of the five-year-olds managed to unhook her bikini top. She was able to hold onto it and prevent the waves from carrying it away, but not before I and a number of five-year-olds got to admire her white breasts.

'Do not believe that I desire to incite you to face dangers which I shall refuse to share with you.'

She told them off and I laughed. Then she laughed and I told them off.

Alana explained that Basil had made a bet with her, worth fifty thousand Lebanese liras, that she could not drown me. She said she would give me half of them if I pretended to drown. I said I did not want half of them. She said she would give me all of them. And I said I did not want all of them. Then she said she would give me another peek at her breasts because she saw how much I enjoyed the first one. She said she needed to get them tanned anyway and that she did not mind a Muslim Lebanese boy perving over them while she did. I said I was not Muslim. She said she did not care.

We swam as far away from the shore as we could. I looked back and the children were little dots in the distance and Basil was a slightly bigger dot – in an unbuttoned white shirt which he had refused to take off all day – and it was winking. Alana unhooked her bikini top, closed her eyes and floated on her back, allowing the sun to kiss her breasts. And I stared at her breasts, unashamedly. I stared at them for so long that I could see them start to turn a different shade of bronze. I mentioned this to her.

'You would know,' she said, 'you've been staring at them for twenty minutes.'

Alana said that I should be an astronaut if that is what I wanted to be. I said I was not so sure anymore. I said that I wanted to be but that if I was not, it would be alright too. She said she had always wanted to be Canadian and now she was.

'Never give up on your dream,' she said, gently removing her aviators even as she lay floating on her back in the murky water.

The oil from the Israeli warships, coupled with the waste from nearby factories and sewage plants, had severely damaged aquatic life along Lebanese shores. We had been instructed not to allow the children to swim for more than one hour a day in the sea. Alana and I ignored this. The sea was littered with empty bags of Fantasia chips and glass Pepsi bottles, and we reasoned that a bit of oil could not have done too much more harm.

'What about you?' I asked.

She wore a silver necklace around her neck. There was no Hilal or cross attached to it.

'I don't want to be an astronaut,' she said, eyes closed, 'it must be the loneliest feeling in the world. Why would you do that to yourself?'

'Perspective,' I said.

I plunged my head underwater then slowly emerged so that my nose rose barely above the warm water.

'Whose?'

I let the salty water be sucked into my gaping mouth, then I spat it out. My eyes were now level with her breasts and I could see the children walking in behind them and coming out the other side. There was a miniature version of myself in space gear landing on her chest, floating past the little spot on her left breast, around the first nipple, into the cavernous valley in between, all the while gaining momentum, then bursting furiously uphill to plant the American flag on her right nipple. It was always the Stars and Stripes that were synonymous with achievement, with overcoming adversity, with a sense of accomplishment, with the act of marking success by planting a flag on a mountain top, or a moon or a nipple.

'I suppose being the first woman on the moon doesn't sound too bad,' she continued.

'The first Arab woman.'

'The first woman, habibi. Even the Americans couldn't get one of us up there.'

She splashed the oily water into my eyes.

'I know.'

'And besides, I'm Canadian.'

'I know.'

There was a long pause for which the waves were grateful.

'You won't be able to achieve your dreams if you spend your whole life in Beirut,' she said.

'I know.'

Behind me was Cyprus, and behind Cyprus was Sicily and behind that was Valencia, and in between all of them and Beirut was the salty water of the Mediterranean, and me. And Alana.

'Not much sun in Montreal?' I asked.

Alana told me about one of the little girls she was looking after who pitied her because she had lived in the West.

'It's so sad,' the little girl had proclaimed.

'Why?' I asked Alana.

'Because the sun always sets in the west,' said Alana, 'she thinks I could only see sunsets in Montreal.'

The sun hovered above the horizon.

'It is a city for the summer and not much else,' she said, opening her eyes and craning her neck to look at me, 'but it is alright in the summer, isn't it?'

'Yes. It is,' I said, nodding my head and squinting to protect my eyes from the sun.

To the casual human observer, I was giving a drowning girl mouth to mouth resuscitation. I was breathing air into her lungs. I was saving a life. I was fighting, railing against death and the mild, gentle waves of the Mediterranean. To Alana, I was giving her a kiss on the lips, at first a soft peck then a deeper more inquisitive exploration of the inner workings of her moist mouth. To the oil-sodden fish, I was in the way.

'When do you think you'll be able to grow a full beard?' she asked, removing her hand from the side of my face.

I shrugged my shoulders. I looked at Alana, half expecting her to morph into one of the mermaids. She did not.

I helped her put her purple bikini top back on then we swam back to the shallow bit. She jumped on top of me and, at first, I let her weight drag me down. I lowered my body so that my shoulders were level with the water.

Alana gave me a gentle push in order to remind me of our agreement but I did not budge. Then she gave me another gentle push to remind me of the fact that she had upheld her end of the bargain. Then she put her knee through the back of my head and I fell face forward into the salty water. The children cheered and Alana raised her right arm in the air. They called her name and she blew them kisses and they skipped up and down the sand, celebrating the conquest.

I stayed in the water for a few minutes afterwards. I looked at the sun, without blinking, until I had tears in my eyes. In the distance, I saw a whale. It was blueish white and not very big. I only saw it for a second. I might have only seen the tail. I plunged my head into the water again, then walked back to shore. Basil, still in his dirty white shirt with the sleeves rolled up to the elbows, extended the palm of his hand and I reached for my wallet, which I had tucked neatly under my blue towel, and gave him two twenty thousand Lebanese lira notes and told him I would cover the rest later.

Basil's dark black hair turned slightly red in the sunlight. I also told him that I had seen a small whale in the sea. He said he had seen a goat.

'I'm serious,' I said, throwing myself onto the sand-covered towel.

He said there are no whales in the Mediterranean.

There are.

I had only just rested my head against the sand when I heard it. A guttural screech emanating from what I knew was the other end of the shoreline. I leapt to my feet and instantly felt Basil's arm around my shoulder. He was both leaning against me and pulling me closer to him.

'Don't react,' said Basil, his beer-breath in my ear.

There along the shore, some way away, was a boy of eight or nine who was barrelling towards us, screeching, kicking sand behind him. Every few steps, he would stop to catch his breath, always resuming his gallop with the same visceral cry and a rigid clenched fist in the air.

I crossed my arms to show that I was unfazed.

'I slapped him,' said Basil, maintaining his gaze.

'What?'

I uncrossed my arms.

'I slapped that boy twice. Knocked him right off his feet in front of all his little friends. Don't react, son of life.'

The boy bent over to catch his breath again then raised his same fist in the air and willed himself forwards, his voice commanding the attention of everyone at the beach except for the seagulls.

'I called his mother,' continued Basil, 'I meant to apologise. She asked me what he had done wrong. I said nothing. She said he must have done something wrong. And I said he had not. And she said she was going to punish him again when he gets home.'

'She's going to beat him.'

'She said she would make him bleed.'

'He doesn't even know it.'

'He knows.'

Basil's eyes were urging the boy, pleading with him not to give up. He explained that the boy, Moustafa, had asthma which was why it was taking him so long. As he drew closer we could see that his fist, unretracted since his last stop, was covered in fresh, glistening blood. I began to take one step towards the boy but felt the weight of Basil's pull.

When Moustafa did finally reach us, the sun had set and he could barely breathe. We washed his face in lukewarm water and patted him on the back. I tried to clean his wound but he would not unclench his fist and instead squeezed harder which caused the blood to gush forward. Then, without further warning, he lashed out at Basil, scratching and kicking any part of him he could get a hold of, smattering Basil's shirt in red. Basil lowered himself to his knees so that he was almost level with Moustafa, who then unclenched his bloodied fist and rammed a jagged piece of broken glass into the slight gap below Basil's cheekbone.

Basil sat on the sand, hunched forward with his feet in the water and his now off-white/ burgundy shirt rolled up and pressed against his cheek. I had spent the evening on the Octo-bus – the Octopus Summer Camp's official choice of transportation – alongside Alana, dropping the children off and explaining to their parents exactly what had happened. Then apologising. A scuffle had broken out immediately following Moustafa's concealed attack. Basil had chucked Moustafa in the air and landed him half a metre away and the kids had then rushed towards Basil kicking and screaming, accompanied by Alana. Most of the parents had not been too concerned. One or two mothers shook their heads or hugged their children a little tighter and asked when we would be picking them up tomorrow. A few told us off then insisted that the culprit – Basil – resign, which we assured them he would do. As soon as the last of them had been returned to their parents, Alana declared that she never wanted to see me or my psychotic friend again. I protested my innocence briefly without conviction. Then I said that I would quit, if she wanted me to, and requested that the bus driver drop me off back at the beach where I knew Basil would still be.

'Where the fuck were you?' he asked, scowling.

My eyes slowly adjusted to the absence of light as I made my way towards his huddled figure.

'Dropping off the kids you nearly murdered,' I said, grabbing his head with both hands and tilting it back to get a better view of the damage to his face.

He slapped my hands away, and blood dripped onto the sand.

'I should have given Moustafa's mother another call,' he said, running his blood-stained hand through his hair. 'She would have finished the job for me.'

'Did she say anything?' he asked, after dabbing at his cut for a while.

'She wasn't there.'

I bent over without sitting and extended the palm of my hand. He placed a single twenty thousand lira note.

'Didn't work out between you and Tariq Bin Ziyad?'

I often wonder if it was he or I who had first compared Alana to the famed conqueror, and whether I had reimagined our encounter based on Basil's remark soon after or my own impression of her at the time. I sometimes believe that I mentioned the resemblance to him just before Moustafa came running at us, but then I remember that I could not have because I had barely rested my head when I heard the boy's cry of war.

'There were two of those.'

He shrugged.

'I'm short on cash. My adulterous bastard of a father doesn't store it in his wallet anymore,' he said, flipping the crunched up shirt and dabbing at his cut again. 'I think he caught on after the missing picture.'

Behind us rose the glass Tower of Dreams I, in which it was rumoured resided several celebrities including former Miss Lebanons and wealthy Saudi oil merchants and a number of gluttonous politicians and their business associates. Hidden behind the Tower of Dreams I stood a bomb shelter which had been turned into a brothel and an old bakery which would soon open its doors and allow the smell of manouche and cheese and thyme and olive oil to overtake that of the sea.

'Why didn't he confront you about the money you already stole then?' I asked, placing my hands in my pockets.

'The pimp's afraid I'll tell my mother about the girl in the picture if he confronts me about anything,' he said, reaching into his own pocket and producing the picture. 'I'm dead certain he's having an affair after this.'

The photograph was smeared with his blood. He raised it up in the air, holding it between his thumb and index, then he gave it a flick with his middle finger and let it drop into the water.

'All those Gauloises, all those olive, lime-flavored condoms, all that cash, and the pimp notices when I take a picture from his wallet,' said Basil, reaching for his Gauloises and placing one between his lips.

As Basil shifted his weight in the sand, the moonlight gently brushed against his bicep and I could see for the first time the reason why he had not taken off his white shirt for the entire day, nor delved into the sea. It was a tattoo of the spinning swastika of the Syrian Social Nationalist Party on his biceps. It appeared to be fresh and raw and protruded, as if it were about to leap out of his left arm and spin wildly out of control.

'What's that about?' I asked, flicking my head in the direction of the tattoo.

'Nothing,' he said, covering it with his bloodied shirt, 'it's the "whirlwind".'

He chucked his transparent green lighter at my chest. I caught it and lit his cigarette for him. I had not held a lighter since Don Amin confiscated mine that day when my father was late to pick me up from school. The act felt natural. I instinctively knew what to do. I imagined that this was how old militiamen must feel when handed a gun.

'It's that spinning swastika on the board in Momo the paedophile's office,' I said. 'Isn't it?'

'It's the emblem of the Syrian Social Nationalist Party,' said Basil, without flinching, 'the "whirlwind".'

'It's the paedophile's swastika,' I said.

I held his gaze for some time as he took a puff of his cigarette.

'It's not a swastika,' he said, baring his left arm with the cigarette dangling between the index and middle fingers of his right hand. 'Look here, it's a combination of the Muslim Crescent and the Christian Cross.'

I could not see it.

'What about the Druze?'

'They're in there somewhere,' he continued, 'the four arms each stand for one of the party's virtues: freedom, duty, discipline and power.'

He attempted to trace the spinning swastika with his index finger, but the tattoo was still sore. He winced and dropped his cigarette. I picked it up, took a puff and gave it back to him. Basil covered the spinning swastika with the palm of his hand.

Looking back, I am reminded of the old Druze saying, which I was unaware of at the time: 'That which shields is that which is shielded. And that which is shielded is that which shields. The former is the latter and the latter is the former. There is no difference between them.'

'Since when are you a fan of duty and discipline?' I asked, coughing and slipping the lighter into my pocket.

Basil's mouth widened. I took this to be a smile. He tapped his hand against the wet sand gently. I took off my shoes, then my socks. I rolled them up and placed them inside my shoes then I dipped my feet in the water and allowed myself to drop back onto the sand so that I was lying right beside where Basil sat cross-legged; and he told me that the SSNP was everything he and I had been looking for. He said that they were a secular party that did not care about who you are or where you come from. He said that they did not care about 'advancing the dogmas' of this religious sect or that, unlike all the other political parties in Lebanon. He said that they were not Sunni or Shiite or Catholic or Druze or Maronite or Orthodox.

'They're not Lebanese, either,' I said, reaching for his cigarette and taking another puff.

His mouth widened once more. This time I did not take it to be a smile.

'They are,' he said, 'they just believe in something greater than Lebanon.'

He said that the SSNP also believed in youth.

'This,' he said, pointing to the tattoo on his biceps, 'was designed at the American University of Beirut by students, like you and me, in secret.'

I asked him where he had learned all this and he said, 'Mr Malik.' Not Momo or the paedophile or Momo the paedophile. Just 'Mr Malik'.

Then he gave me a light slap across the cheek and tossed his bundled-up shirt onto my face.

Opposite the brothel, Candlelight, stood half a building. It was under construction and would rise to twenty-four floors when complete. 'Luxury Furnished apartments for

Rent/Sale' read a large white sign. The future inhabitants of that luxury building would not take too kindly to having a brothel between them and the Tower of Dreams I. Candlelight would become Tasty and Tasty would become Two Cups and Two Cups would become Starlight, which was audacious and older generations would boast about understanding the reference. And the bakery, that would have to go too.

A RIP IN SPACE AND TIME

When I asked my father if he was having an affair, he said 'no'. And when I asked him again, he said he was not. When I asked him for the third time, he said he would say he was if it meant I would stop asking him about it. I did not say anything. And he said he was.

'With whom?' asked my sister, as she sat on the comfortable couch eating her share of Bonjus vanilla ice cream.

The two towering blocks of literature by the door had remained there undisturbed, but beside them and in front of the bookshelves, a wall of old books had been accumulating all along. At first, no one had realised what was happening apart from my father. No one believed that it was even conceivable. And by the time we caught on, the wall was already halfway up and there was very little we could do about it except avoid running into to it so that we did not have to deal with the rubble.

The wall stood between the bookshelves and the rest of the hallway and seemed to have been erected to shield the bookshelves from the outside world, or to keep them from ever venturing out into it. It was like the Berlin Wall, except instead of the Soviets on the Eastern side, we had books. And instead of Checkpoint Charlie, we had three or four gaps in the wall through which my father would slip his hand and reach for his intended reading. Now and then, he would come up with the wrong book and chuck it back over the wall.

'Madame Hafez.'

'Since when?'

'Jesus-Mohammad-Christ. Since the incident with the cedar tree.'

'You're a terrible human being,' said my sister.

'What's the matter with you two?' he asked, his face hidden behind his *An-Nahar Daily*.

Had my father looked up from his newspaper more often than he did, I suspect that he would have had one of those clairvoyant, nebulous stares; eyes that see through and past you into a place where you cannot hope to go. But he rarely did.

My sister said that she would never again climb into the room stacked with books, that he could get his own books and that she was too big now anyway.

Every man suspects his father of having had an affair. Some have pictures of younger women or condom wrappers or an unforgiving memory, others have an uncomfortable glance or an ill-timed clearing of the throat or a cough.

My father's affair with books culminated in a publishing house. The publishing house was an idea which had weighed on his mind for several years, ever since his drunken conversation with Monsieur Mermier, but it was not until what I took to be his midlife crisis, that he felt confident in going through with it. He called it Ninnette Publishing House. The logo was the silhouette of a cat with a tail which resembled a question mark and his first client was Madame Hafez. Madame Hafez was now almost an octogenarian of Armenian descent. Her first name, I learned that day, was Lusine, and her real last name was Sarkissian. Her choice of Hafez was a name she'd used to shield herself from the hostility she perceived she might face in west Beirut. She had resided alone in Bourj Hammoud, the Armenian quarter in Beirut, prior to marrying the doctor and moving in with him.

Before that, however, Lusine had travelled the Middle East. Her parents had been forced out of their homes due to the Armenian genocide in Turkey around the onset of the twentieth century. She had lived in Baghdad with her parents before the Gulf War, Mosul with her first husband before the Iraq war, and Aleppo, with her sister.

'I've written a book about my life, Mr Najjar,' said Lusine, pointing her arthritis-plagued finger in the direction of my father's heart, 'and I want you to publish it.'

My father had insisted upon the whole family accompanying him to the first meeting. He promised us zucchini and vine leaves at my mother's favourite restaurant, Socrates, afterwards.

'It would show that I'm a family man,' he said, 'this business is all about impressions.'

It did not seem to matter that Madame Hafez was the landlord and neighbour, that she had lived a single floor below our own for nearly two decades or so, and that whatever impression she had had about my father, she would have formulated some time ago.

Madame Hafez, or Lusine, offered me a plate of Arabic sweets. I said I did not really like Arabic sweets. She produced a Cadbury bar from a drawer in the living room side table. The doctor had passed away two years before and Madame Hafez was living with her sister again, who had moved in with her recently from Aleppo. Madame Hafez's sister said she did not feel safe in Syria anymore. She said that age had not dimmed her ability to smell a war brewing from afar. She spent her days and nights in bed, except when she felt obliged to attend to the garden/parking lot at the bottom of the building. Lately, Madame Hafez had taken on those gardening duties due to her sister's failing health.

The chandelier was decorated with what appeared to be crystal and hung low from the ceiling. The rest of the furniture did not go with the chandelier and made it look even more impressive than it might have otherwise been.

'Have you titled the book yet?' asked my father, sipping his Turkish coffee.

My sister and I sat either side of my parents. I placed my finger through the crochet on the couch's armrest.

'I have not finished writing it yet,' said Madame Hafez, who had more white hair than grey, 'I thought about titling it: *Sykes-Picot and I.*'

'How about something more straightforward like *From Armenia to Lebanon*?'

'That is possible.'

'Or how about *Through the Middle East*?'

'That is possible, too.'

'Or how about *Wars and Cities of the Middle East*?'

'No,' said Madame Hafez.

Madame Hafez then requested that the defecating cat be excluded from the cover of her book. My father explained that the cat logo would have to be included but that the dot beneath the question mark/tail could be negotiated away if she so wished. Madame Hafez placed her glasses on her nose and scrutinized the paper in front of her displaying Ninnette, the defecating cat.

'I suppose,' she said, removing her glasses, 'if you insist.'

She had two sets of glasses on her at all times. One hung from her neck and another was uneasily balanced on her nose. She was forever removing a pair of glasses to place the other pair on.

My father spoke at length about how vital a book like this is, how it will change the world, how this is exactly the kind of story that literature has been lacking of late. Madame Hafez nodded along, the water in her sea blue eyes responding to the windswept charm of my father's barren words. She may have even smiled at one point. Then my father explained that as he did not yet have the capital to invest in the book, she would have to fund the publication of the book herself but that he would ensure she got a fair portion of the earnings in return. Madame Hafez said she had some gardening to do and walked us towards the elevator.

'What kind of human being are you?' asked my sister, as my mother, father and I squeezed into the old elevator opposite Madame Hafez.

The lift had a Vintage Otis wooden scissor gate which one had to close manually. The mirror was rusted around the edges and foggy, but it didn't matter because the light was too dim for the mirror to be of use.

'Excuse me?' asked Madame Hafez.

'Who uproots a tree that a girl planted in the ground and throws it in the bin?' asked my sister.

There are rare instances when a wronged child speaks and you see the rip in space and time, the affronted adult emerge and the words flow from the coarser lips. If you should happen to miss the rip in space and time, observe the adults in the room. They will squirm. Their noses will shrink, their eyes double in size, their cheeks inflate, their wrinkles fade away and their foreheads enlarge to occupy most of their faces pushing the rest of their features down towards the chin which often takes on a less angular form shedding any residual facial hair and developing a crisp gleam. And once the rip in space and time occurs, reality very briefly manifests itself in unstable form.

'I did no such thing,' said Madame Hafez, squirming.

'It wasn't me,' said a fresh-faced Lusine.

The latter had a lisp.

'It was a tree given to her by the school on Independence Day, a few years ago,' said my mother, 'I don't expect you would remember this.'

'You're lying,' shouted a little brunette girl who resembled my mother, her teeth a pearly white not yet stained with nicotine.

'What kind of tree was it?' asked Madam Hafez.

'What tree?' asked young Lusine.

'A cedar tree and you killed it,' said my sister.

'That's enough,' said my father who had his arm around my sister.

'I don't want to play anymore,' said my young father, his face no longer jowly, his eyes bright and unsaddled with bags, his moustache gone.

'Whoever planted that tree there killed it. I merely cleaned up the mess that was left behind,' said Madame Hafez.

'It was him. I'm telling you. It was him,' said Lusine.

My sister looked up at my father, who placed both his hands on her shoulders.

'You don't know that it would have died,' he said, now staring at Madame Hafez.

'Cedar trees do not belong by the coast. They belong in the mountains,' said Madame Hafez staring back. 'Have you ever seen a cedar tree in Beirut?'

'It would have been the first one,' said my father.

'It would have been the first one,' said my young father, fists clenched, eyebrows furled, teeth grating.

'Don't be ridiculous, Mr Najjar. You're a grown man. It would have died and you know it.'

'Surely, you could have let her find this out for herself,' said my father.

'That's enough,' said my mother.

'It is not my job to teach your children life lessons,' replied Madame Hafez as the elevator arrived at the ground floor.

It is then that my sister's curls began to unfurl. It happened almost imperceptibly at first, then a couple of them would audibly snap into a faultless, listless strand of hair and so dangle from her scalp down to her shoulders, as if exhausted by the sheer outrage. In the following years my sister would begin to use a hair straightener, but long before the BaByliss there was Madame Hafez and her crimes against cedar trees, there was sitting silently in the back seat of the Oldsmobile, there was clinging onto the edge of the bed at my grandparents' place, there was being refused the option to fast by my mother and the opportunity to publish an article by my father, there was getting up to change the channel at our every whim, there was having to navigate the untold horrors of my father's book room, there was being called *Fara* which it would transpire, a few decades later, she did not in fact like.

My father reached for the Vintage Otis wooden scissor gate and slammed it open. Madame Hafez stood aside and my father stomped his way out, adjusting his collar as he did so.

'Everything alright, Basha?' asked Saeed, the porter, who was standing by the entrance to the building in his flip-flops.

'Do you have cedar trees in Egypt, Saeed?' asked my father.

My father's question caught everyone but the porter off guard. The latter had, evidently, never given up hope that my father would one day directly address him again. His answer was succinct and then it was adjusted in order to please my father.

'We do not, Basha. I think it is too hot in Egypt for cedars.'

'But do you think that if you really wanted to, you could grow one?'

'I hear there is snow in Dubai now. You can go and ski there, if you really wanted to. So I don't see why not.'

My father turned on his heel and smiled in the direction of Madame Hafez who was still making her way out of the elevator, while my mother held the door for her. He opened his arms as if he had just conjured a cedar tree out of the ether, as if there was a judge sitting where an old lady was climbing out of an elevator, as if there was a jury lined up on the stairway behind him, as if out there, past the green gate which led into the building, there were cameramen and camerawomen and reporters jostling to get a glimpse of the man who had proven to the world that cedar trees, that *Cedrus libani*, could, if one really wanted them to, be grown in Beirut.

'But I would not go to Dubai to ski,' added Saeed, 'I would not go to Dubai at all.'

Wars and Cities of the Middle East was never published. And *Through the Middle East* was never published. And *From Armenia to Lebanon* was never published. And, perhaps above all, *Sykes-Picot and I* was never published.

The day Mohammad came in to school after his father had disappeared was a memorable one, in that the teachers mostly did not know how to behave. It happened a day after that rip in space and time within the walls of the elevator. I wondered whether his disappearance was an unintended by-product of that tear in the very fabric of the universe, but Mohammad explained that his father had not disappeared at all.

'He was kidnapped,' said Mohammad.

'From his bed?' asked Basil.

'It was a targeted operation.'

Ms Mayssa offered her condolences, to which Mohammad replied that he thought his father was still alive. Ms Mayssa then took back her condolences.

'The Don was right about this one,' said Mohammad, as she left the class.

Mr Abu Alam pretended that the whole kidnapping had not taken place, and Mohammad burst into tears in the middle of the former's explanation of relativity. It was not even on the syllabus for that term but I suspect he believed that Einstein's theory of relativity would prove enough of a distraction for the day.

Mr Malik singled Mohammad out and asked him to recite a poem written by Al Mutanabbi, an egomaniacal, tenth-century Arab poet who had played at being a prophet. He later recanted his claim but the name 'Mutanabbi', which means 'the self-proclaimed prophet', stuck. Under the circumstances, Mohammad did what can only be described as an admirable job. He walked up to the front of the class and stood by Mr Malik's desk. He looked at Mr Malik who nodded then mouthed the words 'go on' without uttering another word.

At first it was incoherent blubbering, and Basil swore he heard him stumble over the words 'I want my father'. Then Mohammad straightened his back and treated us to his own summation of Al Mutanabbi's greatest hits. The structure made little sense and whole poems were reduced to one or two verses, he even modified certain words and arguably added substance.

'I am he whose literature is seen by the blind. And whose words are heard by the deaf.

'The steed, the night and the desert know me. As do the sword, the spear, the paper and the pen – and the eraser.'

The class fell quiet again and you could hear the overhead fan humming its approval.

'Man does not obtain all that he wishes. The winds take the ships where they do not desire to go.

'If you see the lion's teeth displayed, do not think that the lion is smiling – or frowning either.'

Nadine and Wael led a round of applause, Basil and I joined in half-heartedly and so did the rest of the class. Mr Malik shook his head and waved Mohammad back to his seat.

According to Mohammad, a helicopter had descended onto the roof of their building in the middle of the night. A group of armed men had burst through the door and led his father out of there.

'They spoke Hebrew,' he said, during break, as he spread himself along the green wooden bench under the acorn tree.

There had not been a president for so long that the school simply opted to paint over where the portrait once stood.

'So not the SSNP then?' asked Basil.

'This is not funny,' said Mohammad, looking up at us with his hand now resting on his forehead.

Wael smacked Basil across the back of the head.

'Are all Syrian Nationalists idiots,' asked Wael, 'or is it just you?'

The incident had been all over the news featuring Mohammad's mother wailing and Mohammad standing in the background looking perplexed, almost like he was about to recite one of Mr Malik's poeMs His father shared the same name as the leader of Hezbollah at the time. This had been enough to puzzle the Israelis and rush the Mossad into an operation which ended with them in possession of a fairly jovial and clean shaven man. The nation had been caught between a mood of comic disbelief and one of concern for the fate of the unfortunate namesake.

'What's in a name?' the LBC news anchor exclaimed, cocking an eyebrow. 'A lot, apparently.'

I wondered what Mr Aston would have made of that appropriation.

The only self-evident piece of information available was that someone from the Israeli side had committed a mishap. This made the Israelis the butt of a joke for a couple of weeks.

'An Israeli walked into an electronics store to buy a coloured TV,' said Basil, pausing to look over his shoulder,

'When the owner asked him which coloured TV he would like. He said, "An orange one".'

Even Mohammad laughed timidly at that.

'Do you think they'll return him?' I asked.

'Return him?' asked Mohammad in a raised pitch. 'Like he was a shoe that did not fit.'

Basil leaned in and muttered his assessment of the situation in my ear; it was to do with Mohammad being a bit too dramatic, even for a boy whose father had just been kidnapped by the Mossad.

It did not matter whether I agreed, I was glad to have a private moment with Basil. He and I had found our time together constrained now that he was spending more of it after classes with younger boys who would lurk outside school for him to emerge and greet him with a cigarette or two. These new recruits of the SSNP – his own or Mr Malik's, I could not tell – usually nodded in my general direction. Somewhere within the nod there was also a nudge, or on those less subtle days, a shoulder barge. I was never personally introduced to any of them – though I did recognise a regular boy with a pudgy face and dimples who was always the first to spot me – and Basil, sensing that they were not my crowd, would pat me on the back as we approached the school gate and promise to catch up later.

Ms Iman, who seemed to know where on school grounds to find us, walked straight in between Basil and myself and sat on the green bench by Mohammad's head. He hesitated at first, his body stiffened and his hand gripped the edge of the bench. Basil and I both stood over Ms Iman, hands in our pockets, with Wael behind us.

Ms Iman placed her hand on Mohammad's forehead . She shaped her lips to say something but did not. Emboldened by this, Mohammad laid his head against her lap and turned his neck so that he was now facing her Bordeaux shirt. And he sobbed. He sobbed like a man, not a boy. At one point his knee slammed hard against the back of the bench but he did not acknowledge this at all. Basil and I tried to expand our adolescent bodies as much as we possibly could in order to conceal Mohammad from the rest of the school. But we could not.

We looked to Wael for guidance on this matter, but his body contracted instead as if to shield an infant from the weight of the world. Every passer-by would have seen Mohammad that day, his head buried in Ms Iman's lap, his chest heaving, his shoulders shivering, his torso shaking, his voice cracking.

Ms Iman pursed her lips and for some time said nothing. She looked at the three of us and the edge of her mouth dipped.

'Maybe he should have stayed at home,' said Wael, planting his elbows on mine and Basil's shoulders.

Wael was so tall that he sometimes had to duck when Mr Abu Alam aimed his famous Highlanders at us in class. The trajectory of the physics teacher's flying Highlanders was spot on when it came to narrowly, but purposefully, missing most of us. Wael, however, quickly found that he was an exception, a statistical anomaly.

'It happens,' said Ms Iman, stroking Mohammad's hair.

She might have meant the sobbing or the kidnapping. I was back in the bathroom hiding from the bombs.

This encouraged Mohammad who took his sobbing to a more pronounced level.

'Now he's definitely milking it,' said Basil, nudging me in the ribs and squeezing the udders of an invisible cow.

Wael smacked the both of us across the back of the head before I could protest.

For the first week, no one heard anything about Mr Nasrallah. Ms Mayssa refrained from reoffering her condolences and classes carried on as usual. During break, Basil and I speculated that the whole scenario was an elaborate ploy devised by Mohammad's father as a means of escape. We did this away from Wael and Mohammad because we did not want to appear callous.

'He'll have called the Israelis up and begged them to kidnap him,' said Basil, but he did not laugh.

Then on a Wednesday, in the second week, Mohammad did not come to school. We later learned that another helicopter had landed on the roof of their building and dropped off a disorientated Mr Nasrallah. He was escorted, blindfolded, down the stairs and left in the hallway. He staggered into the front door and Mohammad, who had slept in the living room by the door, with his mother, rushed to open it.

The jovial man was no longer so clean shaven.

'He did not know where he was at first,' said Mohammad, in the morning just outside class. 'He shouted something about fucking the mother of the next man who lays a finger on him.'

The man's lip was swollen.

'Was he badly bruised?' asked Wael, placing his hands on his waist.

'Not at all,' said Mohammad, 'once he realised it was me who was hugging him. He calmed down.'

Mohammad chewed his gum thoroughly then he tossed it in the air and swung his foot at it but missed. He winced.

'He must be Mossad,' whispered Basil in my ear. 'How else do you explain him waltzing back into the country like nothing happened?'

'Don't be ridiculous,' I said.

Mr Nasrallah was in his mid-sixties but he stayed up that night telling them how tiresome this whole trip had been and repeating that there truly is no place like home. It was as if he had been to London on a business trip. He refused to do any interviews and when one TV reporter would not leave, he told her that he could arrange for her to be picked up by the Israelis from her place if she really insisted on an interview.

'He's gone,' said Basil, grabbing my arm and squeezing it tightly for a moment.

'Who?'

'The pimp. I couldn't believe it at first. I thought for sure he'd come back. I told my mother about the picture. They had a big row. He's gone.'

'Your father?' I asked, disingenuously. 'When?'

A few weeks prior, I had been helping my mother carry the groceries up the staircase after a power outage, when she ran into an acquaintance of hers who was there visiting Madame Hafez. The acquaintance mentioned Mr Abou Mekhi – and wasn't his son a classmate of your son? That poor fatherless boy. My mother turned towards me. Sweat dripped down the sides of her face and her fingers strained to prevent her palms from opening to unleash bags of onions and bell peppers rolling back down the stairs. She closed her eyes and opened them gently then pushed on, lugging the groceries up the next flight. And I followed.

'Three weeks ago,' said Basil.

He patted his pockets for a cigarette or a lighter. When he could not find what he was looking for, he made his way steadily towards the school gates without another word.

Basil and my father sat opposite one another at the dinner table, between them were stacks of books including one titled *God, Arab Nationalism and the Leader*. I sat on the comfortable couch in the living room. This was the only time they spoke at length. Up to that point, my father would acknowledge Basil by giving him a nod and asking how his father was doing and never stopping to hear the answer. I could see them clearly but they would have had to crane their necks to look at me. A wall of books towered over Basil. It was a business meeting and I was there only to moderate.

Basil had come up to me after Ms Shahab's maths class. The board was devoid of shapes. There were only numbers and radical signs and 'unknowns' symbolized by an X or Y.

'Remind me to get Wael to go over all of this again later,' said Basil. 'Numbers make about as much sense as politics in the Middle East.'

He had become good at interweaving subjects which had seemingly little in common with one another. I suspected that this was Mr Malik's influence but I did not make this known.

Basil went on to explain that Mr Malik had written a book about the political state of the region and that our mutual Arabic teacher's wish was for my father to publish it.

'A revolutionary book,' Basil described it. He said he would be happy to tell me a lot more about it if I had time.

'Don't you have to meet up with the SSNP boys?'

'Not today,' he said. He shook his head and offered a smile which was not his.

It has occurred to me since that Basil was the first literary agent I had ever met, though I was not familiar with the term at the time. I never read the book. I held the manuscript in my hands that day and it seemed heavy enough to start a revolution. When I looked at my father's face, I saw that it would not.

'It is bland,' my father said, leaning closer to Basil. 'It is repetitive Pan-Syrian-light bullshit repackaged to fit the social nationalist agenda of today.'

'That's not true,' whispered Basil through gritted teeth. They were already yellow and stained.

'Worst of all is he hasn't said anything that Antoun Saadeh himself didn't say sixty years ago,' said my father, flipping through the manuscript but barely touching the pages. 'It's the worst kind of plagiarism. The kind that doesn't know it is plagiarism until someone else points it out.'

Antoun Saadeh was the founder of the SSNP. His life was spent between exile and imprisonment. Eventually, he was hanged for treason after launching the armed 'First Renaissance Revolution' against the Lebanese government in the late forties.

'It will start a revolution,' said Basil, gasping for air.

After Saadeh was hanged, the SSNP responded by assassinating the first Prime Minister of the Republic of Lebanon: Riad El Solh.

Basil held my father's stare. It was the longest I had seen Basil go without winking or smiling or sighing or puffing at his Gauloises.

I was unsure whether he had in fact read the manuscript or sat for a summary which Mr Malik would have been more than glad to provide.

'This book wouldn't start a fire if I held it to a flame,' said my father, 'let alone a revolution.'

My father played the role of disgruntled publisher well. Had his intention been to lower the agent's demands he would have succeeded, but Basil had long ago relented. He had offered that Mr Malik pay for the costs of publication in return for the name and logo of the publishing house as well as half the earnings.

'But we are the *Sons of Life*,' said Basil and I looked around because I did not see the words come out of his mouth.

This last phrase was how Saadeh had referred to members of his party. Sons of Life. And he dubbed all the ideologies which he opposed as the 'forces of darkness'. These forces included but were not limited to: feudalism, Christian separatism, Islamic fundamentalism, Zionism and, time permitting, colonialism. There was always a lot more darkness than life.

'Why does Malik want me to publish it, anyway?' asked my father, looking up.

Bits of the ceiling now resembled that of a brothel. The plaster had been peeling and neglected for several winters. There was even a single path which the dripping water had drawn for itself extending from the ceiling to the floor.

'The Don liked you and Mr Malik respected the Don,' said Basil, 'he heard that you were now in the business of publishing books. He wanted this to be a joint venture.'

This was not the reason. My father knew it.

An ephemeral smile sauntered through his face without pausing to acknowledge Basil's words. In its short-lived run Ninnette Publishing House, via the personage of my father, had failed to publish two books: the first for lack of funding and the second for lack of content. From the comfortable living room couch, I could see that my father was prouder of not publishing the second book than he was of not publishing the first.

'Will you publish it?' I asked.

It was not the suspense that was killing me. I knew the answer. It was having to watch Basil struggle under the weight of my father's retorts.

Had Basil asked me whether I believed my father would go along with Mr Malik's proposal, I would have persuaded him to find a publisher with a record for publishing books. Mr Malik and his odd choice of publisher baffled me, but the manner in which he had gone about it – that is, manipulating Basil to go through me in order to get to my father – sat well with my perception of the man.

'Jesus Mohammad Christ,' said my father, with an unusual, and undue, resolve. This was not the almost intuitively dismissive Jesus Mohammad Christ of old. This one was a different breed.

'What?' asked Basil.

'Listen to me, son,' said my father, holding Basil's chin between his thumb and index finger. 'When you see this man next, run in the other direction. And keep running. He won't catch you. He's got a bad leg.'

That my father had felt the need to point out Mr Malik's leg struck me as odd, even at the time, before everything else that would happen afterwards. Possibly, my father thought that Basil was so blind to Mr Malik's tricks that he would not have noticed his bad leg. Or maybe he derived a certain pleasure out of noting that this man, whom he disliked, was in some way disadvantaged.

'You've got it all wrong,' said Basil, pushing my father's hand away, 'I volunteered to bring the manuscript to you.'

'He's a war relic,' said my father. 'He lives for war. The entire party is a war relic.'

'You're mistaken, you'll regret this,' said Basil, now shaking.

And with those words came the end of Ninnette Publishing House, though neither I nor my father knew this at the time.

He stood up and made to reach for the manuscript but my father banged his fist twice in quick succession against the stacked pieces of paper. The first time his fist connected with the manuscript it rose as if insulted by the gesture and a few papers were sent flying across the room. The second time was more final and the towering blocks of literature by the door threatened to tumble.

'He's a pimp,' said my father, looking Basil straight in the eyes, 'a crippled pimp.'

'I'm telling him.'

I never fully knew why my father so despised Mr Malik. He never disclosed this to me or to anyone for that matter, so far as I know. When I think of the article I wrote soon after the Don's death and how Mr Malik used that as a tool with which to insult my father, I feel a measured sense of guilt. Though, even then I believed the matter was much larger than me and my article. I suspected my father saw in Mr Malik everything that was wrong with his Lebanon and I suspected Mr Malik saw in my father everything that was wrong with his. It could have been just that: former members of the same party, now permanently in opposition. Though up to that point, I had not yet been told about Mr

Malik's involvement in my parents' wedding nor that long journey back on the plane from Cyprus.

T-54 AND OTHER STORIES

'How shall I explain my war to you, my son? I am too old to play now but let us start a game of hide and seek. Do you remember that one? Rest your arm against the palm tree there, and your forehead against your arm. Close your eyes, while the war goes to hide, and count aloud: one year, two years, three and, then, fifteen. Where did they go? You want to open your eyes now, but you dare not, because you cannot feel the trunk of the palm tree you once leant against or the promenade on which you stood. And even that little piece of the Mediterranean which you and your friends used to frequent is gone. And now you don't want to play anymore, and now you shout and now scream and stamp your feet and now you wish you had never closed your eyes. You thought it was just your turn and that it would pass. And now it has.'

My father wrote that article the night after he had walked back home across Hamra Street with his rolled-up certificate in his back pocket. He did not know that he would have a son. That night, after Iftar, Uncle Gamal went out for the traditional fireworks to celebrate the end of Ramadan with the boys in the neighbourhood. My father remained seated by the dining room table long after the plates had been cleared. He wrote first about love, inspired by Abdel Halim Hafez's songs, but he said it seemed disingenuous.

Abdel Halim Hafez was an Egyptian actor and singer in the seventies, dubbed the dark-skinned nightingale, and famous for his unique voice and on-screen charisma. At the time, my father sported the very same oily haircut: hair parted to the side, with the fringe pushed backwards. When Abdel Halim died, aged forty-eight, millions attended his public funeral and four women threw themselves off the balcony.

Then my father wrote about the joy of success, also inspired by one of Abdel Halim's songs, but that too seemed insincere. Then he turned off the radio, and Abdel Halim fell silent. He listened to the fireworks and he wrote about the war, and he knew that this was his voice, not Abdel Halim's.

I was in bed when I heard the first few shots being fired. I heard them in my dreams first. I saw them piercing Alana's half-naked body. I saw her purse her lips and widen her eyes and curse Beirut. She said that this would never have happened in Montreal, as we lay in the sand.

It was almost summertime again and I had insisted on using the air conditioner that night even though it had rained not two nights before. I had not seen Alana since that evening on the Octo-bus. I had asked her if she was going back to Montreal and she said she had got used to sunrises after all.

My mother said they were fireworks. She reached for the volume control of the TV set and turned the knob down. My father did not say anything. He looked up at the ceiling, or through it. My sister, who came running into the living room after me, said she did not think they were fireworks. It did not sound like joy, it sounded like anger.

Armed militiamen from the militant Hezbollah had taken to the streets backed by the SSNP and Amal with their AK-47s and RPGs. Opposing parties, the Future Movement and the Lebanese forces, had formed their own token militias too and armed them hastily but they stood very little chance. The army also gave it a go. Soldiers in tanks made it to the middle of Hamra Street in an attempt to try and diffuse the situation. After the first couple of hours, it became abundantly clear that this tactic was not going to yield any results. The soldiers abandoned their T-54s and left to go home to their families.

Amal means hope.

In the beginning, it was dark and no one said a word. Then from the dark came the voice of my father.

'Where the hell is the goddamn candle?'

The electricity was cut off and then the water and eventually after days we had very little toothpaste, or toilet paper, or Head and Shoulders. My father had dandruff and he had passed it on to me.

My mother and sister initially sat on the edge of the bathtub, I leaned against the toilet seat and my father stood over us, cross-armed, listening intently to the sound of gunfire and RPG rockets being launched in the distance. When a bomb went off somewhere very far away, he did not look down at us and smile, like he used to, and ask us about school and deadlines and essays and football and literature and such. He grimaced, he scratched his moustache, he expanded his chest then he retracted it and, once, he sighed and the sigh went on for a couple of minutes.

My sister reached for her toothpaste above the sink and offered it to my father. The rest of us had run out of Colgate, but my sister had her own tube of Crest. She had insisted upon this some time ago because she liked the old commercial with the Crest-coated egg immersed in a cup of acid. The Crest-coated egg did not dissolve, as opposed to the other one, and that was enough to convince my sister that Crest, not Colgate, was the answer to her probleMs My father picked it up. It was new, unopened.

'Where did you get this?' asked my father.

My sister reached behind the sink and pulled out four or five tubes of Crest.

'I wondered where they all went so fast,' said my mother, 'I was beginning to think you ate them all.'

My mother and father laughed.

There was silence. Gunshots. Silence.

'You don't know this, but your father and I almost died before you two were born,' said my mother.

My mother told us the story of how she and my father almost died before we were born. It was Christmas and they were hiding in the very same bathroom. There was no electricity and no heating.

'It was the coldest winter I can remember,' said my mother.

She now had one arm around my sister and one hand on my shoulder. We crouched on the floor and leaned our backs against the white porcelain bathtub and looked up at my father. He was still standing, cross-armed. Once or twice he would rest his elbow against the washing machine or use the door handle to support his weight but he never sat down.

'I wish it was winter now,' said my sister, wiping the sweat off her neck.

My mother had filled the bathtub with water. She reached for the hand towel by the sink, dipped it in the bathtub and placed it on my sister's forehead.

'It snowed, *Fara*,' said my father.

This was a lie. It had not snowed in Beirut since the sixties according to Grandfather Adam.

My sister resembled a desert wanderer with the wet hand towel on her head and my father's dirty white flannel shirt which she had turned into her summer dress and refused to take off since the shelling had begun. It smelled of newspaper too and so did the windowless bathroom.

'An RPG rocket landed on the stairway right outside this house on that night,' my mother continued.

My mother said that she could not hear anything after the explosion. She said she could feel herself scream out empty words but that she had believed she was dead because she could not hear her voice or see my father. She had felt his hand on her face. She swatted it away instinctively. Then she felt his hand on her face again. The first thing she heard was him laughing. She asked what he was laughing about.

'Jesus Mohammad Christ,' he replied, still laughing.

'What?' she said. 'The ringing is too loud, I can't hear you.'

'That's what you were screaming: "Jesus-Mohammad-Christ",' he said, with one hand around my mother's waist. 'How did you come up with that one?'

She read his lips.

'I must have been thinking we need all the help we can get.'

'It worked,' he said, resting his head against my mother's shoulder and placing his hand on her stomach.

'He's kicking,' she said. 'That must have scared him.'

My mother would have a miscarriage later that week.

'It happens,' said Teta Mary at the hospital, wiping the tears away from her face and my mother's. 'I'll ask the Virgin Mary for another favour.'

There was silence again. Gunshots. Silence.

My father leaned against the door. It was a sign that the gunshots would cease for an unspecified period of time. Some part of me believed that my father could communicate this to the militiaman, that whenever he would lean against the door, they would hear the creak of the wooden doorway and stop to listen to his stories and reminisce. That evening, for the first time, my father told us the story of the real Bilyasho, a boy named Ibrahim Bel Adel who sat two desks behind him at the Italian School in Ras Beirut. Bilyasho was the Don's nickname for Ibrahim, who would show up to class with thick blue-rimmed glasses which complemented his curly red hair and his white, freckled cheeks. Only my father called him Bob. I think he was Druze.

Bilyasho would regularly bring Arak to class disguised as water in a small bottle of Soha and pass it around the room until it was empty.

'He took a chicken, from Abu Ibrahim's farm, to class and set it loose,' said my father, arching his back and snorting in a mock attempt to suppress a laugh.

His laugh was the sound of a thousand pieces of paper being ripped at the same time.

One morning, Bilyasho even shot fireworks through the class window from the playground which caused his classmates so much distress that some of them had to be picked up by their parents.

'You think this is funny?' said my father, imitating the Don's scowl and addressing an invisible Bilyasho. 'Terrifying your classmates into believing their lives are in danger. Do you think this is clever?'

'No one was hurt,' said Bilyasho.

'You're a clown. An absolute clown. And if you carry on like this, you'll never amount to anything,' said the Don, a vein bursting through his forehead and spit spewing from his mouth.

Bilyasho smiled and rested his hand on the Don's arm.

'You should learn to take things lightly, Don. You'll give yourself a stroke if you carry on like this.' That, according to my father, is what Bilyasho said to the Don in response.

The Don had curly black hair at the time and he would regularly slip his hands through it when feeling frustrated, or if things did not go his way. After he lost his hair, he would run his hands over his bald head but this did not seem to give him any satisfaction.

'You should learn to take things lightly, Don. You'll lose your hair if you carry on like this,' that, when my father retold the story, is what Bilyasho said to the Don in response.

I heard my father tell that story several times to Monsieur Mermier imitators. After the first ending, the audience pursed their lips, those who knew the Don winced or nodded their heads knowingly and the more pious of them said 'God rest his soul'. After the second, they laughed quietly, shook their heads and the more pious of them said 'God rest his soul'. Monsieur Mermier alone would have raised his glass of Arak and toasted Bilyasho. The story was always about the Don, never about Bilyasho.

My father placed his hands in his short pockets. It was sage green with stripes of grey. His shoulders arched forwards as if they were supporting the weight of his old schoolbag.

'We walked back home from school that afternoon in March,' he said, 'the pimp snatched my backpack and ran off with it.'

In my father's mind, it was the last time he saw Bilyasho, running ahead with his backpack swinging from side to side. In truth, he would see Bilyasho the next day and the day after that, and almost every day for another two months or so. He confessed as much in his later years.

Bilyasho was one of the seventeen thousand Lebanese citizens who disappeared during the civil war. His body was never found and he was never declared dead. Officially, Bilyasho is still alive today and he will live on for many years yet. He will outlive your children and your grandchildren and your great-grandchildren. And if you like you can tell them stories before they go to bed, about Bilyasho, or Pagliaccio or Ibrahim.

My father's backside hovered over the edge of the toilet seat, the weight of the imaginary schoolbag proving too much for his aging limbs. He soon caught himself in the act and stood up as if the toilet seat had bitten him or else stunned him into an upright position. He shook his head and crossed his arms and furrowed his eyebrows at me.

Silence. A loud explosion.

My mother crossed herself. Then she crossed my sister then she crossed me.

'I'm hungry,' said my sister, leaping into the air as if offended by my mother's sudden bout of piety.

She stomped her feet and I anticipated another Dabke, but she appeared not to have the energy for it, and so she slipped back into my mother's arms. My mother said that she would make us a halloumi sandwich each.

'When?' asked my sister.

The absence of natural light into the bathroom blended the days and nights into one. After a heated exchange of gunfire, the city would take a deep breath and hold it in for an hour. My mother cracked the bathroom door open to let the light in.

'Soon.'

'I need to go,' I said.

'Go where?' my mother asked, placing her hand on my moist neck.

'There,' I said, pointing to the toilet seat.

'Not this again,' my father grimaced.

One hand held his chin in position and the other was tucked under his armpit.

Silence again. Then we heard a scream, it echoed in our ears.

My mother told us about the time when she hid under the bed in her parents' house during the civil war. This was the civil war of the seventies and eighties, which included the Israeli invasion of eighty-two, and which followed on from the prelude back in the fifties, and preceded the month-long one with Israel in the mid-noughties and the internal armed conflict between Hezbollah and some other militias in the late noughties. My mother told us about the four militiamen who tried to break down the front door, only for Deddi Nabil to open it for them.

'Your grandfather explained that his home is their home,' said my mother, getting up to light another candle. 'He was a charming man, your grandfather, his hair always parted to the right, and that well-groomed, gleaming moustache, and his jawline alone. He never took his suit off except to go to bed.'

My sister edged her small head across the gap left by my mother's warm body and she rested her mane on my lap.

'Your Teta tucked me under the bed and told me not to breathe whatever happens,' continued my mother, 'she had the largest eyes that will ever see you.'

So large were they that you could swim in them, or swim halfway across them and then float on your back out of exhaustion.

Deddi Nabil asked Teta Marry to make the gentlemen some Turkish coffee, which she did. And he asked them if they would like some biscuits, which they did. And they laid their guns aside and they sat down and they had their first cup of coffee, and their second. They asked to use the toilet and my grandfather showed them where it was. Then they asked to search the bedrooms and my grandfather obliged. They opened all the drawers and threw the underwear and socks in the air and flipped the mattresses and removed all the clothes from the closet and cast them onto the floor and stepped on them and emptied the dustbins over them.

'Couldn't find anything,' said the youngest, who must have been about fourteen.

'No Palestinian flags, keychains, kufiyahs? Are you sure?'

'Yes.'

That was when they heard the scream. It was Yvonne's hollow scream; the elderly disabled woman who had lived across from my grandparents' house and lost her teeth to age, and her children to war. That night she lost her life too.

'May she rest in peace,' said Deddi Nabil, crossing himself.

The eldest militiaman, a bearded man with thick black eyebrows and a cut above his upper lip, produced a rotten tomato from his coat pocket and showed it to my grandfather.

'What is this?' he asked, holding it centimetres away from my grandfather's nose.

'Banadura,' said Deddi Nabil.

'Banadura' means tomato.

'You're not Palestinian then?'

'No, sir. Lebanese. From Tripoli. So was my father and his father before him.'

Had Deddi Nabil opted to say 'Bandura' instead, he would likely have been shot where he stood. And so would my grandmother and so would my mother, eventually.

'Did you check under the bed?' asked the eldest.

'No,' said the youngest.

'Why?'

'I don't know.'

'Is it because you're an idiot?'

Under the bed hid a wooden chest adorned with fragments of seashells, right beside my then fourteen-year-old mother's nimble body. It contained official ownership documents with King George's seal stamped upon them, indicating Deddi Nabil's right to his father's house in Haifa. It contained kufiyahs, a flag, several keychains and the keys to the house which he and my grandmother had vacated all those years ago. Also in that seashell-adorned chest was a bottle of Palestinian sand. My grandfather had managed to procure it from some Lebanese merchant in the south. Teta was unsure whether or not the sand was Palestinian, just as she was, sometimes, unsure whether or not she would return home.

The boy looked at the chest then at my mother, who must have been about his age at the time. She told him with her eyes that there was no chest, that he could not live with himself if there was, that it did not contain flags and documents and keychains and kufiyahs, that he was a good guest and good guests do not kill their hosts. Then, without breathing, she took off her gold cross and slipped it to him.

'Nothing,' said the young boy, as he climbed out from under the bed, 'there is nothing under the bed, I swear on the Virgin Mary.'

Silence again. Then some more gunfire. It was louder this time, like the militiamen were standing behind us. They were not aiming at anyone in particular. They were firing in the air, at the birds or the clouds or God; not their god, the other god.

Silence. Gunshots. More silence.

My father announced that he would like a Cadbury. The Fruit and Nut Dairy Milk Cadbury bar.

He told us about Grandfather Adam, how he did not see him often but when he did, he would always have a Cadbury Fruit and Nut in his coat pocket. He hated the raisins to begin with but he got used to them and began to appreciate their value when he could afford his own chocolate.

'It isn't worth the effort it takes to chew on it without the raisins,' he said, scratching his chin.

Then my father told us about the time Grandfather Adam took him and his brothers to Ramlet ElBayda for the day. It was a hot summer's day in June, and the shelling had ceased for several days. Grandfather Adam wore his white flannel shirt, blue swimming trunks and fake Ray-Ban sunglasses. He had not yet won the lottery. He placed his faded green towel on the sand and lay on his back looking sideways at the occasional bikini. A young woman in a white bikini bottom and black top sat on his towel, had some of his Almaza and talked with him until the sun had almost set. Then my father, who had been carrying Uncle Gamal on his shoulders the whole day, dropped him on his head. My grandfather slapped my father so hard that he flew into both his brothers and knocked them over.

On the way back, Grandfather Adam gave my father a Cadbury Fruit and Nut from his pocket. It was melted and hot, but my father lowered Uncle Gamal onto the ground, leaned against the railings by the promenade and savoured the Cadbury while gazing across the sea. Grandfather Adam lit a cigarette, and leaned against the railings next to my father.

'One day the war will end,' he said, 'and then we'll be able to go to the beach every day in the summer.'

'I'd like that,' said my father, looking down at his own flip-flops and wiggling his toes.

'The Don tells me you're pretty good at this writing nonsense.'

'Did he?'

'Just as long as you remember that no matter how good a writer you become, you'll always be the son of an illiterate mother, and semi-literate father.'

'I'll remember.'

Grandfather Adam paused for breath. He looked around at his younger sons, playing hide and seek along the promenade. One leaned against a palm tree and counted until ten and the other hid behind another palm tree. He looked at the thin golden line. He looked at the spent waves of the Mediterranean, and he heard them too, and he smelled the fish and the rotten towel hanging over his round rock of a shoulder. He ran his hand through his thick black hair. He picked up the faded green towel from his shoulder and swung it around my father's neck.

'If something were to ever happen to me,' he said, lowering his voice and the cigarette from his lips, 'you would take care of your brothers and sisters, wouldn't you?'

'Yes,' said my father, licking the chocolate off the wrapper.

'And your mother.'

My father nodded.

'Good man,' said my grandfather.

'Why? Are you planning on having something happen to you?'

'I've never planned for anything in my entire life, son,' said Grandfather Adam, 'I think that's part of the problem.'

My father nodded again.

'Are you leaving?'

'No,' said Grandfather Adam, 'but if I were to win the lottery for instance, in the future, I might have to leave for a little while.'

'Why?'

'Because that's how it works.'

'Who said?'

'Prophet Mohammad, peace be upon him, said, that's who,' said Grandfather Adam, before flicking his cigarette butt into the sea.

'Who was that woman?'

'A lifeguard.'

'What was she doing sitting on your towel and sipping your Almaza?' asked my father.

'Ask another question and I'll slap the chocolate out of your mouth.'

My grandfather took a deep breath. He had so much hair gel on his head that the salty water of the Mediterranean stood no chance. The otherwise curly hair remained permanently gelled backwards.

'You're a big boy now,' he continued, 'you understand, don't you? Money doesn't just fall from trees. You're not given money. You take it.'

'I think so,' said my father.

Then he spat out the raisins and the nuts, and lifted Uncle Gamal onto his shoulders again.

We heard gunshots. And one big explosion some way away. Silence.

The electricity flickered on. Then the electricity flickered back off. More gunshots.

My mother told us where she had hid the jewellery, this was in case the RPG rocket landed on her but not us. She told us not to tell anyone. She told us about the bank accounts she and my father had set up. She made me repeat the name of the bank and recite the account number.

'Why are you making him memorise the bank number?' asked my sister. 'Where are you going?'

'Australia, *Fara*,' said my father, tugging at one of her ponytails.

A loud bang made my mother leap up into the air. It was not an RPG rocket, it was the slam of a door, possibly Madame Hafez's. After the initial fright, we all realised this and began to take up our previous stances. Except for my sister, who remained huddled in a foetal position with her cheek pressed hard against the cold floor.

My father's voice echoed still and the flame from the candle wavered. It might have been the way the light moved, or her proximity to the candle, but my mother's eyes narrowed and she fixed them on my father with such ferocity that I was sure she was not above pouring the hot melted wax onto his back.

That was the last year my sister would sport her trademark ponytails. One night, she appeared in front of the old TV set with the vinyl wood varnish while we sat there watching *Basmet ElWatan*. She held her ponytails in one hand and scissors in the other. My parents stopped asking her to get up and change the channel after that.

My father crouched down to my sister's eye level and shaped to say, 'Nowhere, *Fara*', but he did not.

'Repeat it, again,' said my mother, standing up and crossing her arms.

'It's not the first time,' said my father, resting his hand on one side of my sister's face.

'My name is Adam Najjar. I am underage. My parents left a bank account in my name, here,' I said automatically, staring at the ceiling.

'Why left?' asked my sister. 'You said you were not going anywhere.'

It was not the sound of bullets or RPG rockets or bombs going off far, far away that frightened me. It was when I could not hear the stories flow from the lips of my mother and father.

'Don't be afraid,' said my mother, 'in a few years, this will be one of those stories which you can tell your children.'

'Then don't make him recite the bank number,' said my sister, eyes held shut.

She refused to be prepared for any other possibility, as if being prepared was itself an invitation.

Silence.

My mother told us the story of Yvonne. Yvonne would sit on the balcony and smoke every day, from morning until late in the afternoon. Then she would take a short nap and resume smoking until late into the night. Most of the time there was no electricity during the war and Yvonne did not have a generator or candles. She had her lighter and her Viceroys and whatever else happened that evening, you could count on that light from Yvonne's cigarette to shine through the night.

'With all those militiamen around, she was asking to be shot,' said my mother, who had resumed her position by the bathtub in between my sister and me.

My father stood cross-armed once again. He looked up. Nothing happened. He was losing his touch.

'Yvonne had a famous blue nylon bag with that raw potato inside,' said my mother, biting her lips.

She was out of cigarettes.

The blue nylon bag was attached to a rope which the elderly woman would lower from her balcony. The function of the raw potato was to prevent the wind from blowing the bag away. She would not shout or call for anyone. Passers-by would toss their change into the nylon bag on their way to somewhere else.

Abou Abbas, the grocer around the corner, knew exactly what she wanted and when he spotted the bag. He would take the money he required and replace it with a box of cigarettes and a bottle of Sohat water and a can of tomato soup, which she would often return.

'I didn't ask for this, Abou Abbas,' she would shout.

'You didn't ask for anything, Set Yvonne,' Abou Abbas would say.

She would regularly throw the tin can of tomato soup out the balcony and Abou Abbas would laugh and say to whoever crossed his path, as he mopped the floor, that he had tried his best. Once, she did not say a word and when Abou Abbas showed up with a mop he did not find tomato soup on the floor.

'How was the tomato soup, Set Yvonne?' shouted Abou Abbas.

'I flushed it down the toilet,' she said, in her coarse voice.

'There is no running water, Set Yvonne,' he said, his hands shielding his eyes from the sun as he looked up. 'How did you manage that?'

The next day Abou Abbas put another can of tomato soup in the blue nylon bag alongside the Viceroys and the bottle of Sohat and the potato and so it went on until one day he replaced the tomato soup with hot dogs.

'I don't have teeth, Abou Abbas.'

'I don't have any more tomato soup, Set Yvonne,' he said.

The next day when Yvonne lowered her blue nylon bag,

she felt that it was heavier and she struggled to pull it back up. Passers-by would drop a pot of yoghurt, or tomato soup, or labneh and some would even drop a Cadbury or a Ras El Abed or zucchinis.

'Yvonne would never have survived as long as she did in today's Beirut,' said my mother. 'They were better times.'

Gunshots. Silence. Gunshots again.

My sister then told us the story of Wahid, a boy in her class who would regularly piss in his pants.

'Is it because he laughs too hard that he can't control his bladder?' asked my mother.

'No,' said my sister.

'Is it because he is scared too easily and can't control his bladder?' asked my father.

'No,' said my sister.

'Is it because he is too lazy to walk all the way to the toilet?' I asked.

'No,' said my sister.

'Why then?' asked my father, impatiently.

'I don't know.'

'What kind of story is this, *Fara*?' asked my father, as my mother lit another candle and placed it by the bathroom mirror.

'It's a story about a boy who pees in his pants.'

'Where is the beginning, the middle and the end?'

'He pees in his pants,' she said.

Silence.

My mother told us the story of how she and my father eloped. My father stared uncomfortably at the ceiling.

'How could you do that to Teta Mary?' asked my sister, whose voice was so far removed from my late grandmother's that it appeared to have gone full circle and taken on her distinctly Palestinian intonation.

As she spoke, my sister rose as if the question itself required the gravitas which only a standing child could accord.

My mother said that it was a different time and stole a glance at her Casio wristwatch to make sure.

She omitted the contents of the 'heat-of-the-moment' letter by my grandfather Nabil. She also neglected to mention the reason as to why she decided to defy my grandfather, to stay on that Cypriot plane heading back to Beirut.

She did admit that she would watch my father drop food in Yvonne's nylon bag from her bedroom window. She looked coyly up at my father as she retold the story as if she had not shared this minor detail with him many, many times before. She said that was why she had not rebuffed him when he first approached her by Abu Abbas's old corner shop. She said it was his generosity, then she shook her head. That and his thin legs, so thin she was worried that they might crack under the weight of his pot belly. That was a new detail. Every time she told us the story there would be a new detail. My father tore his eyes away from the ceiling and attempted a smile in the direction of my mother, who gave him an exaggerated wink and a wolf whistle which set my sister giggling and scratching at her throat.

An RPG rocket landed on someone else's family. Someone else's home. My father looked up again.

'I know it was you who smashed the Captain's windows that night,' said my father, without looking at me.

His hair was as grey as it was black now, especially around the sides, and he had begun to dye his hair brown following in the footsteps of my grandfather Adam. There were permanent bags under his eyes and his eyebrows, once thick and imposing, had thinned and lost their striking charm.

'It was not,' I said.

'That's a lie,' he said.

I shook my head.

'What does it matter now?'

'It matters,' he said, scratching his chin. 'Is my son a coward or not? It matters.'

'No,' I said.

I stood up. My father was still taller than me. He did not tower over me anymore but he would still look down at me when he spoke.

'Life isn't a fat, old bartender with a motorcycle injury.'

The implication was that life, unlike the fat, battered Captain, would catch up with me. I wanted to smile because I knew it would infuriate my father, but I could not.

'Why are you bringing this up now?' asked my mother.

'Because he has nowhere to go.'

'I didn't,' I began, and I stopped when I saw my father place his index finger over his lips.

'You don't want to go to the moon. You never did. You want to run away, that's all. You want to smash windows and run away and never have to face any consequences.'

He stopped because my sister was crying and because we could hear the gunfire getting closer. My father looked up again but nothing happened.

'I want to go,' I said, making a fist with my right hand.

My drenched back arched forwards and began to shake. I made another fist with my left hand in a failed attempt to control it.

'Don't mind your father, he's just blowing off some steam,' my mother said, then she bit the side of her lip and waved her hand dismissively.

'Then go, leave,' he said, 'show me how you are going to run out onto the street with bullets and RPG rockets whizzing, mother and father, past your ears.'

My mother blocked the door with her body. She did not stand up. She crawled towards the door and placed her body between it and the rest of us.

I squeezed past my father, unbuckled my belt, unbuttoned my denim shorts, undid my zipper, sat on the toilet seat and let go.

No man ever remembers the good old days when he used to shit himself daily,. If he did, he would be infinitely more modest.

My mother and sister looked away. My father did not.

He looked straight at me. He did not shout or stomp his feet. He did not say anything to the effect that he would make me wish I was never born. He did not take out his black leather belt, or his Arak. He did not even call upon 'Jesus-Mohammad-Christ'. He allowed himself a half snigger. He removed the *An-Nahar* from under his arm, unfolded it, and then offered it to me. We had run out of toilet paper. I took the newspaper and flipped through the pages. It was five days old and, I assume, my father must have read every page twice, particularly the obituaries section. I looked for his article, I knew it was in there.

'…I am reminded of Ziad Rahbani's answer to a journalist who insisted on prodding him to provide words of advice for the "coming generations" of Lebanese youth. Without skipping a beat, the sardonic musical genius said

"do not come" and I am increasingly inclined to agree…
To be Lebanese today is to take small steps home, with one
hand on your heart and another firmly planted against the
wall. It is to wave to the wars as they pass by, so that you can
plan for a tomorrow that is already gone. It is to be jilted by
sleep, and consumed by fear over everything and nothing.
The world sleeps and wakes, and you float in a permanent
state of restlessness between sleep and exhaustion. It is
to jump to your feet at the slam of a bathroom door, or
clap of thunder in the sky. It is to act natural in unnatural
circumstances; neither a hero nor a victim nor a martyr, just
ordinary. It is to miss your country when you are in your
country, like you miss your children when they are not. It is
to dream the same dream, night after night, that, like in the
Ziad Rahbani song, "our country becomes a country". And
you worry about being arrested on charges of dreaming. It
is to wake up every morning as if it were the first and last
time, to recount your name and age and account number
and walk on coal and fire with the blessings of others
ringing in your ear, all the while repeating this phrase to
yourself: "I am a human being, I am a human being". It is
to know that you are alone, without land or sky or borders
and that it is up to you to recreate the republic, every day.
It is to pay the heavy price of living and being, and not
cower under the weight of it all. It is to learn from time,
hollow wisdom and from space, scathing cynicism. It is to
reinvent hope, when you know you will have to reinvent
it again tomorrow. It is to set up a place for the 'good old
days' on the comfortable couch next to you, feign a yawn,
place your arm around it and say to it: "you should visit us
more often".'

When I was done, I wiped my ass with the words of my father.

Gunfire. Silence. Rebellion. Rebellion, at last. More silence.

My father and I walked past Saeed and onto the main road. Saeed informed us that the corner shop at the end of the street would be open. He said the gunfire had subsided and that he was fairly certain everyone had gone home because they were tired and because it had rained momentarily. This was odd because we had not heard the rain and because it was May, and it rarely rained in May.

'You won't be able to get any bread and the prices will be hiked up a bit, but you can count on Abou Abbas's shop being open,' he said, shutting the gate behind us.

My father's footsteps echoed throughout the hollow street. The smell of dust and gunfire mixed with that of the fresh but feeble rain occupied the air. Black flags and banners featuring the red vortex lined the narrow road on either side. They hung from trees or poles, and across the shattered windows of looted shops. We marched straight down the middle, avoiding the broken glass along the pavement and altering our course only once to circumvent an abandoned sky-blue Nissan Sunny. As yet untrodden German cockroaches scurried around our feet, seemingly lost, daunted by the sudden reemergence of water from the sky.

My father made a fist with his left hand, but not his right, and swung it forward as if to guide his path. The flesh on both sides of his plain gold wedding ring leapt out of his finger and enclosed the ring itself. The ground was littered with empty shells of bullets which had been launched up in the air at no one. I bent down to pick up two or three, always jogging afterwards to catch up with my father's longer strides.

His stronger right foot sank into the asphalt and the cement. I thought that if I got lost or if I could no longer see his soaked blue shirt out of the corner of my eye or smell that whiff of sweat and newspaper, I would retrace his footprints all the way back to our house.

Outside the corner shop stood a tank. Abou Abbas noted that it took up about as much space as the old White American.

'How much for a gallon of water, Abou Abbas?' asked my father.

'Ten thousand liras,' said Abou Abbas.

He was around sixty now, with a white moustache and a belly that meant his face was never within reach of anyone else's.

'How much for the toilet paper?' asked my father.

'Ten thousand liras,' said Abou Abbas.

'Ridiculous.'

'If you don't like it *leave*, Najjar,' said Abu Abbas, his voice quivering, some words only beginning and ending aloud but holding their silence right in the middle.

'You're no better than they are, out there,' said my father.

'They're killing people,' he said, 'I'm risking my life to bring you toilet paper. I'm better. Do you want the toilet paper or not?'

'How much for the Cadbury Fruit and Nut?'

'Ten thousand liras,' said Abou Abbas.

'You're a thief.'

Abu Abbas shook his head and bit his lower lip which I now noticed was also quivering.

Two armed militiamen emerged from the abandoned T-54. The tanks had been given to the Lebanese army by the Soviet Union at some point, possibly because they had very little need for models that were in use during the Second World War. The militiamen wore black tops and army trousers and had bandanas hiding their mouths and noses. But you could see their eyes, and that was enough. Each of them had an AK-47 in one hand and an Almaza and a Cedars in another. The taller one jumped off the tank. The significantly shorter man opted to stay on top of the tank, dangling his legs off the edge.

'Is this man giving you trouble, Abu Abbas?' asked the former, staring intensely at the vendor. 'Do you want us to teach him a lesson?'

His was a more demanding presence. The eyes were wide and large and green but only in the way that the grass throughout a sweltering Lebanese summer is green when there is not a single drop of rain to moisten the earth or wash the dirt off the cars or the windows or off tall buildings almost entirely made of glass.

'No,' said Abou Abbas, 'he was just going to buy a Cadbury Fruit and Nut and be on his way.'

'God speed,' said my father, placing a hand on the man's arm. It was the arm that held the gun. A black armband with the red vortex superimposed clung to his biceps.

My father carried the plastic bag with the toilet paper and the gallon of water over his right shoulder, placed the Cadbury in his back pocket and his left hand on my shoulder.

'I've never tried Cadbury,' said the militiaman, as we turned to walk back home.

'You wouldn't like it,' said my father, squeezing my shoulder.

'That's what I used to think about this,' he said, raising the Almaza as if to make a toast then slipping it under his bandana to take a sip. 'But I have now learned to keep an open mind about things. Where I come from, we didn't get these fancy English chocolates. We just had Ras El Abed, and that was it.'

'Tarboush,' said my father.

Ras El Abed is a cheap, Lebanese variation on the chocolate teacake. It is a chocolate covered, cream filled treat that has been popular among generations of Lebanese children since the fifties. The actual meaning of Ras El Abed is 'head of a slave' and when Gandour, the Lebanese chocolate company, tried to launch a marketing campaign to rename Ras El Abed, the Lebanese public simply ignored the whole thing. Tarboush, or Fez, was the proposed alternative, due to its close resemblance in shape to the traditional Lebanese headwear famously worn by the first prime minister: Riad El Solh. 'Because everyone has tried it on' was the slogan pushed throughout the campaign, as opposed to the implied slogan of the initial name: "Because it is black".'

'What?' asked the militiaman, scratching his neck with his thumb only.

'Never mind.'

'I think I'll try some of that English Ras El Abed.'

'Leave it, Adel. We're not here to sample foreign chocolate,' said the short one, slamming his heel against the tank, 'do your job and let's get out of here.'

'I'll just have one bite,' said Adel.

My father instructed me to reach for the Cadbury Fruit and Nut in his back pocket and offer it to the man. Adel removed his bandana. He looked barely my age.

He took the first bite, he let the chocolate melt in his mouth. He laid his gun against the wall and spat the raisins and nuts out. Then he took a second bite, this time he did not spit anything out. Then he took a third and fourth and fifth and sixth. When he was done he stuffed the wrapper in my father's shirt pocket and he took a sip of his Almaza.

'That was alright,' he said, his voice going up a pitch, 'I want more.'

'I don't have more,' said my father, 'Abou Abbas does.'

'Then go in there and get me some more,' said the unhinged militiaman, bringing his nose close enough to my father's that he could smell the Cadbury.

The former resident of the Ottoman house, which throughout my childhood would have been visible at the end of the street, died on the eve of his centenary birthday. Builders and cranes and drilling rigs and ripped jeans and concrete mixers and dust and construction trucks came and went. In its place stood a sixteen-storey-high building with no balconies and double-glazed glass where the walls should be. This happened while my father and Adel stared at one another.

The glass was not a good idea. The architect was French-Lebanese. She had never lived in Beirut. Though I am certain that my father would have struggled to launch the foldable chair onto the roof of that particular glass tower.

Past Adel, you could see a small part of the Mediterranean which was discernable still from our balcony on the sixth floor. It was forever in the background. And past the Mediterranean, you could see the sun setting. There was a fine golden line now telling the sea not to encroach upon the sky's territory, and telling the sky that it is not as boundless as it might have believed but finite and limited and terminable. And when my father spoke again, the Azan had sounded off and his voice was drowned by that of the muezzin singing God's praises. It was the loudest I had heard the Azan. As if the muezzin believed that if he sang louder, if he made more noise, then maybe he could turn God's attention to Beirut, because perhaps the gunfire and RPG rockets were not loud enough and all he needed was a bearded man with an amplifier to make him stand up and take note.

But Adel heard my father because he picked up his gun by the barrel and swung it at him. My father shielded his face with his arMs Adel put his knee through my father's gut which knocked him on his back. My father raised his hand but Adel swung his AK-47 again, this time in the opposite direction, landing a heavy blow above his left eye. Blood dripped down his moustache and he wiped it away with the rolled up sleeve of his oversized blue shirt.

'I am a human being,' mumbled my father, as he rolled on the ground.

I watched Adel swing his AK-47 in the direction of my father's red-stained forehead. It did not belong in his hand. He knew it, my father knew it, I knew it, Abou Abbas knew it, Mohammad knew it, Jesus knew it and God knew it.

'What's that?'

'I am a human being,' mumbled my father, as he stumbled to his feet, 'I am a human being.'

Except he did not say *human being*, he said *baniedam*. It means son of Adam.

He clutched at Adel's army pants. But he did not look at Adel. His eyes were fixed on the sky. Adel grabbed my father by the collar and dragged him upwards.

248 A. Naji Bakhti

Once my father stood upright Adel aimed the back of his gun against my father's kneecap and the sound of the Azan stopped long enough for me to hear it break.

'Jesus-Mohammad-Christ,' said my father, clutching his thigh and falling back.

I did not cry. I said something about Cadbury. I sat down and scraped my knees against the melting asphalt. I said I have some or I can get some or that it is not that good. I wrapped my arms around my knees. I said that I like Ras El Abed more, or that I did not think that raisins or nuts had any business being in a chocolate bar anyway. Cannonball. I said that he should try Swiss chocolate or Belgian chocolate, because that is what chocolate is about. Cannonball. Not Cadbury. Cannonball. Not fucking Cadbury.

'That's enough. Respect your elders, boy,' shouted Abou Abbas, flailing his arms and hobbling out of his shop.

Adel placed the gun between his thighs and slid his unbuttoned shirt off his back to reveal his tattoo of the spinning swastika on his bicep. Even amidst the chaos, I remember thinking that the armband and the banners and the flags had rendered the tattoo redundant.

Adel wrestled the gun out of Abou Abbas's hands, who had made a symbolic attempt at seizing the weapon, and pushed the grocer's sizeable frame to the side. Abou Abbas shouted abuse at him, telling him how worthless he was, how he would never amount to anything, how incompetent he had made himself appear and how ignorant and immature it had been of him to beat the blood out of a man for a Cadbury Fruit and Nut.

'Your grandmother must have been raped by the dumbest fucking Crusader of the whole lot,' I heard myself stutter, as

I wiped the snot off my upper lip.

It was a schoolboy retort and my father, who was looking up expectantly, grimaced and dug his nails into his thigh.

'Not him,' shouted the other militiaman when Adel aimed his gun at my mouth, 'he'll kill you if you harm him. Not him.'

I saw the chaos in Adel's eyes, the sense that all was not well with the world, I saw that paradox of youth which Mr Abu Alam had once ranted about many years ago in Ms Iman's office, the black hole and those young stars at the centre of the galaxy. And I waited for an explosion, I cleared my head. I believed in a Big Bang, that's how I believed it would end, with a bang. I pressed the palm of my hands against my ears. Adel swiftly pointed the AK-47 at my father instead. Had I not gone to the toilet earlier, I would have wet myself and my father would have cringed and looked Adel straight in the eyes and told him to pull the trigger.

A cockroach slithered past my foot, and with no recourse to bodily fluid or excrement, I instinctively stomped on it with my heel. It was, I had hoped, a sacrifice of some kind so that my life and my father's would be spared in return for that of the cockroach.

The shorter man pulled at his khaki vest. Bits of skin protruded from the gaps between the strained buttons. He climbed up into the T-54 and whistled for Adel to follow him. My father groaned through gritted red teeth.

Adel, now standing over him, leaned in and whispered someone else's words into his ear, and smiled. He, too, had dimples.

I could not hear the entire line, but I managed to make out the words 'Ninnette' and 'done for good'. And due to my dumbfounded state of mind in that instant, all I could think about was that poor old cat and why these militiamen had gone through such lengths to murder the zucchini-loving, Cadbury-Fruit-and-Nut-licking, former inhabitant of a broken down Oldsmobile. The rest, in a twisted way, seemed to make sense. After all, my father was a known Ninnette sympathizer, and if these men had had it in for the cat then they would have naturally opted to go after my father next.

Then the unhinged Adel fired his AK-47 in the air and flung his visceral, black army boot through my father's head. My father went limp but he did not die.

I was standing on Westminster Bridge watching the fireworks when he died. It was a cold November evening in London, more than a decade later. I still could not grow a beard. I had one arm around a German girl called Lisa, whom I had met two years previous, when I received the call from my mother.

I would tease Lisa about Hitler and she would tease me about bin Laden. I said bin Laden was not Lebanese, he was Saudi Arabian, and she said Hitler was not German, he was Austrian.

At first the doctors thought it was just an infection. When he coughed, they gave him an antibiotic and my sister patted him on the back and my mother made him tea and I spoke to him on the phone and wished him well. I asked him if I should come to Beirut for a visit, and he said he would never forgive me if I did. It was not an infection. It was lung cancer in the end.

I could hear my sister suppressing sobs in the background over the phone.

'What are we going to do with all those books?' asked my mother, her coarse voice cracking.

Over the years, her voice had come to resemble that of Teta Mary. She said it was as if the books had lost their purpose. The ink faded and the paper hardened and the covers discarded their colour and assumed more sombre attire instead.

In his final few days, he was put into an induced coma. The doctors said it was the humane thing to do. My mother placed the phone against his ear. Talk to him, she told me. I stayed silent throughout until I heard my mother's voice again.

'Adam,' she whispered, 'what did you say?'

She said he was weeping in his sleep. It sounded like a line out of the very many obituaries he had written over the years.

'Weeping?'

'Tears hanging off the edge of his moustache,' she said, 'I can't explain it.'

She explained that his head was propped up with pillows because the doctors were afraid that he might choke on his own fluids.

I squinted to shield my eyes from the cold and buried my nose behind my thick, hoary scarf. Lisa had both arms wrapped around my waist and her sharp chin resting on my chest. Her long brown hair smelled of coconut oil. She bit her chapped lips, and though she did not speak, vapour escaped her mouth. It was her idea to watch the fireworks from Westminster Bridge. I had been pacing the flat in Battersea, which was not a sea at all, waiting for the news from Beirut when she announced that I needed a change of scenery.

'I'll call you back,' I said.

I tucked the phone into my coat pocket.

Just below the pupil in her right eye, Lisa had a little black spot which almost resembled another eye. It stared at me even when she was not. It held my gaze at any given moment and for as long as necessary

'I'm sorry, leibling,' said Lisa, and she kissed my neck and she pulled tightly at my waistcoat.

Her nasal voice was forever on the verge of erupting into sincere but inappropriate laughter.

The fireworks were launched into the air, above the River Thames, but soon hid behind the fog and the clouds. We watched the clouds and heard the explosions and felt the rain as it fell on our unfettered heads.

THE GOAT

Abou Abbas's voice seemed to come from across the sea at first. I heard it, like I had heard the first few gunshots days earlier, in a state of semi-consciousness within which only the sounds were real but not the images. Abou Abbas had carried my unconscious father over his shoulder and into the back seat of his car. He drove us to the hospital in his rusty old Honda Civic hatchback which he had painted himself and you could tell because he had not done a very good job of it. The original colour was blue but it had since been painted silver, all over including the side-view mirrors and the tail lights. The faint blue exposed itself through the murky greyish-silver. A large arabesque sticker spread across the top of the windshield read: 'There is no god but God.'

The Honda only had two doors. Abou Abbas shoved my silent father into the car while I adjusted the front seats and held the door open. I sat in the front next to Abou Abbas so that we could spread my father's body across the back seat.

'I will step on the pedal and take my foot off for nothing,' warned Abou Abbas, adjusting the steering wheel, 'do you understand?'

I nodded. On the other side of the street, a cat lay in a puddle of its own blood. He placed his hand on the back of my neck.

'One hundred and eighty kilometres per hour. Checkpoint or no checkpoint,' he said, handing me a pistol which he had tucked under his belt, 'barrier or no barrier. I drive, and if anyone tries to stop us, you shoot. Do you understand?'

I nodded. I placed the pistol on the dashboard. There was pubic hair stuck to the barrel of the gun. I grasped it tight with both hands. It was warm and smelled of sweat.

'Keep your head down. Our lives are not cheap, son. Do you understand?'

Abou Abbas talked nearly the whole way through, he did not stop to breathe or bite his lip and he did not puncture his speech with laughter or a sigh or two.

'This is why the country has gone to the dogs, you see,' he said, taking one hand off the wheel to roll down the window. 'People like this. They make the country what it is – duck, son, duck. Our lives are not cheap – and people like you, they leave. And why wouldn't you? If the Queen of England had need for a grocer like me, I'd be in London selling Ras El Abed and toilet paper to Sean Connery and Paul McCartney. You know, I once had tickets to go see McCartney in Dubai. This was after his Beatles days. After John died. What was the name of the fourth one? I could never remember. It was when I was still working as a cab driver. I wasn't always a grocer. Sometimes, I think to myself, I think, Abou Abbas, you should have left when you were younger. You should have sought asylum. And why not? I could have said, I've pissed off Hezbollah or the Syrians, by kissing some Israeli ass. Who would care? I would know it wasn't true. I could live with that. With being a traitor.

Or I could say I pissed off the Israelis because I helped the Syrians, but I doubt they would take too kindly to that at the British embassy. Imagine that. Can you imagine that? Young Abou Abbas, at the British embassy. Asking the British to hide him from the Israeli's? Or the Americans? They would call your Uncle Sharon on the phone and say, "We've got something that belongs to you, you want to send someone to pick him up?" Imagine that. And the Israelis would say: "Abou Abbas, that bastard, he cost us Beirut, we could have had Beirut if it weren't for Abou Abbas", because they would not want to sound incompetent in front of the Americans or the British.

And your Uncle Abou Abbas, he would spend fifteen, twenty years in prison until some reporter from somewhere finds out about my story, or Angelina Jolie might find out about me and my conditions. She would say something about this being a violation of human rights, and I would be out and I'd come back here to open a grocery shop right here. Right where it is, right now, except I'd be a different man. A different man to the man I am today.

And maybe I wouldn't be Abou Abbas, because I wouldn't have had the time to marry Em Abbas, and father Abbas. But that is alright, because I would be a hero. Wouldn't I? A hero for trying to run away. I find the world often works like that. It confuses you about things you thought were clear and pure and obvious. Don't you? I do, anyway. I do.'

'I do,' I said, as Abou Abbas drove into a ditch in the road, then out of it and into another one. He went over speed bumps as if their entire purpose was to give the Honda some elevation. My father appeared undisturbed by the turbulence. The grocer glanced at his rear-view mirror.

'I'll tell you, for instance,' continued Abou Abbas, as the Honda shook violently and he lit a Cedars with one hand on the steering wheel, 'there was this man who lived on my street when I was growing up. He was a handsome man, old enough to be married and old enough to be divorced, but sane enough to have done neither. Which was odd enough because in general, he was nuts. Crazy, I tell you. Whenever he asked for money, the adults would ignore him, you know, tell him go away. I didn't know why.

My parents, God rest their souls, were generous people, to everyone except this man. Then my friends and I were playing hide and seek once on the street, we must've been about ten, and we saw him. It turns out, he had a habit of putting the money he had collected down the sewer hole every day at five in the afternoon. That was why the adults ignored him. He thought he was saving them. He thought he had an entire life's worth of savings down the sewer hole. And in fairness, he probably did. My friends and I kept giving him krouch just to watch him drop them down the same sewer hole, every day at five. And all this is fine and well, you know, but that is not the point of the story. The point is, pretty soon, people started speculating. They must've thought: no one is that crazy, no one is that nuts. It must be an act. And you know what? They said he was Mossad, a traitor. Because if I were Mossad, that is what I'd want to be doing all day, you know. Collecting money from kids and then dropping it down the sewer hole. But I knew he wasn't Mossad. I knew it. That smile. That was clear and pure and obvious. Then one day he just did not show up at five in the afternoon. For the next few days, I kept dropping those krouch into the same sewer hole for him. But it wasn't the same, you know. He was gone, in the past. I didn't believe in the sewer hole, like he did. Maybe, he was a Mossad traitor, maybe I am, maybe you are. Are you?'

'No,' I said.

'The past is like a rear-view mirror,' he said, his eyes flickering in the direction of the erstwhile metaphor-laden object, 'if you fix your eyes on it too often, you'll crash.'

The Honda backfired. I fired my pistol in the air, twice. The bullets pierced the roof of the car.

'What the fuck are you doing with that, son?'

Abou Abbas had kept his foot against the pedal even as he turned his head towards me.

'I thought we were under attack,' I shouted back.

'Give it here,' he said, extending the palm of his dry hand.

I fired two more shots through the roof of the Honda.

'Keep your head down, son. Our lives are not cheap,' said Abou Abbas, taking a sharp breath for the first time and retracting his hand. 'Would you ever consider it, though?'

'Consider what?'

'Joining the Mossad.'

We could hear gunshots echoing throughout the deserted street. They were louder than the roar of Abou Abbas's Honda Civic but distant. He leaned forward and dug his foot in and placed both hands on the steering wheel. There was more purpose in his driving, a more focused intent, though still not urgent. It had stopped raining and militiamen were done with their smoke break.

'No,' I said.

'That certainty,' he said, 'that is the certainty of youth. It will desert you. And then what will you do?'

'I don't know,' I said.

'Exactly.'

I placed my head between the front seats in order to get a better look at my father. The fact that he was still breathing was of little comfort to me. The car shot forwards and I realised that I had been inadvertently pointing my gun at Abou Abbas. He had not uttered a word for fear that I might pull the trigger in response. I sat back and resumed pointing the gun at the roof of the car. Abou Abbas remained silent for the remainder of the drive to the hospital.

As my father was being carried off into the emergency room, Abou Abbas put his hand on my neck and pulled me closer to him.

'It wasn't a coincidence,' he whispered. 'That boy Adel was outside my shop waiting for your father. He knew your father would come at some point and he waited there for several days. Someone from the SSNP wanted to teach him a lesson.'

I tried to tell my father. But Jesus Mohammad Christ said never to mention it again.

Abou Abbas later complained that he was finding it very hard to wash the blood off the back seat and that the bullet holes in the roof were leaking water into it. He hinted at this every time my father passed by his shop until finally my father relented and bought it from him. Abou Abbas claimed that he had only wanted my father to pay for it to be properly cleaned and patched up, but my father insisted that Abou Abbas was looking to get rid of his Honda and that my father's blood, and my bullet holes, were the perfect excuse. My sister dubbed it 'the Muslim car'.

Abou Abbas drove me back home. I shook his hand. He gave me a kiss on the cheek and a pat on the shoulder and followed me up the stairs. There had been no electricity for the entire day. And the phone lines were dead. I walked into the apartment. My mother stood behind the door, right beside the two towering blocks of literature, and my sister was crouched on the floor leaning against the wall. My mother wrapped her arms around me and kissed my chest and neck and cheeks. I made my way towards the kitchen.

'Where's your father?' she asked, as Abou Abbas panted his way towards the door.

I laid out the flatbread on the kitchen table and I began slicing the halloumi. I placed the pistol by the halloumi.

'Adam. Where's your father?' she said, her voice high-pitched and her breath short.

She clutched the back of my shirt and pulled at it with a firm grip. I lost my balance momentarily then steadied my knife hand.

'He is fine, Mrs. Najjar,' said Abou Abbas, laying a still blood-stained hand on her shoulder. 'He is a strong man, your husband.'

I sliced my finger. She shoved me aside and took the knife from my hand and continued slicing the halloumi.

'I knew it. Did I know it? I knew it,' she told the cheese, slicing away at it with force, 'I said we should leave, years ago.'

Then she made me a sandwich and I sat down on the remaining foldable kitchen chair. I wiped the blood on my pants. My mother handed me a towel. I wiped my pants then my hands then my face with the towel. I wrapped the damp towel around my thumb. She watched me eat the halloumi sandwich, all the while tapping her foot. And Abou Abbas watched me eat it too, as he filled my mother in on the vague details. My sister hid behind Abu Abbas which was not hard. She stared at my now blood-smeared face and he turned his attention to the pistol.

'It's not my place,' he kept saying, in between the fragments of his newfangled story, 'it's not my place.'

It was in that same rusted old Honda civic, a couple of years after my father had been kneecapped by the militiamen, that Basil announced he would soon make his way to Syria to join the 'revolution'. My mother had placed a navy-blue tablecloth with a sprinkle of smiling suns on the back seat to cover the blood stains. My father had not bothered with patching up the bullet holes. Damp books and soggy newspapers soon found their way onto the back seat. I had my foot on the brakes and was willing the red light to turn green. Traffic lights had always been more of a suggestion in Beirut. I could hear the honking behind us.

'Some of us have things to do,' shouted the cab driver in the nineteen-seventy-something Mercedes model.

His cigarette hand dangled outside the window and was reflected in the side-view mirror.

To our right was the large, green campus of the American University of Beirut and to our left was the Mediterranean. The campus was one of the few green spots left in Beirut. All four windows were rolled down and Basil's shirt had turned from beige to charcoal grey. The air conditioning in the Honda had long since ceased to work.

'You and whose army?' I asked, but I already knew the answer.

'The SSNP,' he said.

'You can't be serious,' I said, the car spluttered.

'Put your foot through that gas pedal,' shouted the cab driver, now sticking his head out the window, 'may you bury your mother.'

This last wish expressed by the moustached cab driver was not a curse, it was a pleasantry. It implied that he hoped I would live long enough to bury my own mother; and that he trusted I would step on the gas pedal long before that eventuality.

'I have been for a while now,' said Basil, falling silent for a moment, 'this is our chance to stop talking about a unified Syria and do something about it.'

'Is that what he told you?'

Basil let out a sigh. He gazed out the window at the Mediterranean. We could smell the dead fish and some living ones too.

As we drove north alongside the sea, the sparkle of lights from the houses in the mountains blended in with the stars, forming clusters which seemed to float just above Beirut and fade into the light at sunrise.

My father would point those mountains out as my sister and I sat in the back seat of the Oldsmobile complaining about the density of the books and the smell of the damp, rotten newspapers. He started off with the white tops of Mount Sanine and Tanourine, which had both been trademarked for brands of bottled water. Then he would squint, reach out with his right hand and point out Rim and Sohat and Nestle and Perrier, which were brands of bottled water too but not mountains.

A child, no doubt a refugee, leapt onto the hood of the Honda and pressed the side of his sun-kissed but water-spurned face against the windshield. I took my foot off the brakes, the car edged forward, the child slid off the side.

'Buy me a manouche,' he demanded, banging his fist against the window

I sped past the red light.

'Mr Malik did not have anything to do with that incident involving your father,' said Basil, without turning.

It was the first time the subject had been broached. Neither he nor Mr Malik had come to visit my father at the hospital nor had they brought up the 'revolutionary book' again. Ms Iman showed up with a bouquet of flowers on behalf of the school. My sister pulled at the white petals, and proclaimed that they were real not fake despite the lack of fragrance. Abu Abbas passed by the hospital every other day for a week. Mohammad and his father dropped by with a box of chocolates. Not Cadbury. Wael's mother, who accompanied him to the hospital, made him write a 'get well soon' card which he delivered by hand to my father, who whistled and tapped Wael on the back of the head lightly. The Captain made an appearance too and he promised my father his coldest Almaza. He gave me a nod and a transient, wry grin.

'I don't doubt it,' I said, with eyes fixed on the road.

I did doubt it.

'I'm telling you. I know for a fact,' said Basil, 'it wasn't him.'

My father had ordered me never to bring it up again to

anyone, including himself. I never spoke of Adel or the T-54 or Abou Abbas, even to my mother and sister. Everyone who came to visit him at the hospital had some idea of what went on that afternoon, but no one knew about the blood, the Azan, that resounding crack, the cockroach and the four or so bullets which I had fired through the roof of the very car I was now driving. More importantly, no one suspected Mr Malik's involvement: the man whose classes I had trudged through over the past couple of years with gritted teeth and a newly acquired defiance which, to my surprise, he begrudgingly accommodated. Never once was I called out on my willfully disengaged, bordering on disruptive, demeanour. Perhaps even an ex-militiaman like him understood the need for the sons of battered fathers to spread their feathers a little in the face of the aggressors, even if nothing were to come of it, or rather especially because nothing would ever come of it.

I looked in the rear-view mirror, the cab driver was gone.

'You want to get yourself killed by ISIS or the Americans,' I said, 'is that it?'

He told me that I was naïve, that Estelle always said I was, that he knew I would not understand, that I was a dreamer not a fighter. He said he had supported my dream, believed in me, even when everyone thought I was ridiculous. He said that just because I would never achieve my dream of becoming an astronaut, it didn't mean that he should not try to achieve his own dream. He said at least his dream was realistic, noble, not selfish and unattainable. He said at least he believed he had something to offer.

'Grow up,' he said.

He said he was fighting alongside a dictator not *for* him. He said he was fighting the terrorists. He said he was fighting for a cause. The dictator would be next, he said. After the terrorists.

'Seriously, grow up,' he said.

I found a parallel parking spot by the promenade and had begun to reverse when Basil flung the door open and jumped out of the car in an attempt to help out. The moon was nowhere to be seen.

'Back, back, back, back, back, back, back, back,' droned Basil with admirable consistency.

I hit the kerb.

'Stop,' said Basil, barely suppressing a laugh.

I laughed too. My laugh was deeper than his.

'I saw this in a movie once,' said Basil. His hand covered his mouth.

His hair had begun to recede but it had lost none of its shine. It was gelled back now. He had matured into a handsome man with high cheekbones and thick lips and eyelids which acted as curtains shielding a precious stone or two. He had also grown a goatee. I asked him if it was ironic; he shrugged his shoulders.

'Forward,' said Basil waving his hands, with the Honda perfectly positioned between the two cars, 'just a bit more, a bit more, bit more, more.'

I slammed my foot against the gas pedal and the Honda crashed hard into the Chevrolet in front of it. The glove compartment flung open and a batch of cassette tapes, which I was not aware of, fell onto the floor. Basil howled, he lowered his hand from his mouth and knocked his head back. The sound of his laughter was louder and shriller than that of the Chevrolet's car alarm. He hopped back in and we found a quieter parking spot.

We leaned against the rusted blue railings, each holding a bottle of Almaza. Basil scratched at the label then at the peeling blue paint. There before us again was Gibraltar. Behind us was the palm tree, the one my uncles had played hide and seek around, or some other palm tree. It looked young. Younger than the civil war.

Basil lit a Cedars and offered me one. I thought of Yuri Gagarin. Much later, I would come across a little known picture of Gagarin smoking a Papirosa, a cheap Russian cigarette with no filter.

I drank Almaza and smoked Cedars and coughed and spat out phlegm and when I gazed at the sea I could scarcely make out the Rawche Rock.

'Come with me,' Basil said, his eyes struggling to make out Nicosia.

'And do what?' I said.

'Fight,' he said.

'I can't see it.'

'Report. Be a journalist,' said Basil, 'remember that article you wrote once. That was alright.'

'There's nothing for me there.'

'Your father would completely flip, Gagarin.'

He had not called me that for some time.

Basil leaned back with his left hand on the railing and looked up. Then he swung his right arm and let the bottle slip from his fingers. It flew farther than we both had anticipated and landed so far away in the Mediterranean that two Cypriots reported a UFO that night and twelve Sicilians thought it was the second coming of Jesus Christ and three Spaniards shouted 'Hijo de puta!' and heard the blop as it sank away. Basil turned his head towards me, opening his dark eyes wide as his greasy, oily, royal hair fell onto his face.

'You astronauts,' he continued, straining to open another bottle of Almaza for himself using his lighter, 'you see the world and nothing in it.'

He bit his lower lip.

I felt a sharp tug on my elbow. It was a woman in a burka carrying an unwashed infant in one hand and a single packet of Chicklets in another which she kept rattling to the infant's amusement. Basil handed her a thousand lira note.

'God keep your parents,' she said in a Syrian dialect.

'When do you leave?'

'Not for a while. I'll finish school. Get my diploma first. Mr Malik says that is important,' he said, 'we start training in the south in a couple of weeks.'

'God keep your youth,' said another woman in a burka who stood behind the first.

Basil waved them away. Told them that he did not have any money to give them, and that he had spent it all on beer and cigarettes. Then he folded up the sleeves of his light pink shirt and I could clearly see the spinning swastika as he strained to open the bottle. Wristbands, both cloth and rubber, hung around his left wrist. No watch.

One wristband in particular stood out. At first, I mistook it for a rainbow of sorts. I quickly realised that it was familiar, that I had seen it before. I did not initially understand what it stood for and it was not until sometime later, after the complete collapse of my father's 'Berlin Wall', when I spent that uninterrupted night in our house on Sadat Street swimming amongst the books, drowning in their pages, that I accidentally came to understand the meaning of the rainbow bracelet, having literally stumbled upon a book about Druze symbolism. And it was not until then that I recalled how Basil had refused to take it off when we were at the beach or even when he was taking a shower. It was strange for me to come to terms with this idea of Basil as man of some faith, any faith, no matter how small it may have been. I believe still that it was sentimentality, as opposed to any real religious conviction, which kept the wristband permanently around his wrist.

The green stood for the universal mind, or so the book about Druze symbolism declared, the red for the universal soul, the yellow for the word, blue for the past and white for the future.

I smiled then pursed my lips. He smiled back.

'Why don't you get a tattoo of a cedar tree to go along with that spinning swastika?' I asked.

'The cedar tree was chosen by the French colonialists. The first flag of the "Lebanese republic" was the French one with the cedar tree in the middle,' he said, flicking his unfinished cigarette into the sea and lighting another. 'And it's not a spinning swastika. It's a vortex.'

There is a line in the Bible, which Teta Mary would read to me in my younger years, about the righteous man flourishing 'like the palm tree and growing like a cedar in Lebanon'.

I raised my bottle of Almaza and Basil raised his.

'It's a swastika however which way you spin it,' I said, as the two bottles came together.

'Were those your words or the words of your father?' he asked, and he gave me a wink.

'His,' I said, dropping the cigarette butt onto the floor and stepping on it.

Basil shook his head then he laughed then he shook his head some more.

'I think in a previous life your father and I were good friends.'

I imagined the swastika spinning right where I had stood that night by the sea, searching in vain for blond and blue-eyed men and finding only tanned, dark skinned, thick browed, black-eyed men staring back at it. Where am I? It would ask.

'Stay here,' I said.

'I've made up my mind, son of life,' he said.

'Alright.'

'Good.'

'Fine.'

'Do you believe in this Arab Spring that everyone's talking about now?'

'You're the one going off to fight a war that is not yours, not me.'

'Do you?' he insisted.

'No, I suppose not. Maybe,' I paused, searching his face for clues, 'maybe not. Do you?'

'I don't know. Sometimes I do, when it is not raining outside and the weather is not humid, not so warm that the asphalt melts beneath the soles of your shoes, just a light breeze and you can smell the cypress trees and foliage around the old houses with the red-brick roof and the hollowed out buildings and you can feel the sun on the back of your neck but only in as much as you want to feel it, and only in as much as it wants to be felt. And early in the morning, always early in the morning but not before the call to prayer.'

'Isn't that just spring?' I asked, taken aback by the sincerity of his musings.

'It is,' he stared at my mouth as if it and not I was responsible for my words. 'Isn't that what we were talking about?'

Then, I told Basil about Bilyasho. I had never shared my father's stories with him. I chose the lighter ending.

'You should learn to take things lightly, Don. You'll lose your hair if you carry on like this,' I said.

I put on a high-pitched voice and I blinked repeatedly. It was my best impression of a young boy with red hair and freckles whom I had never met.

'A Lebanese boy with red hair?' asked Basil.

Basil turned his back on the Mediterranean and leaned his elbows against the railings. He ran his fingers through his oily hair.

'Aren't you afraid?' I asked.

'No.'

'Alright.'

'I could always come back if I wanted to.' He looked up in that same way my father would look up as we hid from the bullets and the bombs in the bathroom.

'To life?'

He laughed.

'To Beirut,' he said.

Then I started spinning on the spot; I extended my arms out and started whirling like a Sufi.

'Stop whirling like a Sufi,' said Basil, with a snort.

I did not know why I was spinning. I did not know much about the Sufis either. I knew that they are a sect of Islam which does a lot of whirling as a form of meditation. This whirling, Mr Malik had explained, is a means to achieve a higher form of enlightenment, to be in touch with the 'perfect man' spiritually.

As I spun, I saw nothing, and if there was a perfect man then I must have missed him or he must have missed me, and I did not know which way to look, for when I looked west onto the sea I worried that he might have drowned on the way; and when I looked east onto Beirut, I worried that he might have been shot because he was in the way, and pretty soon I could not tell east from west nor north from south and I imagined that this was how it must feel like to be perpetually falling into a black hole.

'What are you doing?' came the echo of Basil's voice.

And I knew that Mr Malik had little to do with Adel's attack on my father. The tattoo on Adel's arm, his youthful zest, his lack of education, his inexperience with an AK-47, that other militaman's unmistakably mountain Druze accent, those were not the hallmarks of the older man's influence. And that face, Adel's face. I realised that I had encountered it intermittently after school in amongst a crowd of other faces which would wait by the school gate for Basil to emerge. It was younger then, fuller, a little pudgy even and it rested on a shorter body.

When Beirut stopped spinning I saw Basil and his Almaza.

THE ASTRONAUT

'To Syria?' my father raged. 'You want to go to Syria?'

He launched the nearest book he could find in my direction. I ducked and it smashed against the shelf in the living room knocking the graduation picture onto the ground and shattering the frame again. It was titled *The Literature of the Lebanese Diaspora: Representations of Place and Transnational Identity.*

My mother and sister came rushing in. My sister's hair was almost apologetically curly and she had from time to time, begun to wear one ponytail instead of two.

'Your son thinks he is an upper middle class European white boy,' shouted my father.

'What?' asked my mother.

'He wants to go on an adventure in Syria.'

I explained that I wanted to be a journalist, a reporter. I said I wanted to cover issues that matter.

'There are plenty of those here,' said my mother, 'I did not raise you so that you would go chasing the war.'

I said I wanted to go to Syria, cover the war.

'Go to Thailand,' he said, flinching or winking to himself. 'Cover the mistreatment of elephants.'

'What are you saying?' she asked, her eyes pleading with mine as she sat down on the ground.

'They're majestic creatures,' he said. 'They whip them every day. It's a travesty.'

'How would you even get there?'

'I'm going,' I said.

Silence. No gunshots. Just silence.

'It is that Druze boy, isn't it?' he howled.

I said that I did not necessarily have to go to Syria at first. I would work my way up through the newspaper then gradually make my way there.

'Don't be stupid,' said my sister, scratching her chest. 'Why are you being stupid?'

'Go, leave, then,' he said, 'show me how you are going to march into a war zone armed with your unsharpened pencil.'

I had long since learned to resent my singular *An-Nahar* article and the manner in which my father would weaponize the words of my younger self for his purposes.

'I will,' I said, as I turned my back on him.

My father flung another book towards me. I felt a sharp pain in the back of my shoulder as *The Arab Spring Today* landed with precision. Then he got up and limped past the towering blocks of literature. He reached for a book behind the wall shielding the bookshelves from the outside world. For a while, my sister, my mother and I observed as he struggled to fit his hand through the window of space which he had created for himself. Then the ground shook, my mother and sister ducked and the wall came tumbling down.

He grabbed a falling book in midair and hurled it at my nose, then he reached for another and he aimed that one at my chest. This went on for some time. The wall, the bookshelves, the towers, even the floor came alive. The books leaped out of their place, and launched themselves in all directions. Some books rose out of the ground and smashed against the ceiling and fell back down. Some twirled eastward, others twisted and turned westward. A few of them crashed into one another, their pages interweaving, their covers falling back to release the ink and the paper and that distinct smell of the old: old books, old furniture, old men. The walls collapsed, the room danced, shifted and grew, contracted and expanded, so that I doubt even my father could still make sense of that random grand pattern.

'Read,' he barked, spit flying from his mouth.

I dodged *Syria Under Islam*, I skipped past *The Rise of Assad*, I sidestepped *Syria and Iran*, I flinched when *The Cedar Revolution and the Consequences in Syria* flew past my left ear, I winced when *Lebanon Under Occupation* smacked against my ribs, I screamed when *Your Syria and My Lebanon* made contact with my forehead. I sat on the floor and I felt warm blood make its way past my right eyebrow and I shut my right eye and I placed my right hand over my head and I wrapped my left arm around my legs and I heard my mother plead with my father to stop and I heard my sister wrestle a book or two off him. I heard my father order her to stop biting him.

'Stop biting me, *Fara*,' he exclaimed, struggling to push her aside with his free hand, 'stop biting me, I said.'

'That's enough,' said my mother, her strength and that of my sister now overwhelming my father.

My father's moustache remained a curious black, well into his sixties. His hair eventually turned grey then white then, to everyone's relief, began to fall out. He fought it at first. There was a point when his hair was brown, his moustache black, his stubble white and his eyebrows peppered with grey, and I wondered whether he might now wear blue contact lenses in one eye to complete the abstract self-portrait that his face had become. I suggested this to my mother and she giggled and told me not to repeat it to my father because it might hurt his feelings. Then she corrected herself.

'It might hurt his pride,' she said.

I walked into my parent's bedroom one evening, years before Monsieur Mermier moved into the opposite flat, hoping to find my father sprawled on the bed with his *An-Nahar* shielding his face. I did not. Instead, lying on my father's nightstand, I found a small diamond-shaped plastic box with a protruding sponge on the end of it. Impracticality aside, it looked like it belonged more in a shoe shiner's tool bag than amongst the toiletries. It was without colour, without odour, without brand. A plain white label read 'Brown hair'. I lifted the bottle closer to my eye level then against the light. It was unopened. Beneath it was a lottery ticket and beside it was a hastily folded newspaper. I tucked the lottery ticket into my back pocket and left everything else as it was. I saw my father turn over newspapers and books, I saw him crouch on his hands and knees to look under that comfortable couch in the living room, swearing and patting his shirt pocket as he stood up. He glanced at me, acknowledging my brown hair, but I did not ask what he was looking for and he did not ask if I had seen it.

Initially, just before informing my father of my plans regarding Syria, I told him that I wanted to be a journalist, a reporter. And I stopped there. I had learned to time my pauses to perfection.

'That will do,' said my father, his voice did not crack nor his eyes tear up. But I saw his chest heave. His words were carried on the back of one long sigh. My father's sigh was entrenched before the birth of time, before the opening of the eras, before the pines, and the olive trees and before the grass grew. He had held his breath for the duration of space-time, and now that he had finally exhaled, he appeared smaller, his shoulders less broad, his chest less pronounced, his neck slightly thinner and even his rigid spine gave way.

He did not mention the first Arab astronaut, he did not bring up the space shuttle or the Hubble telescope, he did not berate my flat feet. I imagine it was a peace offering.

It was then that I said I wanted to cover Syria. I did not really; and not only because Basil was there. I never did. I had every intention of running as far and as fast as possible away from the crack of bullets piercing the air and echo of RPG rockets landing on cement and burnt flesh.

And in any case, there were many practical and logistic problems with my hasty, makeshift plan. For one, I was not sure whether *An-Nahar* would hire me to report in Syria. I was also not sure whether they would have the means to smuggle me into Syria. I expected my father to pinpoint those flaws. He did not.

Had my father not sighed, I suspect he would have found the strength to burst past my mother and sister. But

he had sighed. He stopped resisting and my sister slowly
unclenched her jaw, releasing his forearm from the grip of her
teeth. He dropped *Standing by the Ruins: Elegiac Humanism
in Wartime and Postwar Lebanon*. He muttered something, he
cursed someone.

There was another rip in time and space, and I saw
my father, the moustache-less boy, who had emerged in
the elevator momentarily to argue with Madame Hafez or
Farhat. He shook his head, he stomped his feet, he ground
his teeth then he scrubbed his eyes with his knuckles.

'Curse this country of pimps and prostitutes,' said my
father, and his voice tailed off, 'mother and father.'

When he limped towards my huddled figure, he did
so calmly, stepping over the hills of now stationary books
without looking down. He placed his hands underneath
my armpits and he lifted me against the wall. It must have
taken every remaining ounce of strength he had, because I
offered him no help. That was the closest I remember my
father's face ever being to mine, his flat, flaring nose almost
touching my own. His unyielding hair, his thick lips, the
dimple parting his chin and that moustache. It was not as
full as I had always assumed it was. There were little gaps
in between which he had hid well. I wondered whether, like
my sister in her early years, I would fail to recognise him
without his moustache.

That night, after my father and sister had gone to bed,
my mother and I sat on the comfortable couch in the living
room. She made me a halloumi sandwich and I ate it. Then
she made me another with tomatoes and I ate that one
too. Then she took out the Arak. It was a tall and thin blue
Massaya bottle. She poured me a glass.

'One third Arak and two thirds water,' she said, as the Arak turned white, 'the ice goes in at the end. Never before.'

Unlike my father, my mother had lost weight then gained it back then lost it again. Every autumn, her freckles would grow stronger, and fade again in the summer. Her teeth were now stained with nicotine but it did not matter because when she smiled all you could see were her dimples and the way her wide eyes instantly watered, as if mistaking the parting of the lips for a quiver.

We talked about what it would have felt like to be in space, to walk on the moon, we talked about my grandmother, we talked about the weather and we talked about my father but only fleetingly.

'He's a human being,' she said, biting her lip and waving her hand as if she were dismissing a fly.

I asked her if she'd ever seen him cry.

'No,' she said softly, her eyebrows furrowed, 'but then your grandfather never smiled.'

And was it not better to have a father who is incapable of producing a tear than a father who is incapable of producing a smile? And maneuvered into choosing between those two mutually exclusive alternatives, I was forced to concede that, yes, it was better. Which is why, when I received the phone call from my mother, years later, describing the state of my withering father in his final days and the tears which had made their way down to his moustache, I could not but dwell on her words with scepticism. I was certain that she remembered our conversation and wondered whether this was her attempt at giving me the closure which she thought I needed.

'It doesn't mean that your father cares any less about you or your sister,' she continued in her gentlest voice.

'I know.'

'Is this what this whole Syria thing is about? Getting a rise out of your father?'

'No,' I said, 'I really do want to be a reporter.'

'Not an astronaut?'

She smiled wistfully as she said this, as if I had just conceded defeat, and she glanced up to where there were no stars and she indulged, for the last time, in that childish fantasy which it now appeared she had also allowed herself to believe in.

'Did you ever regret it?' I asked, and she understood what I meant.

'They were different times, habibi. You have to remember that. Your grandfather did not know any better. Your father and I did not know any better. I did what I thought was right.'

She told me about the time my father went to my grandparents' apartment and asked them for my mother's hand in marriage. My Grandfather Nabil was welcoming and gracious, as he always had been. And my grandmother was occupied but polite, she accepted the bouquet of red flowers which my father brought and placed them in a vase. Just before my father left, he remarked to my mother that he thought grandfather Nabil was receptive and that they would soon be able to marry one another. My grandfather escorted him towards the lift, kissed him on either cheek and bid him goodbye. Just after my father left, Grandfather Nabil smashed the vase against the floor and declared loudly that he forbade it.

'A Muslim husband?' said my mother, putting on her best impression of her father. 'Muslim grandchildren?'

My grandmother told my grandfather off for smashing the vase, but not for forbidding the marriage.

'But what made you stay in your seat on the plane?' I asked, hurriedly wiping the snot off my nose with the sleeve of my shirt.

'The truth?'

I nodded.

'It was Malik, more than anything else that day. It was Malik.'

'Mr Malik? Momo the paedophile?'

'Don't call him that. He is a nice and gentle man. I know things have been rocky between them since, I don't know exactly why. I also know that he had something to do with that incident with your father and Abu Abbas and the pistol and the Honda, but I also know that he would never have intentionally harmed your father. I know it.'

'Why was he there on that plane?'

'We needed a witness for the marriage registration to take place in Cyprus. Malik was a close friend of your father's, they were both members of the SSNP at the time, and he agreed to come with us. By the time your father and I got on the plane, we had already been married, and the plane was supposed to have taken off half an hour earlier but it hadn't. Which is when that damn letter from your grandfather arrived. Your father was stunned, he just would not move. I thought he would beg me to stay, throw himself at my feet, or at least kiss my hand and tell me that he too was scared, that we had done a dangerous but brave thing together and that we love each other, which is what I thought. I thought everything would be alright in the end, I told him so, but I wanted to know that he thought this too. I was risking a lot more than he was, I wanted to know that he was going to be there for me when it mattered. But your father did not say or do a thing. He stayed there in his seat motionless, with his eyes opened wider than I have ever seen them. I think he finally felt the weight of it, I think he went into the whole thing without really realising the burden of it, I think the letter helped hammer it home, which is the only thing that damned letter was good for anyway. And we were so young, Adam. So young. You won't understand now, but we were. But it rocked him, that letter, and he handed it back to me and just stared blankly out the window. And it was Malik who acted on impulse. He knelt to the ground, with his bad leg, and grabbed my calf with both hands and he wept like a baby, like a little blubbering baby. The whole plane was watching us. And he begged me not to go, he said that we were very brave and that we were changing the world, that not many people could do what we did and that he knew how much your father and I loved each other, and that would never change. He was sure of it. And he said that my father would speak to me again, and never forgive himself for what he wrote. Which was true, you know. He never did, your grandfather never forgave himself.

'Then Malik looked up at me with those wet round eyes and runny nose, and he did not bother to wipe his round face, and he asked me if I would please stay. For him. If I would please, please stay. For me. That's when I looked at your father, and now I could see he had forgotten about the letter completely and he was staring at Malik in disbelief, his mouth hanging half open and his eyes narrow. And I told your father to stand up and let the poor distraught man sit in his place, which your father did without objecting. And Malik and I sat next to one another for that entire flight, and we talked about everything and we laughed and drank

Ksara. The hostess kept coming over to beg us to lower our voices, but we were having none of it. And your father found a place, two seats behind mine by the window. And we kept sneaking glances back and laughing at him for the whole trip.'

My mother was laughing, wiping her tears away. And so was I. Smoke swirled around the room.

Then we talked about my aunt and uncle in London and she said I should go visit them. As she spoke her freckles danced, unsure of the season.

'You won't like the weather,' she said, 'and, you know, it's not a coastal city.'

'I know,' I said, 'Teta Mary always said that she felt trapped there, like she couldn't see the end of it.'

'Just follow the great river out to the coastline.'

I expected her to be hurt; her blood ties to Beirut being thereafter indefinitely reduced to two. She was not, or if she was then she did not show it.

The conversation went on past midnight, and by the time we were done, she, cigarette in mouth and all, had managed to turn a short visit into a student visa.

'You will love it,' she said, smiling and raising her glass of Massaya, 'you'll come back a proper journalist.'

I stayed up until sunrise reading fragments of the books which had been the subject of my father's rage and made firm contact with my forehead and ribs. I did not mind the unperturbed sweat making its way down my spine. The daylight crept in through the shutters, past the comfortable couch in the living room and into the hallway as the dust settled on the bookshelves and the piles of books on the floor. The tiles had always been cracked, and the longest one

extended from the window in the living room and loosely
resembled the shape of Madame Hafez's arthritis-plagued
index finger. There was a story in there that I never asked
about and was never told. I sat on the hard floor coaxing
the words out of my unwitting transgressors. In amongst
those battered book covers, I came across Basheer Gemayel
and his father the football captain, Antoun Saadeh and his
forces of darkness, Habib Shartouni and his poetry, Riad
El Solh and his Tarboush, the Druze and their colours,
the Sufis and their dancing, the SSNP's decorated history
of assassinations, the Phalangists, the Sabra and Chatilla
massacre, the Syrian regime, and others.

I looked up from the pages of the books which smelled
not of paper but of my father's flesh to see the man himself
standing cross-armed, eyes shut listening intently to the
sound of pages being turned. His forearms alone were
caught in a beam of unusually harsh morning light such
that the hairs on the back of them appeared to blur into a
black flame.

On our high school graduation night, I did not see Basil.
He had stopped attending classes but I had hoped that he
would still make it to the after-party at the private beach
resort anyway. Mohammad, Wael and I stretched our lean
bodies across the sand. All three of us were dressed in
white shirts with the sleeves rolled up to the elbows and the
buttons undone down to the chest. Mohammad's chest hair
protruded through his shirt. He was always a growth spurt
ahead of the rest of us. His thin, red tie still hung loosely
around his neck and he held a 961 in his hand. I dropped
my tie by the bar and decided to leave it there. I had taken

a dislike to the chequered pattern and in any case I had borrowed it from my father who was unlikely to miss it. My mother had picked it out, my father nodded his approval without lifting his head above the newspaper.

I balanced an Almaza on my chest, with the label now scratched off, as Wael knocked back the rest of his Beirut Beer, a recent, unimaginative addition to the market. The moon was full and it shined brighter than the spotlights at the beach and louder than the sound of the bass emanating from the bar behind us. We owned the shoreline. The pool was theirs and the sea was ours.

Mohammad said that he was definitely in Syria, probably Homs.

'Who?'

'The goat-worshipper.'

Wael said that he could imagine Basil riding a goat into battle. Of the four of us, Basil had been the shortest. To Wael, from his elevated point of view, it must have seemed like Basil and the goat were about the same height.

I dug my left hand into the sand.

'He might find his way back,' said Mohammad. 'My father came back when everyone thought he was gone for sure. But I believed.'

I had not had much contact with Basil since that night by the Rawshe Rock. He came to my house once and asked my mother, through the intercom, if I would like to come out and play. My mother laughed at this. I said I was not feeling well and my mother invited him to come up anyway. He declined. My mother insisted.

'I made stuffed vine leaves and zucchini,' she said, 'you must try them. They're Adam's favourite.'

'Another time,' said Basil, and he must have been relieved that it was my mother's and not my father's voice through the intercom.

I had not confronted him that night.

I like to think that, when I steadied myself after my bout of Sufism, I chose not to, that I was being the bigger man, but my reaction afterwards makes that perception difficult to maintain. He must have realised, the way the smile faded from his face, that I had found him out as a thug. For a long time, I convinced myself that it was pity not fear which had kept me from confronting Basil. That I was not a coward who would smash windows and run. After all, I told myself, I was speaking to a dead man and it is petty to hold a grudge against a dead man.

'Where's your date?' asked Mohammad, for once looking sideways not upwards at Wael.

Wael's date was a thirty-something-year-old woman who promptly discarded Wael the moment we arrived at the Pangea beach resort.

'Where's your father?' replied Wael, which was so unlike him that Mohammad ended up snorting his 961 between fits of laughter and coughing.

Wael tipped the last drop of lager down his throat. He reached for my Almaza but I snatched it away and nudged him off with my elbow.

'It was never going to happen,' said Wael, sitting up and resting his elbows on his knees.

I exchanged quick, baffled glances with Mohammad. The Muslim pursed his lips and lifted an eyebrow. Wael looked down at the sand between his feet.

'What? You sleeping with the thirty-year-old?'

'You becoming an astronaut,' he continued, 'I sat down and calculated the odds one night. A while ago. It was not long after we were suspended from school for starting that playground revolution.'

He paused to allow himself a sigh.

'The chances of you becoming an astronaut are about one in twelve million. And that's not accounting for the fact that you are an Arab.'

I said that it was in the past now. As he spoke the thud of the bass and the whoosh of the waves blended into one indistinct din.

'Adam,' he said, 'you are more likely to be struck by lightning, twice.'

I knocked my head back and poured the lager into my gaping mouth.

'You are more likely to win the lottery twice.'

It burned its way down my throat. Mohammad said that astronauts don't come from warm countries anyway.

The outline of a man carried the outline of woman into the sea. He threw himself into the water or she threw him. Then she ran back up towards the swimming pool, across the sand, with her wet hair flickering in the night light. He stumbled after her, stopping every so often to pull up his heavy pants. The cold bottles soon turned warm and sweat stains swiftly appeared under our armpits.

'Where are those mermaids you and Basil used to speak of all the time?' asked Mohammad, lager dripping down his chin and sweat down his forehead.

I shrugged my shoulders. Mohammad did not see this. We heard the dull thud of the bass again, glass shattering, and smelled the sambuca and the vodka but not the good stuff.

'Another round?' I asked, pushing my palms against the sand.

I made my way across the bridge which arched over the pool and led straight to the crowded bar. The bridge was the only way to reach the bar, which was otherwise stranded in water. There was no Arak. This was not the place for it. Behind the bottles of Johnnies and Jacks and Jims, there were blue lights and red lights and green lights which shone through the glass and the alcohol and through the back of bartender's head and out of his eyes and into mine. I closed my eyes and gripped the towering white pole which rose straight through a hole in middle of the bridge. It was cold and wet and I pushed my torso and my cheek against it. It parted the stars and I counted forty-one of them. Forty-two with the sun which I knew was there but could not see because it was too dark.

I spotted Nadine amongst the stars and she was with a Christian boy with a cross the size of Dr. Antoine's swimming pool hanging around his neck. I nodded.

Nadine came over and I asked how she was. She said she was fine. She looked fine. I said I was fine too. She did not ask. She said she was glad to see me.

There was a change in her smile which I did not recognise. Not that she smiled. But I imagined that she had, and I still could not recognise it.

'The nose,' I shouted.

'I had an accident,' she said.

'While doing a cannonball?'

'What?' she asked, pretending to lean in but ensuring she kept sufficient space between us.

She wore a loose, silk Bordeaux dress which rose above her knees and would have flapped behind her had there been any wind. Instead it hung from her shoulders and tickled her virescent thighs which glistened from the light reflected off the pool and off her champagne glass and my Almaza and the towering pole and the parting stars and off the cross around the Christian boy's neck and the bartender's eyes and mine.

The Christian boy, whose navy-blue tie was still tightly knotted around his thick neck, whispered three words in her ear. What-an-asshole or I-love-you. It could have been either.

Christian boys wore navy-blue ties. Muslim boys wore carpet-red ties. It was an unspoken nationwide agreement.

I pointed my Almaza at the resort pool.

'Cannonball,' I said.

My stomach felt heavy with food and beer. I pinched my forearm.

'What?'

'Cannonball,' I shouted.

The bottle flew out of my hand and into the pool. Nadine took two steps back.

'I can't hear you the music is too loud,' she said caressing her eyelashes with her index finger, then, 'congratulations.'

'You too.'

It was the same tone with which Ms Iman had uttered her 'congratulations', reserved, almost apologetic. Perhaps both of them had believed at the time that I had lost more than I had gained and they were caught between having to offer their commiserations and their congratulations all at once.

In the distance, Mohammad and Wael stood side by side with their feet in the water staring out into the pitch-black night of the sea. Beirut might as well have burned behind them. Cranes rose into the moonlight and dwarfed the palm trees beside the escalating Tower of Dreams II. The music blasted so deafeningly into the sky that I feared the future residents of the tower would be jolted awake. Wael had his arm around Mohammad's neck and Mohammad had his arm around Wael's waist, and their legs were spread apart and their hips thrust forward and their slim fit, striped, black pants pulled down to their knees. And though I could not have heard it that night, there echoed the unmistakable sound of piss coming together with sea water.

'Nadine,' I shouted after her, cupping my hands so that my voice would carry further, 'you deserve better.'

They were halfway across the bridge when they heard my raspy voice. I meant that she deserved better than her father, better than that day by the swimming pool and the Roman columns, better than whatever accident which had resulted in the irreversible alteration to her smile. The Christian boy did not understand this.

He turned around forcefully and made his way towards me. Nadine held the sleeve of his shirt but he pulled it away. His upper lip thinned and retreated into his mouth as he made his way forward.

'I was not referring to you, George,' I said, backing into the waist-high metal railing on one side of the bridge.

His name was not George. This angered him further.

He flicked his floppy hair to the side and seized my creased shirt in one swift move. His teeth came together as if he were biting off the head of an ant.

In the time it took for his fist to connect with my eyebrow, I realised that it was an easy enough mistake to make. I reasoned that it could be imminently resolved were there enough time to resolve it and had the music not been so loud and the bridge so wet and slippery and my left eye so warm and soaked in blood.

I pushed myself backwards, over the railing and into the gently lit pool. As I fell back, I glanced another star which I believed I had not counted before and I was gripped by the fear that I had made a grave error in failing to account for the twinkle of the stars.

I shook Ms Iman's right hand coldly and snatched the certificate from her left hand, without looking into her eyes. She had dubbed us 'the graduating class of heroes' presumably because the vast majority had managed to avoid getting ourselves shot or blown up in the intervening years between the Israeli bombardment of Beirut and our own graduation. Doubtless there were many such classes of 'heroes'. I suspected that she had known about the extent of Mr Malik's influence over Basil throughout. She had done nothing and I held that against her for the duration of the ceremony, and for the rest of her life. Mr Malik resigned himself to the fact that I was never going to speak to him again, though I doubt that it mattered much to him. In the final few months of class, he would repeatedly call out my name for recitation and I would repeatedly ignore it. He did this until the final class of the year, never once telling me off for my deliberate waywardness.

The first time I ran into Mr Malik on Hamra Street, two weeks after graduation, it was dark and Sabah could barely see the cars beneath her. I did not wave to him and he did not nod. I walked straight past him, picking up the pace as I approached his round, limping figure.

'I did not make him go,' he shouted after me. 'He wanted to go. It was his idea.'

It was not a shout in anger. His voice was calm but loud. I should have walked, but I figured I owe him something. After all, I thought, what if he had never thrown his sizable figure at my mother's feet and begged her to stay on that plane? I never thought that I owed him my life in any way, but a 'listen'. I owed him a listen. But I was wrong about that too, looking back. I suspect I misunderstood my mother's story at the time. She had already made up her mind to stay.

'I won't tiptoe around this. It is not my style. I'll say it straight. It'll be best for all concerned if you were to leave the country, Mr Najjar,' he continued, 'I say this to you out of concern for your well-being. Abu Mekhi – Basil – would have agreed. Adel is not a stable boy.'

The massive, uneven figure of Mr Malik appeared, for the first and only time I can recall, to be uncertain how to proceed.

'It seems he has gotten it in his thick head that he has some unfinished business with you. Something you said to him apparently about a Crusader raping his grandmother? He just will not get it out of his head. I mean of all the things…'

I nodded. Some part of me enjoyed watching him flounder to explain that my life was in some danger, that he was powerless to prevent this and that, though he would never utter those words, he was sorry for his role in the way things had turned out.

'Basil could talk to him. Calm him down whenever it was necessary. I don't know how he did it. I have tried. But with Abu Makhi gone, I cannot guarantee your safety. Adel is a troubled boy.'

I nodded again. This revelation changed nothing for my part. I had already made up my mind, with the help of my mother and Arak, to leave the country and Mr Malik's words had little effect on my resolve. The tickets had been booked and arrangements had been made.

'He might be off to Syria soon, but there is no way of knowing how soon. And he's only a boy really, barely sixteen.'

I stared at Mr Malik without blinking and my eyes burned and I clenched my fists inside my pockets, and ground my teeth. He fell silent for a few seconds.

'The manuscript,' he said, clearing his throat as if taken aback by his own words. 'We had always said that we would write a revolutionary book together, your father and I. To start revolutions. And finish them. Back when he was still SSNP. Back when we were both students of the Don.'

'But do keep writing,' he said, starting a thought which he had not fully formulated in his head and so abandoning it midsentence. 'I read your father's article about being Lebanese, a few years back. It was a good article, I thought. I meant to tell you this at the time.'

After that, I would wave to him and he would nod. I did this to keep him from uttering any more words in my direction. I felt that if I acknowledged him early and without any visible angst across my face, then I might avoid any further exchange between us. It was a meek position, I suppose, but the realisation that Basil and not Mr Malik was directly responsible for my father's injury, had knocked much of the defiance out of me. Amongst the people you loathe, there are those upon whom you might wish the most permanent of deaths but not desire to see die, and there are those whom you would desire to see die but wish a most speedy recovery. I was never sure to which category Mr Malik belonged.

I went back for my father's chequered tie. When the party was over, and the music had died down, I walked past the inebriated young men and women in one another's arms, or lying flat on their stomachs or their backs, clinging to a bottle or a glass, or a plastic bag into which they had emptied the previous contents of a bottle or a glass, or else floating dizzily in the dimly lit pool into which they had also unloaded. The smell of piss and vomit overpowered that of the previously impenetrable airborne cocktails of sambuca and tequila. Shards of glass cracked under the soles of my formal black shoes. It was as if the Israeli army – and not a rabid group of sexually volatile Lebanese teenagers – had made its way through the beach resort. My steps felt heavier, due in no small part to the sticky cocktail/puke laden floors and my soaked trousers, but also steadier. The fall from grace into the chlorinated water had done me well.

The tie itself had a noticeable, finely shaped shoe mark, an oversized man's, but remained otherwise unscathed, miraculously immune to the stench of the now ruined beach resort. It was still on the floor by the bar where I had dropped it at the beginning of the night without intending to go back for it. I wore that same tie to my father's funeral many years later. I liked the symbolism, the coming full circle, the wholeness, the completeness of it. I had not intended it this way, but it struck me as a worthy gesture on the day of the interment and I went with it. I said to myself: if I find it, I'll dust it off and wear it, and if I do not then its understandable disappearance will be a sign that it was a ridiculous idea to begin with, born of a misplaced and belated bout of sentimentality. But I found it.

In spite, or rather because, of my father's stubborn protestations, I had made my way back to Beirut not long after that phone call from my mother, at his sick bed. And despite the fact that I had never divulged the conversation between myself and Mr Malik to my father, his insistence that I never return to Beirut grew stronger with every year. I often wondered whether he later had a similar conversation with the Arabic teacher himself, or whether it was mere instinct which guided his thinking. The moment he passed away, the weight of his words seemed to lift, and I was able to reinterpret his requests in such a way as to suit my own peace of mind. I had found it difficult to book a ticket to Beirut while he, with his increasingly sparse breaths, urged me not to. But I soon came to the conclusion that it is a simple thing to mask your own thoughts with the voice of a deceased loved one, and so bless in their name what they would have cursed in their life.

Strange men would hug me and cry, or pronounce that my father was a decent man, a good man who did – had done – good things for good people in good silence, knowing that all will be revealed in good time. It was essentially a litany of mechanics, Saeed and a few dishevelled, once familiar faces (Abu Abbas, Dr. Takkoush, even Mr Malik in a curious sunglasses and oversized charcoal black suit combination, etc.) I say men, because I never saw the grieving women, including my mother and sister who sat in a separate, smaller, room and received the condolences from strange women who must have, I presume, also pronounced that my father was a good man who did good things, etc. Apart from that external, omnipresent weight of grief, several thoughts flickered, with various levels of gravity, through my mind on the day as I stood beside my uncles at the mosque's comfortably spacious reception hall, hugging and kissing strange men. The first thought was how dry my throat was, and how much I thirsted for a gulp of water.

This first thought was accompanied by a sense of guilt, which soon subsided and began to resemble not shame exactly but a mild, self-aware embarrassment, the sort felt by conscientious rich kids when their parents flaunt their wealth in front of their less materially endowed friends. The second was not so much a thought as an image of the remains in five years' time, ten years' time, fifteen years' time and so on. This I countered, or learned to counter, with the image of my father in his forties smiling and winking to himself or scratching his ear with the car keys. The third was a wallowing sense of self-pity and utter loneliness which I like to think was uncharacteristic, but cannot say with certainty.

This last sorry state of mind was, I believe, not helped by the fact that my father wasn't there beside me to receive the condolences of strange men at his funeral. And nor were my mother and sister for that matter, with whom, needless to say, I wanted to be most. It was true that I had hardly spoken to him over the past ten years since I had left for London, and that as it so happened we had very little left to say to one another towards the end, but I had still expected him to be present on such occasions as this. The fourth was twenty years' time, twenty-five years' time and thirty years' time. The fifth was Basil. The sixth was how much facial hair my uncles had managed to produce over the days since my father's death, compared with my own wispy beard which still did not resemble that of my father. The seventh was how hot it was that day. The eighth was how cold. The ninth was how barbaric the whole ritual was of having to wash the naked remains of my father before his interment. How cold.

And why had my mother yielded to my uncles' requests to give him a 'proper Muslim' burial when he was never, nor had he ever aspired to be, a proper Muslim? And what were the words to the Fatiha prayer? And where would my Christian mother eventually be buried? Not beside him.

And would she even want to be? And had they not spent an entire lifetime quarrelling and throwing all manner of print in anger across a coffin-sized, book-infested, smoke-filled apartment? And, Jesus-Mohammad-Christ, would that loud obnoxious man of the cloth shut his yapping mouth so that I could think for just one second? The tenth was forty years' time, forty-five years' time. The eleventh was my own mortality. The twelfth was the passage of time and wounds. The thirteenth was Heraclitus and his river and stepping in it twice. The fourteenth was water, and thirst. The fifteenth, I cannot remember. The sixteenth was the theory that if you toss an infant into a swimming pool he'll come out the other side kicking. And on and on.

And the seventeenth was my grandfather Adam's funeral some years before and had my father not shed a tear then? And eighteenth was the time he and I visited my grandfather's grave alone, and how he had filled a gallon of water from a nearby cistern to the rim and doused the tombstone and the ground with it, splashing his khaki trousers and my white shirt in the process.

And nineteenth was I think he *had* cried, shed a tear or two then, and read the Fatiha too with the wrinkled but not calloused palms of his hands open before him, the battered pages of an unread book, and placed roughly at waist height before making as if to wash his face with imaginary water. And twentieth, why had he never taught me how to recite the Fatiha or performed it in front of my mother and sister. And twenty-first, Buddhism. And twenty-second, I looked over at my uncle Gamal whose round and formidable shoulder was now pressed against my own, and who despite his slightly less rotund figure and marginally less plump cheeks still vaguely resembled Buddha himself. And twenty-third, I think I smiled sparingly which made me thirst all the more.

BEIRUT INTERNATIONAL AIRPORT

Gone were the days when people would have to sit on broken, plastic chairs in a tattered cafeteria awaiting their loved ones arriving from France or Germany or England or Brazil or Canada or the USA, or lean on rusted rails to wish them a safe journey back to wherever they came from while they smoked their Cedars or Viceroys or Gauloises or Marlboroughs. This cafeteria was bold and new and knowingly charged extortionate prices for a bottle of Tannourine and a croissant. The airport was renamed Rafic Harriri Beirut International Airport after the assassinated prime minister and former millionaire businessman who had, with some personal financial benefit, pushed for the rebuilding of the airport.

My mother stubbed out her Marlborough when news broke that the prime minister had been assassinated only metres away from the defunct St. George Hotel by the Mediterranean. The windows rattled and the books edged forward, and the chandeliers swung and my father cast the newspaper aside and turned on the TV. This was before the Israeli bombardment and Monseiur Mermier and the Don and the White American and Adel. The aftermath of the car bomb was broadcast live. There were burnt, scorched bodies everywhere, cars on fire. The cameraman spotted a man ablaze, he was still alive and kicking around trying desperately to put the fire out or kill himself. A reporter rushed past his cameraman, swearing loudly and audibly. He took off his coat and placed it around the burning man and pushed him to the ground.

I was too young to truly understand most of this and my mother covered my eyes with her soft hands at first, then she reached for a tissue and began to wipe her own tears.

'He was so young,' said my mother, caressing my four-year-old sister's hair. She had been sleeping for at least an hour, her head resting on my mother's lap and the rest of her small body stretched across that comfortable couch in the living room.

'Not that young,' said my sister.

'Is it back?' my mother asked.

She meant the war.

'No,' said my father, running his fingers through my sister's curly hair, and staring into the empty void that is tomorrow.

He meant to sound certain.

'If it is, we're leaving.'

'Where would we go?'

'Australia. I don't care.'

At the Rafic Harriri Beirut International Airport, there were people dressed in suits running around convincing you that the Phoenicia not the Hilton, that the Movenpick not the Four Seasons, were best in case you still had not reserved a place to stay. And no one mentioned the Holiday Inn or the St. George Hotel. And if you said you were leaving Beirut to live abroad, they rested a hand on your shoulder and said, 'your poor mother, now why would you do that to her?' because you were not just a customer to them, you were a future customer who would come back home and need a place to stay long after your mother departs. And all the while on loop in the background, you could hear the tune to Fairuz's songs at her melancholic worst. You did not need the lyrics, or Fairuz's voice, you knew them both by heart. Your mother made sure of it.

I waved to my mother as I entered passport control dragging my black, second-hand luggage behind me and she waved back and cried. She breathed in through her mouth and blew a kiss and I dropped my hand baggage, with a green ribbon tightly knotted around the handle, and tilted back to catch the kiss. A luggage handler brushed past me pushing five or six trolleys in front of him. He was bald and wore faded blue overalls. I waved to my sister and she waved back, moving only her wrist not her arm. Her ponytails were gone now, and instead she had devoted a large part of her mornings to making sure that her once wild hair was irreversibly straight, undisturbed by the curls which would bounce along as she defied gravity on a springy mattress, on the sixth floor of a small apartment in Ras Beirut, just off Hamra Street. My father nodded and raised a clenched fist in the air. It reminded me of Mostafa at the beach. It meant stay strong, do not let the world change you or if it must then let it be for the better. I thought that is what it meant. It could have meant start a revolution. My father was capable of articulating these things with clenched fists and clenched jaws and black leather belts which lashed against air and freshly made bedsheets. I put my thumb up and shut one eye, and my thumb blotted out my mother and father. I didn't feel like a giant. I felt very, very small.

ACKNOWLEDGMENTS

I am grateful to Kit Caless, at Influx Press, for his patience and time spent pouring over the book, and Jordan Taylor-Jones for his enthusiasm towards it. I am indebted to my friend and erstwhile Professor at the American University of Beirut, Dr Robert Myers, who believed in my work many years ago; and my former supervisors at Lancaster University, Dr Zoe Lambert and Dr Lindsey Moore, for the afternoons and mornings spent in their offices talking about the novel, Beirut and everything in between.

I am also grateful to Dr Monica Germana, and the University of Westminster which gave me the chance to try my hand at writing in London via fee waiver. Furthermore, I would like to express my sincere gratitude towards Toby Litt, for his friendship, his guidance, and for bringing the manuscript to Influx Press' hands and making the publication of this novel possible.

Lastly, I'd like to thank my mother, father and sister, Rinad, without whom these pages, and many others, would be neither 'whole' nor 'complete'.